Prince Edward's Warrant

The chronicles of Hugh de Singleton, surgeon

The Unquiet Bones
A Corpse at St Andrew's Chapel
A Trail of Ink
Unhallowed Ground
The Tainted Coin
Rest Not in Peace
The Abbot's Agreement
Ashes to Ashes
Lucifer's Harvest
Deeds of Darkness
Prince Edward's Warrant

Prince Edward's Warrant

The eleventh chronicle of Hugh de Singleton, surgeon

MEL STARR

LION FICTION

Published by
Lion Hudson Limited
Wilkinson House, Jordan Hill Business Park,
Banbury Road, Oxford OX2 8DR, England
www.lionhudson.com

ISBN 978 1 78264 262 6
e-ISBN 978 1 78264 263 3

First edition 2018

A catalogue record for this book is available from the British Library

Printed and bound in the UK, March 2019, LH26

For John Kwilinski
Welcome to the family

Acknowledgments

Several years ago when Dr. Dan Runyon, Professor of English at Spring Arbor University, learned that I had written an as yet unpublished medieval mystery, he invited me to speak to his fiction-writing class about the trials of a rookie writer seeking a publisher. He sent chapters of Master Hugh's first chronicle, *The Unquiet Bones*, to his friend Tony Collins at Lion Hudson. Thanks, Dan.

Tony has since retired, but many thanks to him and all those at Lion Hudson who saw Master Hugh's potential. Thanks also to my editors, Jan Greenough for the first nine books, and Penelope Wilcock for the most recent, who know Master Hugh as well as I and excel at asking such questions as "Do you really want to say it that way?" and "Wouldn't Master Hugh do it like this?"

Dr. John Blair, of Queen's College, Oxford, has written several papers about Bampton history. These have been valuable in creating an accurate time and place for Master Hugh.

In the summer of 1990 Susan and I found a B&B in a delightful medieval village north of Lichfield named Mavesyn Ridware. Proprietors Tony and Lis Page became friends, and when they moved to Bampton some years later invited us to visit them there. Tony and Lis introduced me to Bampton and became a great source of information about the village. Tony died in March 2015, only a few months after being diagnosed with cancer. He is greatly missed.

Ms. Malgorzata Deron, of Poznan, Poland, offered to update and maintain my website. She has done a marvelous job, while working as a university professor of linguistics and also battling illness. To see her work visit www.melstarr.net.

Glossary

Alaunt: a large hunting dog.

All Saints' Day: November 1.

Almoner: responsible for a lord's charity, or a monastic official responsible for gifts to the poor.

Aloes of beef (or lamb): meat sliced thin and rolled in a mixture of egg yolk, suet, onion, and various spices, then baked.

Angelus Bell: rung three times each day – dawn, noon, and dusk. Announced the time for the Angelus Devotional.

Babewyns: figures of fun, often of grotesque monkeys, which was likely the case at Kennington Palace.

Bailiff: a lord's chief manorial representative. He oversaw all operations, collected rents and fines, and enforced labor service. Not a popular fellow.

Banns: a formal announcement, made in the parish church for three consecutive Sundays, of intent to marry.

Baxter: a professional baker, often female, who regularly sold on the street.

Book of Hours: a devotional book, usually elaborately illustrated.

Bowls: medieval bowling.

Braes: medieval underpants.

Burgher: a town merchant.

Burgundy: the eastern section of what is now France – also the wine produced there.

Butler: manorial official in charge of the buttery.

Butt: a barrel for the storage of wine and ale.

Buttery: a room for beverages stored in butts.

Candlemas: February 2. Marked the purification of Mary. Women traditionally paraded to church carrying lighted candles. Tillage of fields resumed this day.

Capon: a castrated male chicken.

Chamberlain: the keeper of a lord's chamber, wardrobe, and personal items.

Chicken in kyrtyn: poultry in a cream sauce spiced with ginger, cinnamon, cumin, saffron, and sugar.

Complexio: the combination of the four humors (hot, cold, moist, dry) which made up a person's life and health.

Cormarye: pork roasted after marinating in red wine and spices.

Coronel-tipped: a blunt lance for use in jousting. The lance had generally three or four small projections at the point.

Cotter: a poor villager, usually holding five acres or less. He often had to labor for wealthier villagers to make ends meet.

Crécy: In 1346 an English army, greatly outnumbered, won a victory there in northern France.

Crispels: a pastry made of flour, sugar, and honey, and fried in lard or oil.

Cyueles: deep-fried fritters made of a paste of breadcrumbs, ground almonds, eggs, sugar, and salt.

Demesne: land directly exploited by a lord, and worked by his villeins, as opposed to land a lord might rent to tenants.

Dexter: a war horse, larger than a runcie or palfrey. Also the right hand direction.

Dighted crab: crab meat soaked in wine, then chopped fine to make a paste. Mixed with ginger, cinnamon, and sugar, the mixture was then replaced in the shell and boiled.

Eels in Bruit: eels cut into small pieces, then cooked in white wine with onions, parsley, sage, breadcrumbs, pepper, and cinnamon.

Farrier: a smith who specialized in shoeing horses.

Farthing: one-fourth of a penny. The smallest silver coin.

Fast day: Wednesday, Friday, and Saturday. Not the fasting of modern usage, when no food is consumed, but days upon which no meat, eggs, or animal products were consumed. Fish was on the menu for those who could afford it.

Fewterer: keeper of a lord's kennel and hounds.

Fifth hour: about eleven a.m.

Fraunt hemelle: a pudding made of beaten eggs, cream, breadcrumbs (old, dry bread was rarely just thrown out), minced meat, and spices. The mixture was placed in a bag and boiled, then grilled just before serving.

Gaunceli: a sauce made of milk, flour, garlic, saffron, and salt. Simmered until thickened.

Gentleman: a nobleman. The term had nothing to do with character or behavior.

Gongfermors: men whose occupation was the emptying of cesspits.

Groat: a silver coin worth four pence.

Groom: a lower-ranking servant to a lord. Often young, outranking a page but beneath a valet.

Hamsoken: breaking and entering.

Hemlock: also known as poison parsley. Not to be confused with the coniferous hemlock tree.

Hypocras: spiced wine. Sugar, cinnamon, ginger, cloves, and nutmeg were often in the mix. Usually served at the end of the meal.

Infangenthef: the right of a lord of a manor to try and execute a thief caught in the act.

Jelly de chare: a meat jelly. Calves' or pigs' feet were boiled for three hours, then the surface skimmed. Wine, spices, salt, almonds, and pork or poultry were then added. The mixture was simmered until the meat was tender. Generally served cold.

King's Eyre: a royal traveling court, presided over by a visiting circuit judge.

Knight's fee: the number of men at arms a knight was to provide in time of war. Also the one hundred shillings a knight owed the king to possess a deceased father's lands.

Knucklebones: a game similar to jacks played with the knucklebones of pigs or sheep.

Lady: a noblewoman. The term had nothing to do with character or behavior.

Lammastide: August 1, when thanks were given for a successful wheat harvest. From Old English "Loaf mass."

Larder: a room or structure where meat and fish were stored.

Let lardes: a type of custard made with eggs, milk, bacon fat, and parsley.

Liripipe: a fashionably long tail attached to a man's cap.

Long worts of pork: a meat stew made with breadcrumbs, cabbage or spring greens, and seasoned with saffron and salt.

Lychgate: a roofed gate in a churchyard wall under which the deceased rested during the initial part of a burial service.

Lymer: a tracking hound.

Maintenance: protection from punishment for misdeeds – provided for knights who served powerful lords and wore their livery.

Malmsey: the sweetest variety of Madeira wine, originally from Greece.

Marshalsea: the stables and associated accoutrements.

Maslin: bread made from a mixture of grains – commonly wheat and rye, or barley and rye.

Matins: the first of the day's eight canonical hours (services). Also called Lauds.

Mercer: a dealer in silk and linen.

Mess: diners were not served individually at a meal. Portions for two to four were placed upon the table – this was a "mess."

Nine Man Morris: a board game similar to tic-tac-toe but much more complicated.

Page: a young male servant. If from the upper classes, a youth learning the arts of chivalry before becoming a squire.

Palfrey: a riding horse with a comfortable gait.

Pannage: a fee paid to a lord for permission for pigs to forage in his forest.

Pantler: a manor official, usually a valet, in charge of the pantry.

Pantry: a room for the storage of bread, dining utensils, and linens for tablecloths. From the French word for bread: *pain*.

Particolored: of several colors. Men often wore chauces (tight-fitting trousers) of more than one color.

Penny: the most common silver coin. Twelve pennies equaled a shilling, although in the fourteenth century there was no one shilling coin. Twenty shillings made a pound, although there was no one pound coin, either.

Plate: domestic dinnerware made of silver.

Porre of peas: a pea soup made with onions, olive oil, and saffron – seasoned with salt and sugar or honey.

Portpain: a linen cloth used to carry bread from the pantry to the table.

Privy chamber: a lord's private room.

Quarter-noble: a gold coin worth eighty pence; one-third of a pound.

Ravioles: pastries filled with cheese, beaten eggs, occasionally minced pork or poultry, and spices. Generally boiled.

Reeve: an important manor official, although he did not outrank the bailiff. Elected by tenants from among themselves, often the best husbandman. He had responsibility for fields, buildings, and enforcing labor service. Also called a hayward.

Remove: a dinner course.

Runcie: a small, common horse, often used as a pack animal or to haul carts and wagons.

St. Edmund's Day: November 20.

St. Stephen's Day: December 26.

Screens passage: a narrow corridor which screened the hall from the kitchen, and from which the buttery and pantry were often accessed.

Scrofula: a tubercular swelling of lymph nodes on the neck.

Shambles: an open-air slaughterhouse to the north of St. Paul's Cathedral, not to be confused with the better-known street of the same name in York.

Shilling: twelve pence. No shilling coin existed in the fourteenth century.

Sole in cyve: fish broiled and served in a yellow onion sauce.

Squab: a young dove about four or five weeks old.

Squire: a youth who attended a knight, often in training to become a knight.

Stag: a male red deer, sometimes called a hart.

Stews: a brothel district.

Stockfish: inexpensive fish, usually dried and salted cod or haddock, consumed on fast days.

Stone: fourteen pounds.

Subtlety: an elaborate confection served between courses or at the end of a meal. Often more for show than consumption.

Tenant: a free peasant who rented land from his lord. He could pay his rent in labor or, more likely by the fourteenth century, in cash.

Theriac: a compound of viper's flesh and other ingredients considered a poison antidote as well as a remedy for diseases caused by melancholy and phlegm.

Tournament: war games. Often lasting three days. Jousting was but a part of the event.

Tun: a large cask capable of holding over two hundred gallons. A ship's "tunnage" did not refer to the weight it could carry or its water displacement, but the number of tuns that could be loaded.

Twelfth Night: the evening of January 5, preceding Epiphany.

Valet: a high-ranking servant to a lord – a chamberlain, for example.

Villein: a non-free peasant. He could not leave his land or service to his lord, or sell animals without permission. But if he could escape his manor for a year and a day he would be free.

Void: dessert – often sugared fruit and sweetened wine.

Wardrobe: the department of a noble household entrusted with the care of apparel, jewels, and personal articles.

Wattles: interlacing sticks used as a foundation and support for daub (plaster) in forming the walls of a house.

Whitsuntide: "White Sunday," ten days after Ascension Day, seven weeks after Easter. Also known as Pentecost.

Wimple: a cloth covering worn over a woman's head and around the neck.

Winchester geese: prostitutes licensed and taxed by the Bishop of Winchester to ply their trade in his enclave of Southwark.

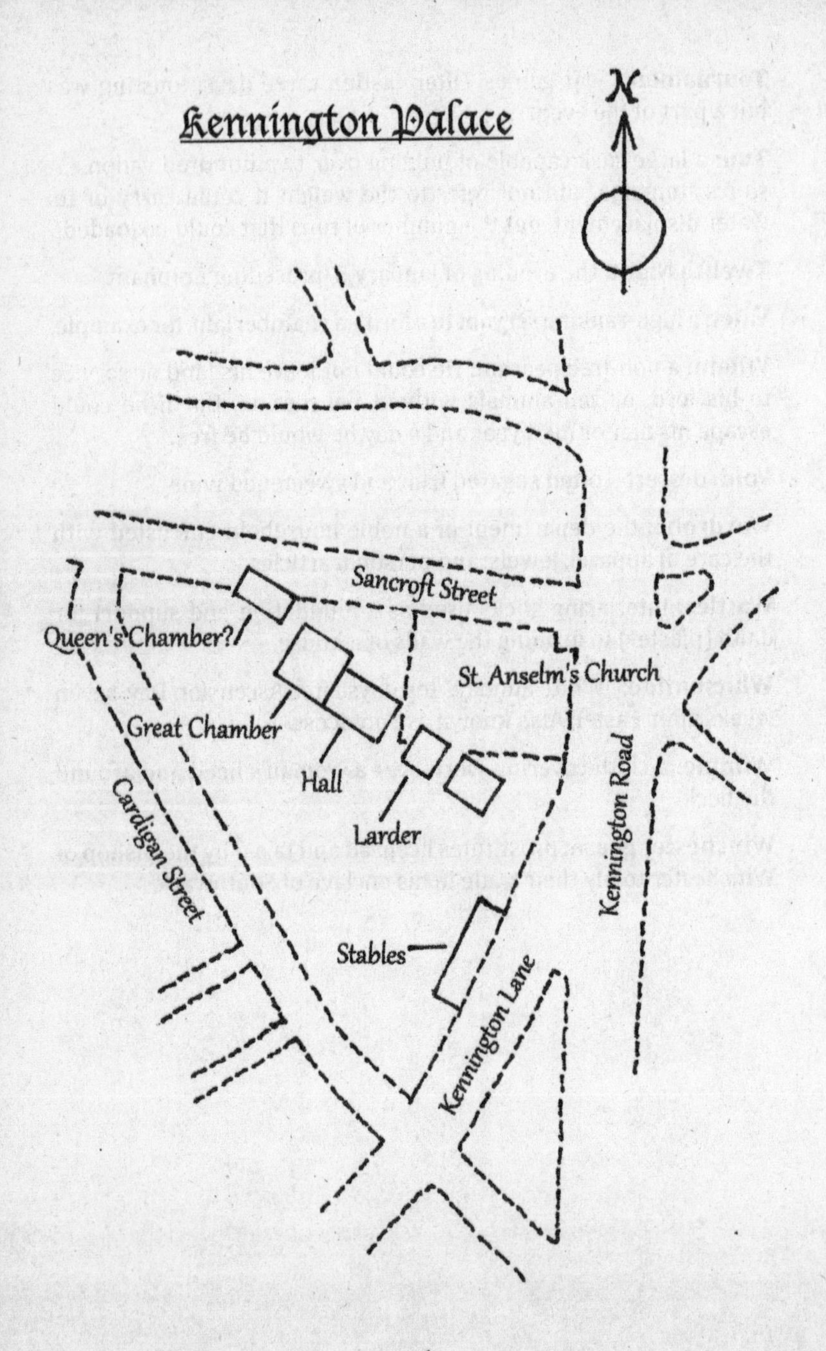
Kennington Palace
N
Sancroft Street
Queen's Chamber?
St. Anselm's Church
Great Chamber
Hall
Larder
Cardigan Street
Kennington Road
Stables
Kennington Lane

Chapter 1

Our party reached Aldersgate after the curfew bell had rung. We could not enter the city, but rather sought refuge for the night at the Priory of St. Bartholomew. I traveled with Sir Giles Cheyne, his two grooms, Milo and Thomas, his squire, Randall Patchett, and Arthur, a groom to my employer, Lord Gilbert Talbot. That we were too late to pass the Aldersgate Sir Giles laid against me. I accept the blame.

I had attempted to avoid this journey, pointing out to Lord Gilbert my duties to him and his manor at Bampton. He replied that my duty to my future sovereign transcended obligations to him. Bampton's reeve, John Prudhomme, could assume my duties while I was away in London.

Sir Giles had arrived in Bampton with his grooms and squire on the fourteenth day of October on a mission for Edward of Woodstock, Duke of Cornwall and Prince of Wales. Edward, he said, wished for the services of Lord Gilbert's surgeon, who had eased his illness at Limoges. I am the only surgeon in Lord Gilbert Talbot's employ.

"When the prince commands me to send you to him," Lord Gilbert said, "your service to me as bailiff here must be dispensable."

Edward, Sir Giles said, was weak, in much discomfort, and perhaps near to death. With his father, the king, the prince had embarked in August from Sandwich with four hundred ships, ten thousand archers, and four thousand men at arms intending to retake Edward's possessions in France lost to the French king.

For six weeks foul weather prevented a landing in France, and the expedition was compelled to return to England. A failure. A costly failure. Six weeks at sea in storms of wind and rain will tax the healthiest of men, which Prince Edward was not. The experience worsened his illness, Sir Giles said, and he required my service as once before at Limoges.

I am no physician, but know enough of herbs that when I met Prince Edward at Limoges I told him that his symptoms might be relieved if he consumed tansy, thyme, cress, and bramble leaves crushed to an oily paste with root of fennel, then mixed with wine.

The prince suffered from numerous maladies: a bloody flux, fevers, then chills, and passing wind so foul that folk despaired to be in the same room with him. These ailments had begun whilst Edward was in Spain, winning honor at the Battle of Najera. At Limoges he was so weak he could not sit a horse. The herbs I suggested seemed to improve his health, enough that with his father he embarked upon the ill-fated attempt to reclaim his patrimony in France. But now, in the year of our Lord 1372, his affliction was returned. So Sir Giles said. The duke desired me to attend him as at Limoges. He had lost faith in William Blackwater, his physician.

I was loathe to leave Kate and our children. The last time I did so, when Lord Gilbert required that I accompany him to the siege of Limoges, I returned home to loss and sorrow. Sybil, our second child, perished while I was in France and now with the Lord Christ awaits her mother and me and Bessie and John. The babe was not yet one year old when she died. Might I have saved her had I not been in France? Unlikely. I am a surgeon, not a physician. And if physicians could cure a babe's fever, few infants would perish.

But Bessie and John are thriving, and Kate's father promised to look after my family while I was away upon the prince's business. A year ago my father-in-law was skin and bones. I thought him ill and close to death. His business in Oxford was failing, and he was near to starvation. I convinced him to leave Oxford and live with us, at Galen House, in Bampton, and Kate's cookery soon had him hale. His locks are grey, but he is once again strong enough to see to the care of his own.

Lord Gilbert agreed that I could take with me to London Arthur Wagge, a groom of Bampton Castle who has proven useful to me in Lord Gilbert's service. Dealing with miscreants does not trouble Arthur. He outweighs most men by two stone, possesses arms as thick as most men's legs, and although no longer young, can with a scowl convince rogues to give up their felonies when I command them to do so.

The journey from Bampton to London may be completed in three days, but not if a cold rain pours down upon a traveler as he ascends the Chiltern Hills and a child requires a surgeon's care. So it was that darkness overtook us before we reached London and we spent Monday night at the Priory of St. Bartholomew.

The delay disappointed me. The sooner I gained Prince Edward's presence and prescribed some physics for his ailments, the sooner I could return to Bampton. And I had found Sir Giles an uncongenial travel companion. My rank was beneath him, and he felt it undignified that his prince would send him to bring me to London. A man of lesser station could have done so. This he remarked upon often. Sir Giles talked much on the journey but said little.

As we passed through Stokenchurch a child of no more than three years stumbled in a muddy rut in the road before our party. Rather than drawing upon the reins Sir Giles, with a curse, spurred his beast – to leap over the boy, so he later said. The animal's iron-shod hoof struck the lad's arm. I wonder if Sir Giles would have behaved so had he known in how few hours he would greet St. Peter?

I halted my palfrey and dismounted to comfort the howling child. The lad's cries drew his parents and siblings from their house. Indeed, half of the homes in the village emptied, their occupants pressing about me, curious as to what harm I had done to the child. Had not Arthur's thick arms, neck, and chest been behind me I believe the boy's father would have thrashed me before I was able to explain what had occurred.

When the crowd quieted I told the babe's parents of the reason for his wails, and explained that I was a surgeon and could deal with the injured arm. Each time I touched the appendage the lad howled anew, but I was able to satisfy myself that there was no broken bone. There was, however, a laceration and red bruise, which would soon darken to purple.

The cut must be closed. My instruments sack was slung across my palfrey's rump, behind the saddle. I unfastened it and withdrew from a small box my finest needle and a spool of silken thread. Had I more time, and was I dealing with an adult, I would have asked for a cup of ale and into it poured a mix of crushed hemp seeds and powdered lettuce sap. An hour or so after drinking this concoction a man would feel less pain as I closed his wound.

But Sir Giles sat scowling upon his horse, impatient to be away, and I was uncertain how a child might cope with crushed hemp seeds and powdered lettuce sap.

I instructed the lad's father to hold his child tightly, and told the mother to grasp the lad's arm and under no circumstances allow it to move. The parents seemed reluctant to do this until I spoke firmly to them about the calamity which might come to their child if his cut was not closed properly.

Tenants on a manor such as Stokenchurch will have no wine. I asked for a volunteer to seek the manor house, explain the need, and return with a cup of wine. A village matron bustled off and I set to work threading my needle.

I took six sutures and with each the babe wailed anew. When I was satisfied that the cut was closed well I took the cup of wine, which had appeared at my elbow while I attended the wound, and bathed the laceration. The lad bawled again as the wine stung his wound. I would have spared him this, but wounds bathed in wine heal more readily than those not so washed. No man knows why.

Generally I follow the practice of Henri de Mondeville, who taught that wounds left dry and uncovered heal best, but in the case of a child I thought it likely the lad would pluck at the wound and sutures if my work was left open. I asked the lad's mother for an old kirtle or chemise. She produced one which seemed clean, and I tore it to strips with which I bound the cut.

I told the child's father that he could sever the stitches with his dagger and pull the threads free on All Saints' Day. The fellow nodded and thanked me for my service to his child. I decided as I mounted my beast that when I returned to Bampton, in but two or three days, I hoped, I would travel this way to learn how the little lad fared. This episode is why we came to the Aldersgate too late to enter the city and waited the night at the priory.

Kennington Palace is south of the Thames, so to reach Prince Edward's home we had to cross London to approach the south bank across London Bridge. We had passed the Goldsmiths' Hall and turned on to Cheapside when a gathering mob of London's inhabitants began to impede our progress.

"Hanging today," Sir Giles said.

He was correct. We spurred our beasts through the crowd, receiving black looks as we did so, and came to the Standard as a noose was being draped around the neck of a lad of perhaps sixteen years.

"Wonder what 'e done?" Arthur said above the clamor.

"Apprentice to a mercer what stole a bolt of silk from 'is master," an obliging onlooker replied.

The lad stood in a cart as the noose was placed about his neck, and when the hangman was satisfied, he slapped the rump of the runcie which then drew the cart from under the apprentice.

He was a slight lad. The taut hempen rope did not break his neck, so he kicked as the tightening noose slowly strangled him. After a few moments the constables relented and allowed the boy's friends to rush to him and pull upon his ankles to end sooner his agony.

"Welcome to London," Arthur said grimly.

We were welcomed again after crossing London Bridge. Winchester geese accosted us as we entered Southwark, rightly identifying us as travelers upon the road. Sir Giles forgot his impatience and would have dallied with one of these strumpets but I told the knight that whatever he chose to do, I would journey on to Kennington Palace, the ramparts being now visible above the trees to the southwest.

Sir Giles scowled and apparently decided that if he was to escort a man to Prince Edward he should probably enter the prince's presence with the man he had been assigned to accompany.

Chapter 2

Our horses clattered across the wooden bridge which gave access to Kennington Palace, and grooms from the marshalsea took the beasts in hand. We entered the hall from the porch, between the babewyns. We were in time for dinner.

I was assigned a place beside William Blackwater, and his disdain was immediately made clear. He slid sideways upon our bench to avoid brushing my elbow.

Between the first and second removes I attempted to begin a conversation. I reminded Blackwater of our previous meeting, at Limoges, and our surgery upon the wounded when the city wall was finally breached. I should say "my surgery," for he had contrived to be otherwise engaged when gore was splashed about the tent where the wounded were brought.

"I know who you are," the physician said, "and I know why you are here. What do you know of men's humors and their treatment?"

"Very little," I admitted. "But Prince Edward has called for me and I must come at his bidding. If he asks me that question I will answer truthfully."

"His ailment requires treatment from a skilled physician," Blackwater continued, "not some mechanic who repairs what is broken, which a man's body will do without a surgeon's attention."

"Indeed," I replied. "If you were to slash your arm with an accidental thrust of your dagger, the cut may repair itself. No need to call upon me to stitch the wound closed."

The physician made no reply, but turned his attention to the second remove. I did likewise, for roasted goose in gaunceli and let lardes was served. As I consumed my portion I glanced to the high table where the prince, Lady Joan, and Edward's household knights and their ladies enjoyed the roasted goose and additional dainties which we lesser folk did without. I looked in the other direction and saw Arthur, with other grooms, consuming long worts of pork. He was stuffing his mouth enthusiastically, unaware, or uncaring, of the fare consumed at the higher end of his table.

'Twas while I chewed my roasted goose that I glanced again to Prince Edward. He had been sallow complected, with sunken cheeks, at Limoges. He was now even more so. As I watched, he picked from his trencher a pale piece of flesh and gnawed listlessly upon it, occasionally watching others of his retinue as they enjoyed their fare.

Blackwater evidently saw my gaze linger upon the high table. "Boiled rooster," he said. "Of course, you would know nothing of the reason for such a diet."

I did not answer or act as if I wished an explanation, as I felt certain the physician would supply one. He did.

"The prince's complexio is out of balance, about which you surgeons know nothing."

He was correct concerning my knowledge of boiled roosters. Physicians hold that the qualities of heat and cold, wet and dry, determine a man's health, and that these four are influenced by the stars and planets, especially upon the day a man is born, and also by his diet.

I hold with St. Augustine, who wrote that astrology strikes at the root of human responsibility. It says, "It wasn't my fault – Venus caused it, or Saturn or Mars." The creator of the sky and stars is to be blamed for my decisions and errors and sins. And Prince Edward's illness. But I held my tongue.

"M'lord prince is a man of courage," the physician said. "This is an attribute of hot, thin blood, as in youth. As a man grows older his blood cools. This, with the moistness of males, may cause the humors to be unbalanced. Prince Edward suffers from too much black bile."

"So he must gnaw upon a boiled fowl while we consume roasted goose and let lardes?" I said.

"Rooster flesh is dry and hot," Blackwater said. "Especially one which crows little and is chased about to tire it before it is slaughtered. Physicians know that such a fowl is recommended for men of old age, in winter, and in northern climes."

I did not think Prince Edward, being forty-two, would appreciate being prescribed a diet suitable for the elderly.

"And under no circumstance must he consume fresh fruits or vegetables. Such must be cooked, and even then consumed in small amounts."

"Has this treatment improved the prince's health?" I voiced the question in innocence. Blackwater did not take it so.

"It did," he growled. "After Limoges his complexio began to improve. He attributed this to the herbs you suggested, but anyone who has studied Galen and Averroes would know that the improvement could not be due to such herbs. They have little effect upon the humors."

"So the prince continues to dine upon boiled roosters and yet grows weaker?"

"He would not but for the sea voyage which cooled his blood and made his humors more moist. This is why he must consume foods hot and dry to restore the balance."

"And yet he sent for me."

"He is so ill he grows impatient for a cure, even when he knows I do what is best for him. He has suffered for so long he will seek succor even from charlatans. Grasping at straws."

When a man is ill to death he will grasp at anything, or chew upon anything, I suppose. Even a tough old rooster. I glanced again at Prince Edward and watched him tear a piece of flesh from the carcass and chew the tasteless mouthful.

The third remove was aloes of beef, cyueles, and apple fritters, which Blackwater found so pleasing that he left off berating my profession and concentrated on adding to his already substantial belly. I did likewise. Although surprisingly, despite my Kate's cookery, my paunch as yet shows little sign of her skill. Consuming such fare is more gratifying than conversation with a man who knows all that is worth knowing and is willing to share his wisdom with the ignorant. And of many things medical I am ignorant. No man can know everything, regardless of what a sophist may claim, but any man may know more. A man knows much who knows how little he knows.

If Prince Edward did not enjoy his dinner, others at the high table did. Sir Giles seemed especially delighted, laughing and exchanging apparent witticisms with his table companions. I saw a valet refill his wine cup several times, which likely added to his mirth.

The clatter of a wine cup falling to the floor interrupted the background chatter which had accompanied the meal. I looked up to see who had dropped his cup, and saw Sir Giles rise slowly from his bench. His wine cup lay upon the tiles before the high table.

The hall fell silent. All turned to Sir Giles and watched transfixed as he stood, swayed, sank to his bench, and then fell back from it to disappear behind the high table. Lady Joan shrieked, and Prince Edward kicked back his chair and went to aid Sir Giles. I thought to do likewise, but decided 'twould be best to wait. The prince would call Dr. Blackwater, or me, or both of us as he saw fit.

I watched as the prince disappeared from view behind the high table. He quickly reappeared and called another knight to assist him. Together they bent over the stricken man and disappeared again as Sir Giles was laid out upon the tiles behind the high table.

A moment later Prince Edward stood, looked to me and Blackwater, and motioned vigorously for us to approach. Or for one of us to approach. Because we stood together it was impossible to know which he desired to tend the fallen man.

As we hurried to the prince the hall became again filled with conversation as folk asked one another what might have caused Sir Giles to fall violently ill. Blackwater and I pressed through the crowd of knights and their ladies which had gathered about Sir Giles's prostrate form.

"He complains that his feet will no longer support him," Prince Edward said when we drew near, "and his hands grow cold and he can feel nothing."

I took Sir Giles's hand and pinched his arm near to the elbow. "Do you feel that?" I asked.

"Feel what?" the knight whispered.

I poked a finger into his ribs and asked again if he felt the jab.

He saw what I did and so knew what he should feel. "Nay," he murmured.

A moment later the knight lifted his head as if to view the world one last time, for he knew, I believe, that he was about to depart it. His head fell back and his breath stopped. I placed a finger to his neck but could detect no pulse. I stood and crossed myself. Noble onlookers did likewise.

"What has happened?" Prince Edward asked. "He was fit when we sat to dinner."

"Poison," Blackwater exclaimed, "or an excess of black bile. A theriac is needed. I have a supply in my chamber."

"His heart has stopped. He can drink nothing," I said. "Mix your theriac with wine if you wish, but he'll not drink it."

"What is to be done?" Prince Edward asked.

"When he first fell from his bench, did he complain of a bellyache or any other infirmity?" I asked of the circle of gentlemen and ladies that surrounded me, William Blackwater, Prince Edward, and a corpse.

All the living shook their heads as I looked about the circle. The sudden death of a companion had brought to each man and woman now present thoughts of their own mortality. Most folk trust that before death comes for them they will have time – days, or at least hours – to amend their ways and seek God's grace. Such an adjustment of attitude and behavior, men believe, will guarantee heaven even if only after a term in purgatory. And this ordeal may be abbreviated by contributions of land or coin to priests or monks who will pray to the Lord Christ to free them from that malignant place. If such a place there be.

'Twas too late for a theriac mixed with wine. Sir Giles Cheyne was beyond all earthly cures. Was the reason for his death mixed with his wine? Like his august companions at the high table I had thought the knight in excellent health when we rode through London in the morning. And what man feeling himself unwell would consider dallying with a prostitute as Sir Giles had but two hours past? No. Whatever slew the man came upon him suddenly. Perhaps after he sat at the high table, which likely meant poison. Or a heart which suddenly failed him. How to know which?

None of the others who had been placed at the high table seemed ill. How could it be that food and wine prepared for all dispatched but one? If Sir Giles was poisoned, the fatal dose must have been added after the food was prepared and presented to him, but before he consumed it. He shared his mess with Sir Humphrey Downey, whose name at the time I did not know. But I recognized him, as he stood behind Prince Edward, as being Sir Giles's companion at table. The knight showed no sign of illness or discomfort, although he stood close enough to hear the word "poison," and must surely be considering the meal he had just consumed.

The only part of the meal which the two men did not share was wine. Each drank from his own cup. I rose to my feet, turned to the table and Sir Giles's place, and lifted his wine goblet to my nose.

Some poisons produce an odor, or taste, which makes them less effective as a way to slay a man. Sir Giles had consumed nearly all of his wine, but a trace remained. Try as I might I could detect no aroma unusual to a wine cup.

Prince Edward saw me hold the goblet under my nose and immediately divined the purpose.

"You believe poison was mixed with Sir Giles's wine? How could this be? We have all drunk from the same butt."

"But perhaps not from the same ewer," I replied. I turned to Sir Giles's dinner companion. "How many times was Sir Giles's wine replenished?"

The man frowned in concentration. "Four times, I believe."

"And each time was your cup also filled?"

"Nay. Second time the valet apologized, said his ewer was empty, and that he would return anon with more wine for me."

"So the valet emptied his ewer when he poured more wine for Sir Giles then?"

"Aye."

Prince Edward is no dolt. He immediately turned to his marshal and spoke. "Who served us wine? Which valet had the duty? I paid the man no attention."

"'Twas Arnaud."

"Fetch him," the prince commanded.

The marshal turned and disappeared into the screens passage. William Blackwater, who all this time was kneeling over the corpse, stood and spoke.

"'Twas an excess of black bile. Travel in the rain yesterday surely brought it on. Was he poisoned, his wine would surely stink from the toxin." Blackwater then took the cup that I had replaced upon the table, and held it to his nostrils. "Nothing," he said. The physician then lifted the cup to his mouth as if to taste it. Before he could do so I reached out a hand and swatted the goblet from his lips. He glared fiercely at me.

"If 'twas poison which ended Sir Giles's life I believe hemlock the toxin. Plato records the death of Socrates, how after he drank from the fatal bowl first his legs, then hands went numb and cold. Within a few minutes his breath was stopped and also his heart. Sir Giles's death seems much like that of the great philosopher. If so, the slightest few drops might kill you. Men have been known to die from consuming a dozen leaves crushed to a juice."

"Bah. Hemlock has a bitter taste," Blackwater said. "If some man put enough of the stuff into Sir Giles's wine to slay him he would have tasted it. His complexio was unbalanced, causing his heart to fail him."

"Indeed," I said. "Hemlock and monkshood, we are told, have an objectionable, pungent flavor. But this may be disguised in spiced food or strong wine. M'lord prince would serve Sir Giles only the best burgundy. Such wine, I think, would cover the bitter taste of poison. No man I know of has survived the consumption of such adulterated wine to report if 'tis so."

From the corner of my eye I saw the marshal appear at the opening to the screens passage. He held his hands out, palms up. "No man has seen Arnaud these past few minutes. He was to serve hypocras at the high table, but is now nowhere to be found."

Did the valet know that the wine he served to Sir Giles was poisoned? Why else would he not be found? Did he flee the palace after serving the fatal draught? Hemlock and monkshood may kill within an hour if the dose is large enough, and a thimble can contain a dose large enough. The fellow would have an hour, perhaps less, to escape the palace and discovery if he delivered the poison.

"Seek him in the valets' chamber," Prince Edward said. "Perhaps he also is ill."

The marshal hurried away to do his lord's bidding.

It occurred to me that if Sir Giles's wine had been poisoned it would be wise to keep the offending ewer at hand, in case something might be learned from it. What this might be I could not say. I spoke to the prince.

"And lest any further harm be done, may I suggest, m'lord, that you instruct your butler to keep separate all of the wine and the ewers it was served in at dinner until they might be examined?"

Prince Edward turned to a valet and said, "See to it." The man hastened to the screens passage and disappeared.

No man or woman in the prince's hall seemed eager to resume a seat and consume hypocras and the void. All of those standing near to me had heard the word "poison." And those who had not heard it from our lips heard it from others as people whispered the word among themselves. In a hall where a man lies dead perhaps of poison few folk will feel themselves hungry or thirsty.

I could think of no way to know for certain that Sir Giles had died of poisoning. But his behavior as he died suggested it was so. The disappearance of the valet who had poured his wine lent credence to the conjecture. And Arnaud had indeed disappeared. The marshal reappeared and announced that the valet was not lying ill in the valets' chamber, nor was he to be found anywhere in the palace.

Chapter 3

Prince Edward directed his chaplain to see to the corpse: to have Sir Giles washed and prepared for burial and set before the altar of the prince's chapel. He then turned to me and said, "Come with me."

I followed the prince as he crossed the hall to a circular stairway built into the east wall. I was not alone. William Blackwater and most of the prince's retainers who had dined at the high table did likewise.

Prince Edward stopped at the base of the stairs and turned to see a confused throng in his wake. Perhaps when he spoke the words "come with me," the others assumed he spoke to them. Perhaps he did, and I had wrongly supposed he addressed only me.

Not so.

"I wish Master Hugh to attend me. No other," the prince said.

Prince Edward climbed the stairs slowly, and his breath was labored when he reached the last step. I followed, and feared he might weaken and topple back. I prepared to catch him if this happened.

Three steps up the incline I glanced back over my shoulder and saw more than a dozen open-mouthed faces staring up at me. What the prince had in mind for me was a mystery – to me and his puzzled retainers.

At the top, the stairs opened into a great chamber lit on one side by colorful stained-glass windows. On the far side of this chamber I saw a set of oaken doors where two liveried valets stood watch over the prince's private rooms. Prince Edward pushed through these doors, motioned for me to enter, then peered out at the great chamber as if to be assured we were not followed. Satisfied, he swung the doors shut.

We had entered the privy chamber. Valets had kept a fire burning upon the hearth, so the room was warm. The walls were of a light grey stone, cut so cunningly that the joints were all but invisible.

Four tall windows illuminated skillfully embroidered tapestries with silken scenes of battle and the hunt. Diamonds of glass as clear as water made up the lower half of each window. The upper halves were of stained glass illustrating saints and tales from Holy Writ.

Climbing the stairs had taxed the prince. He walked slowly to a chair, sat heavily upon an embroidered cushion, and indicated that I should likewise sit. All this time, since his commands to the others at the base of the stairs, he had not spoken. Now he did.

"This is an ugly business."

I did not reply. No words were necessary. I was in agreement.

"Arnaud has gone missing for a reason, I think," Prince Edward said. "He placed poison in Sir Giles's wine. Perhaps Sir Giles slighted him in some fashion, or he is now not to be found because he was paid to do this and has fled with his coins. Or mayhap the man who paid him for the deed has slain him, and his corpse will be found if we seek it.

"I remember two years past, at Limoges, you discovered who had slain... what was the knight's name?"

"Sir Simon Trillowe."

"Ah, just so. Sir John's lad."

"Aye, m'lord."

"As I remember the matter Sir John charged you with the felony, did he not?"

"He did, m'lord."

"You found out the felon and suggested to him he might prefer to die in battle a hero, rather than at the end of a hempen cord. Is this not so?"

I nodded agreement.

"I brought you to London to advise William Blackwater as to my affliction, but now I would have you also deal with this death."

I had hoped, even planned, to suggest helpful herbs to the prince as I had done before at Limoges, then after a day or two bid farewell to London and return to my family. How long might it take to discover who had slain Sir Giles? And was he indeed murdered? I thought so, as did the prince, but this conclusion was not a certainty. Men's hearts do fail them.

Prince Edward saw the consternation on my face. "I require this of you because I cannot trust other men. Sir Giles made enemies. I might select one of them to oversee my constables and serjeants in this matter and it might be that the man I choose is the felon."

"How did he make enemies?" I asked. I had not been long enough in Sir Giles's presence to know the man well. What I had learned of his character during the journey from Bampton had not impressed me, but I had seen nothing in three days which would have created in me a desire to slay him.

"If there was a way to make an enemy of some man Sir Giles would find it. You are perplexed at this. I see it in your eyes. Why then did I keep the man near? Because he supported me when I was in dire need. At Crécy my father the king put me in command of the center, awaiting the French attack. I was but sixteen. When the battle commenced our line held firm, but King Philip's force outnumbered us and we were hard pressed. Sir Giles was but three years older than me, and fought like a demon at my side. Together with Sir John Chandos, Thomas de Beauchamp, and the Duke of Oxford we rallied the center, held fast, then threw the French back down the hill."

I remembered the tales told of the fight, how when King Edward learned that his son was badly put upon he chose not to send men to bolster the center, but rather said, "Let the boy win his spurs." The prince did so, and has done so many times since. But unless his health can be restored he is unlikely to lead men to battle again.

"So although Sir Giles was oft ill-natured I would not desert him, as he did not desert me. Someone must take word of his death to Lady Juliana."

"His wife?" I said.

"Nay. His lady died, what" – the prince drew upon his beard – "ten or eleven years past. Lady Juliana is a widow and the banns are to be read soon. His behavior has been so often repugnant that few women would have him." Prince Edward shook his head, then continued. "Lady Juliana did not need to wed for wealth, I think. Sir Henry left her and his son a castle and lands in two shires."

"Perhaps his behavior to the lady has been more solicitous than to other folk," I said.

"Must have been. Most folk were surprised when they learned of the match, and some others disappointed."

"Disappointed? The lady had other suitors?"

"Hah! A beautiful widow of twenty-seven years with lands in two shires?"

"Oh, aye. I see. A full purse never lacks friends, nor a wealthy widow suitors."

Once before I had been required to seek a felon who had slain a man with many enemies. I did not relish the thought of being required to do so once again. And this time 'twas likely that the killer was a man of rank who, with his noble friends, would place every possible impediment in my path. I explained this to Prince Edward.

"Ah, you speak true. Most of my knights are irascible fellows, especially if called upon to yield to an inferior. Well, they must submit to your investigation. I will make this plain to all of my household, pages and grooms, gentlemen and knights. Sir Giles did not leave me when I needed him, and I will not leave him now, even so he is but a corpse. You are to be my chief constable and discover what befell him.

"Now, upon my other matter. You named some herbs when with the army before Limoges which you said might cure me."

I did not wish to contradict the man who would, unless his malady ended his life, one day be my sovereign. But neither did I wish to set false hope before him. "Not cure, m'lord. Relieve."

"Relieve? Is that not what a cure does?" The prince frowned. This was not a good sign.

"Indeed, m'lord. A cure will relieve, but relief does not necessarily cure. I suggested herbs which I thought might give you some relief."

"Are there no physics which will effect a cure? Blackwater says that if my complexio is adjusted, and the humors of my body are put right, I will be cured of my affliction."

I did not immediately reply, and the prince continued.

"But you do not believe it so. Your silence betrays you."

"I am but a surgeon. I do not wish to contradict a learned physician."

"Go ahead. Contradict him. He has me eating boiled roosters, may the Lord Christ have mercy on him. If his tough old fowl work no improvement he will soon seek his living elsewhere."

Certainly Blackwater would do all to avoid that eventuality. I had heard that the prince paid the physician forty pounds each year. A princely sum indeed.

"Dr. Blackwater believes your improvement before Limoges two years past due to his changes to your diet," I said.

"So he tells me. Regularly. I am too hot and must consume cold stuff. Or I am too cold and must change to a warm diet. Or my complexio is moist and I must consume drier food. I asked him once, if 'tis a fowl I must have for my dinner, why a roasted squab or two would not serve."

"What did he say?" I asked, curious myself about the distinction.

"Couldn't tell you. 'Twas all prattle to me. But the end of the matter is I have not roasted squab upon my trencher. What were those herbs?"

"Tansy, thyme, cress, and bramble leaves crushed, and an oil made from the root of fennel. These should be mixed with wine."

"Blackwater says this potion should be spread upon my belly. That's all 'tis good for."

"Time will tell. Drink two or three cups of the concoction every day."

"This is no cure, you say. If not, what is? What is your opinion of boiled roosters?"

"As for roosters, I think they will do you as much good crowing at dawn as boiled and on your trencher. If there is a cure for your affliction I do not know of it. I am a surgeon. If you were to fall upon the stairs to your hall and break an arm I could deal with the fracture. But your illness requires the attention of a learned physician, which I am not."

"Bah. I have the attention of a learned physician. Blackwater tells me so daily. Little good it has done me. I gnaw upon boiled roosters and waste away, my humors no more balanced than ever."

"Will you continue his advice and consume a boiled rooster each day?" I asked.

The prince pursed his lips and said, "What else am I to do? I'll require of Blackwater that he prepare the physics you recommend, and consume them as well as the roosters." Prince Edward stood. "But for now we will return to the hall, and my household will be told of your warrant."

I bowed to the prince as he passed, and followed him through the doors leading to Kennington's great chamber. The two valets stood guard at the doors, bowed as the prince passed, and stared at me quizzically. There will be gossip in the servants' quarters this night, about the commoner who spent time with Prince Edward after the death of Sir Giles at dinner.

The prince made his way cautiously down the stairs. He knew that his weakened condition might cause his legs to collapse under him and send him plunging to the flags of his hall. Although this slow descent was quiet, those who remained in the hall heard, and these knights and ladies hurriedly gathered at the base of the stairs, bowing as the prince approached. I followed him at a respectful distance.

The hall had been cleared in our absence, tables dismounted and stacked against a wall, and benches drawn to one side. Musicians stood at the far end of the hall with their sackbuts and gitterns, awaiting Prince Edward's return and his command to blow and pluck upon their instruments. The order never came.

The prince halted upon the second step, where he could gaze out over the upraised faces surrounding him. I cannot guess what they expected their lord to say, but I'm certain 'twas other than what they heard.

"Sir Giles may have been poisoned," he began. "Within my hall. Such a thing is a grievous sin, if poison it truly was which took his life. If Sir Giles was slain I intend to see the felon rooted out. Behind me stands Master Hugh de Singleton. He did me good service before Limoges, discovering a murderer and easing my bellyache. I have this day made him chief constable of Kennington Palace and given him warrant to determine the cause of Sir Giles's death and find who has slain him, if indeed murder was done.

"Likely Master Hugh will wish to ask questions of those who dined in my hall this day," he continued, "as well as others not present. You are instructed to provide him with whatsoever aid he requires of you."

This last sentence the prince spoke in a low voice, slowly emphasizing each word. No man or woman present could mistake his meaning. The knights and gentlemen standing in the hall cast surreptitious glances at each other, perhaps wondering who the felon might be, or if they might be the next to imbibe a fatal draught, and one lady smiled behind a lifted hand. I wondered if 'twas me or my warrant she found amusing.

Her smile was warning enough that the inquiry laid upon me would not be well received by those whose station in life made them intolerant of lesser folk. Most men, regardless of rank, seem intolerant of lesser folk. Especially lesser folk who might seek from them information they would prefer not to divulge.

"You will keep me informed of your investigation," the prince continued, turning to me. This was a command, not voiced as a question. When he had spoken he turned and began to laboriously climb the stairs. A valet saw and leaped past me to follow his lord at a discreet distance, but close enough that he could arrest a fall should the prince stumble and topple back.

Sir Giles had enemies, Prince Edward had said. I thought it likely that his squire would know of these, and the reason for the enmity between his master and those who were his foes. From my vantage point on the stairs, behind Prince Edward, I had seen Sir Giles's squire, Randall Patchett, standing at the fringe of those assembled to hear the prince's announcement. I approached the lad. "We will walk in the privy garden," I said, and led the way through the hall to doors that opened onto a walled enclosure filled with walks and hedges and beds of flowers, of which Lady Joan was fond. As we crossed the hall I saw Arthur standing apart with several other grooms, and motioned for him to follow. He had been an observer of events and I thought to enquire later of him of any remarkable occurrences he might have witnessed while I was with Prince Edward in his privy chamber. Grooms, when in the company of gentlemen, learn to keep eyes and ears open and mouth shut.

Chapter 4

The afternoon was cool and cloudy. A light mist dampened the grass. Randall shivered, and I wondered if the cause was the chill or the death of Sir Giles.

"What will you do now that Sir Giles is dead?" I asked.

"Don't know. Haven't thought much on it. Mayhap there are knights at Kennington who will have me. I could serve Prince Edward," the lad said hopefully.

"Indeed. A great prince seems always to need more servants. You heard him speak of my charge. If I find your assistance of value in discovering if Sir Giles was slain I will tell Prince Edward of your good service."

I had no reason to think that the lad would not be forthcoming when I asked questions of him, but thought a bit of honey might sweeten his inclination. Indeed, I saw his downcast features lighten.

"Prince Edward has told me that Sir Giles was not an easy man to like," I began.

"I see that you are a tactful man," Randall replied. "He was easy to dislike, if that's what you mean."

"How about you? Did you find him easy to dislike?"

"I didn't slay him."

"Not what I asked." I said no more, but awaited his next words.

"Didn't much like him. But he dealt with me no worse than other knights with their squires, I think."

"How so?"

"Required of me that I serve him at his foulest tasks. When the cesspit at Wiching Castle needed to be emptied he set me to work with two grooms and a page to do the work. Knights were once squires and were likely treated the same, so now they do as was done to them. Could've hired gongfermors to dig out the pit, but set us to it to save six pence."

"Was that the worst you received at his hand?"

"Nay. I could wash away the stink of a cesspit. 'Twas his mocking. That was the most hurtful."

"How so?"

"I am not a great swordsman. When he saw that I had little skill with a blade he no longer spent time trying to teach me. Rather, he would scorn my lack of ability, most often when in the company of others, especially maids.

"I am a competent horseman. But Sir Giles would never comment upon that before other folk."

"Not before fair maids, eh?" I asked.

"Nay. Never then. When Amabil's friends were about he could be especially rancorous."

"Amabil?"

"His daughter. Sir Giles's wife died just after I came to his service as a page… ten years past. Maud was not as he is."

Randall's eyes seemed to lose focus, as if he attempted to see into his past. "She was kind, was Maud. Not like Sir Giles and Amabil."

"The daughter is much like the father?"

"Very much so. Folk say Sir Geoffrey will need to rule his house with a firm hand."

"Who is Sir Geoffrey?"

"Sir Geoffrey Paget. He will wed Amabil in a fortnight. The banns have been read."

"Prince Edward said that Sir Giles was also to marry."

"Aye. Next month. Lady Juliana Pultney, widow of Sir Henry Pultney."

"A prize catch, the prince said, with lands in two shires."

"Aye. And a beautiful lady. Could have had her pick of other knights."

"Your words and tone indicate surprise that she would have Sir Giles."

Randall said nothing to this, perhaps yet feeling some loyalty to his deceased knight.

"What other suitors did the Lady Juliana have?" I asked.

"I know of but one. Sir Arthur de Lisle. For sure there were others."

"Is Sir Arthur at Kennington?"

"Aye. He has a knight's fee of Prince Edward and is oft at Kennington."

"And is a disappointed suitor to Lady Juliana Pultney," I added.

The squire was silent for a moment. "You think he might've slain Sir Giles?"

"Men have slain other men for a woman's favor."

"And her lands," the lad added sagely.

"And her lands," I agreed. "Sir Arthur would have dined at the high table, I think. Which was he?"

"Wore a pale green cotehardie and sat to the dexter side as you would have faced the high table."

"The knight whose beard is nearly white?"

"Aye. The same. No older than Sir Giles, for all his beard makes him seem a grandfather."

"So there was bad blood between Sir Giles and Sir Arthur?"

"They would not speak... nor would one doff his cap to the other."

I wondered if Sir Arthur's lands were prosperous. A knight who found his purse nearly as empty as his bed might consider murder in order to fill both.

"What do you know of Sir Arthur? Where are his lands?"

"Gloucestershire. He spends little time there, I think. Whenever Sir Giles came to Kennington Sir Arthur was likely to be here already."

Would a knight abandon his own manor to dine at the prince's table if his lands were prosperous? He might. But perhaps Sir Arthur was a knight who needed both a wife and funds. Lady Juliana could provide both.

"What other men did Sir Giles dislike, or disliked him?"

"Sir Humphrey Downey and Sir Giles did not get along. Just after I entered Sir Giles's service King Edward authorized a tournament. Sir Giles and Sir Humphrey were paired against each other in a joust."

"And Sir Giles prevailed?" I asked.

"Aye. 'Twas to be a ceremony, they were told. Each knight

shattering a coronel-tipped lance or two against the other man's shield."

"The contest turned out differently?"

"Aye. Sir Giles unhorsed Sir Humphrey."

I could imagine how it happened. The knight's squires – Randall would not have been party to this, being at the time barely old enough to be a page – would have met beforehand and set the terms. Their masters would mount their dexters and pound toward each other, lances couched, and take careful aim at their opponent's shield. After breaking a lance or two the knights, honor satisfied, would retire to the king's pavilion and enjoy cups of wine and the praise of ladies.

But likely Sir Giles behaved treacherously, aiming his lance not at Sir Humphrey's shield, where it would be deflected and perhaps fracture harmlessly, but at Sir Humphrey's breastplate.

Would a knight slay another for such perfidy? Surely. The unhorsed knight would have injuries to both pride and body, and neither would be quick to mend. But would the affronted knight wait ten years to take his revenge?

"Did Sir Giles speak of this joust later, in your presence?" I asked.

"Aye, often. Liked to tell the tale. Would laugh about how he had deceived Sir Humphrey and pitched him to his rump."

Word of such hilarity at his expense would most likely return to Sir Humphrey. He would take offense anew each time he heard of it. Knights do not take insults lightly. 'Tis a wonder a decade had passed with no response to the slight. At least no response that Randall knew of.

Once or twice during this conversation I glanced over my shoulder and saw Arthur following at a discreet distance – not close enough to hear all that was said, but near enough to be of assistance should he be needed. He told me later that he was concerned about two possible events. That the squire might take offense at my questions, being guilty of Sir Giles's death, or that whoso had slain the knight might believe the squire would share evidence with me, and therefore seek to slay us both as we walked in the garden.

"Were these two Sir Giles's only serious enemies?" I continued.

"Oh, nay. There were others."

"Who?"

"Sir John Pedley hated Sir Giles fiercely. They've exchanged blows."

"Recently?"

"Aye. In Prince Edward's hall little more than a fortnight past."

"What cause?"

"Same as always. Sir Giles charged Sir John with cowardice at Crécy."

"As always? Sir Giles had made the charge before?"

"Aye."

"The battle was more than twenty years past," I said.

"The issue is yet fresh for Sir John."

"Did Sir Giles raise the accusation often?"

"I've heard him speak of it several times. Liked to tell of how he and Prince Edward stood shoulder to shoulder at Crécy. The memory would bring thoughts of Sir John to him and he would remark then upon Sir John's flight."

"Was Sir John assigned to the center, under the prince?"

"Aye."

"And he fled when the issue was in doubt?"

"So Sir Giles has claimed. Sir John protests 'twas not so. Says he rode to the king's position in reserve to seek help."

"Sir John did leave the combat, then?"

"Aye. And he did return, with twenty or so men at arms."

"No knights?"

"Nay. The king would not permit it. Sir John says when King Edward refused to release knights to Prince Edward's aid he set off to rejoin the prince and found on the way a small band of pikemen awaiting orders to reinforce whichever part of the army might be hard pressed. He told them to follow him. Sir John claims this reinforcement was crucial to Prince Edward being able to hold the center firm."

"But Sir Giles says otherwise?"

"Aye. Said the situation was well in hand when Sir John ran to the rear and mounted his beast."

"One man's word against another's. Do most men," I asked, "believe Sir Giles's version of the event, or Sir John's?"

"Hard to say. Sir John fought alongside the prince at Poitiers and I've heard no man speak ill of his valor on that field."

"And Prince Edward," I mused, "welcomes Sir John to Kennington." I thought that if the prince considered Sir John to have fled the field at Crécy when the battle was in doubt the knight would not be welcome in Kennington's hall.

"So there are three knights who will not mourn upon their pillows this night that Sir Giles's corpse lies under a shroud in Prince Edward's chapel. Is there a fourth, or more, who had cause to hate your master?"

"Hmmm. There are many, I think, who disliked Sir Giles. But hated him? Not enough to slay him and risk their own necks."

"Who are those who disliked him? Perhaps name one or two who disliked him most."

The squire rubbed his beardless chin for a moment. "Richard Rowell disliked Sir Giles and would have no more to do with him."

"*Sir* Richard Rowell?"

"Nay. No knight. Rowell is a mercer. Keeps a shop on Gracechurch Street, near to St. Peter's, Cornhill."

"Why would a mercer be set against Sir Giles?"

"Owed Rowell for linen and silks he'd not paid for."

"How much?" I asked.

"Don't know of a certainty. A few months past I overheard hot words exchanged between Sir Giles and Rowell. Sir Giles wanted more silks and the mercer would send him none 'til he paid his debt for the goods Rowell had already provided."

"Was the amount mentioned?"

"Aye. Mayhap near to twelve pounds, although I couldn't hear plainly enough to swear to it."

A man who cannot pay his mercer is likely to be indebted to grocers and glovers and butchers and other such folk. It was no wonder that he sought the hand of a rich widow, and became genial in her presence, if such was required to woo and win the lady.

But would a man slay another if in doing so he would lose all hope of recovering such a debt? Dead men pay no accounts, and good luck to a burgher who goes to court against a knight's heirs.

Of course, the mercer had not been present in Kennington's hall when Sir Giles died, but if the death was due to poisoned wine, as I thought likely, he would not need to be. A valet could have defiled the fatal draught, bribed to do so, and this exchange could have been accomplished just as easily by an absent London burgher as by some antagonistic knight present in the hall when Sir Giles entered into St. Peter's presence.

"Are there others who come to mind who might be pleased that Sir Giles is no more?"

"None he had so vexed that they would slay him, I think," Randall replied.

During our discussion we had circled the palace garden and now found ourselves back at the door which led into the hall.

"If another adversary occurs to you, I would hear of the man," I said, and pushed the heavy oaken door open. The mist had become heavier, and I was pleased to return to the hall. Fires blazed upon the three hearths which heated the great hall, and knights and ladies who warmed themselves before them turned as one and fell silent as we entered. Few men can enter a room and terminate a conversation as well as he who is assigned to send some man to a scaffold.

Arthur had followed our circumnavigation of the garden, and when we entered the hall and I dismissed Randall he touched me upon the shoulder and whispered in my ear.

"You was followed," he said.

"When? In the garden?"

Arthur nodded.

"By whom? Do you recognize him here?" I motioned to the knights and ladies who were gradually returning to the conversations my appearance had interrupted.

"Wasn't a him. 'Twas a her."

"Some woman followed me... us in the garden?"

"Aye. Kept herself hid. Made sure you never saw 'er. Stayed behind hedges. Not close enough to hear what you was sayin', I think, 'cept mayhap once when she got one side of a hedge when you an' that squire was close by on the other."

"Is she present now in the hall?"

Arthur glanced over my shoulder, scanned the gentlefolk warming themselves near the hearths, and shook his head.

"What was her appearance?" I asked. "Young, or a matron?"

"Young. No lass, but not wed. I was close enough that I saw she'd no ring upon her finger. Not the finger what would tell folks she'd a husband. Black hair, not braided nor worn up, but loose."

Here, in addition to the absence of a ring, was further evidence that the young woman was unwed. Did she follow because of an interest in Randall Patchett, or in me? I resolved to learn more of this maiden and her furtive presence in a wet garden.

Chapter 5

But first I wished to learn what I could of tainted wine, if indeed 'twas the wine which brought Sir Giles to rest upon a bier before the altar of Kennington Palace chapel.

While walking with Randall, a possible way of discovering if Sir Giles's wine had been poisoned occurred to me. The garden wall is not high, and from a rise in the path I could see over it to a meadow where sheep grazed. Could a lamb be persuaded to drink from a pan of wine set before it?

The butler had done as Prince Edward required, and six ewers rested upon a table in the buttery. The butler had heard the prince's command that I was to be given all cooperation in the investigation of Sir Giles's death, and was eager to please.

"The sheep in the meadow beyond the garden wall – whose are they?" I asked him.

"Prince Edward's. The meadow and forest beyond are all a part of Kennington Palace and devolve to the Duke of Cornwall," the butler replied.

"Send a groom to find the reeve," I said, "and require of him that he bring six lambs to the palace. Tell him to bring them to the gate in the garden wall, and make haste."

The butler tugged his forelock and called to a lad who had just then emerged from the pantry. He relayed my instructions to the youth and the boy scurried off. The butler seemed puzzled.

I went to the table to inspect the ewers. Five of the six were about half full. One was nearly empty. I asked the butler which of the ewers the missing Arnaud had used to fill Sir Giles's cup. I received a shrug in reply. This I expected.

The ewers were of a matching set, in silver, as would be expected of a royal house. A skilled silversmith had cunningly engraved St. George and the dragon on each, and the representations were so much alike 'twould be impossible to identify one ewer from another by the designs.

Arthur peered over one shoulder and the butler over the other as I sniffed at the contents of each ewer. I could detect no difference in the six ewers. I wished that Kate might be present. My wife has the nose of a lymer and can detect from a hundred paces an odor which would not offend my nostrils at an arm's length. I have heard other men say the same of their wives. I thought of the ladies in the hall and considered asking if one of them would consent to holding her nose above each ewer, seeking some off-putting scent, but quickly dismissed the thought as impolitic.

A small window illuminated the buttery. I held each ewer close to the glass to learn if the contents of one of them might be slightly different in color. I could discern no change from one ewer to another.

There was one test I would not make. I would not touch my tongue to the wine in any of the ewers seeking some bitter flavor. Perhaps had I allowed Dr. Blackwater to taste the wine which remained in Sir Giles's cup I might now know if 'twas poisoned wine which took the knight's life or the failure of his heart. But Blackwater might now also rest before the altar in Kennington's chapel.

As I set the last ewer back upon the table, the youth sent to deliver my message to the reeve returned.

"Reeve says he'll have six lambs at the garden gate betimes."

I told the butler that I would need a shallow pan, and the six ewers brought to the garden gate. The puzzled expression returned to the man's face, but he did not question my request. He told me that he would gather a few grooms and return anon. He did so.

Once again the gentlefolk gathered in the hall had cause to interrupt their conversation. I led a parade from the screens passage across the hall to the garden door. Behind me came Prince Edward's butler carrying a copper pan. Behind him were three grooms, each carrying two silver ewers, and behind them Arthur. I bowed as I passed the knights and their ladies, and received open-mouthed stares in reply.

The garden grass was wet, but the misty rain had ceased. The reeve and three assistants appeared on the outer side of the gate as

I approached from the garden side. I raised the latch and opened the gate to the reeve, his men, and six protesting lambs.

I soon learned that sheep have no interest in wine, not even the finest burgundy. I poured wine from a ewer into the copper pan and set it upon the grass before a lamb. The creature wriggled its nose and turned away. Stronger measures would be required.

I explained to the reeve what I intended. He grasped the lamb tight, and I pried open its mouth and poured wine into the protesting animal's throat. Some of the wine dribbled over the lamb's chin, but most was swallowed.

I told the reeve to release the beast and explained what I had done. He knew of Sir Giles's death, so was quick to comprehend what I was about.

Hemlock can kill a man in minutes if the dose is strong enough. How much of the stuff would be required to kill a lamb? I knew not. A man may weigh ten or twelve stone or more. The lamb weighed little more than two stone. Did this mean that one-fifth of the poison required to slay a man would have the same effect upon a lamb? Who could know? I thought it likely that I was about to learn.

The lamb scampered off, then sensing no further threat began cropping the wet grass. We six watched the animal intently. It showed no sign of distress even after half an hour had passed.

To pour wine from six ewers down the gullets of an equal number of lambs, then wait to observe the results, would take 'til near dark. I considered the five remaining ewers.

If I had been paid to poison a man's wine I would be careful to collect only enough wine from the butt to destroy one man, I think. If wine remained in a tainted ewer there would be a chance – nay, a likelihood – that the defiled wine would eventually be consumed, and another, unintended, corpse would be found in Kennington Palace. And if only a small flask of poison was available to the killer, to add the stuff to a full ewer might dilute it enough that the intended victim might suffer but a terrible stomach ache or swoon, but then recover. This might depend upon the toxin used.

I selected next the ewer which was nearly empty. A lamb was chosen, and proved as obdurate as the first when confronted with wine. As before, the reeve held the animal tight while I poured wine into the lamb's throat.

When the work was done and the lamb released, it snorted with displeasure, trotted to its companion, and soon forgot its pique, joining the first lamb in cropping the moist grass.

One lamb is much like another. As we watched them it occurred to me that if one should collapse and die I might confuse the second lamb with the first. I told the reeve to seize the first lamb and put it outside the garden gate. He did so.

A few minutes later the second lamb looked up from grazing and began to walk in a circle. The creature stopped this after two or three turns and shook its head. A moment later the lamb took a step, stumbled, and dropped to its knees. It tried to rise, but could not. Within moments the lamb lost all sense of balance, fell to the grass, then lay silent. I knelt over the animal and saw its chest heave, then become still. The lamb was dead. Sir Giles's wine, as I had suspected, had been poisoned. The knight's heart had not failed him, nor were his humors out of joint.

The valet Arnaud had disappeared. The conclusion of the matter was plain, as was the poison. 'Twas surely hemlock. Arnaud had placed poisoned wine before Sir Giles. I needed to speak to Randall Patchett to learn if there was some reason the valet might have done so of his own volition. I doubted this was so. He was surely hired to do this evil, and likewise paid to disappear. The fee was likely significant, for Arnaud would be risking a noose and abandoning a lucrative post. Find Arnaud, and with the proper encouragement from Prince Edward's serjeants he would likely divulge his employer.

"Do not permit anyone to consume the flesh of this lamb," I said to the reeve. "The wine was poisoned, and the lamb's flesh may now be also. See that it is burned, immediately."

I did not know if the lamb's flesh was now contaminated, but did not wish to risk some other man's life to learn if this was so.

"And pour out the wine from the other ewers also," I said to the butler. It was unlikely that the wine in those ewers was tainted, but who would want to risk discovering if it was or not?

I left Arthur in the hall and sought Prince Edward's chamberlain. I found the fellow in the prince's wardrobe, advising two seamstresses upon the creation of a silken doublet for the prince. 'Tis unlikely they needed instruction from him for the work, and I conjectured that his discourse would be the subject of some merriment in the servants' hall later that day.

I told the fellow I had news for his master and required him to accompany me to Prince Edward's presence. The fellow had heard his lord announce my warrant, and so turned without a word and led me from the wardrobe. I saw the seamstresses glance up from their labor with gratitude in their eyes.

Two valets, as was usual, stood at the door to the privy chamber. They stood aside as the chamberlain approached and rapped upon the door. The door opened immediately. The valet whose duty this was recognized me, turned, and said, "Master Hugh, m'lord."

From the privy chamber I heard, "Bid him enter," in a voice barely above a whisper. The chamberlain would have followed me into Prince Edward's presence, but the prince waved him off. He bowed and backed through the door to the great chamber.

When Prince Edward had wed Joan, Countess of Kent and his cousin, she was known throughout the realm as the Fair Maid of Kent. That was eleven years past, but the duchess had lost little of her beauty. She sat upon a cushioned chair beside her husband. In a corner a fair-haired child played with wooden knights and horses. Here was Richard of Bordeaux, now five years old, and heir to the throne of England since the death of his older brother Edward to plague two years past.

The little lad looked up from his play as I entered. I removed my cap, bowed to Prince Edward and the duchess in turn, and hoped the sequence was according to court proceedings. I am not well versed in courtly manners.

Evidently the order was appropriate, for the duchess gave no sign of disapproval.

"Here is Master Hugh, the surgeon to Gilbert Talbot I told you of," the prince said to his wife with as much strength as he could muster.

"I am in your debt," the lady said, "for the relief you provided my husband two years past. I pray you will be able to do so again." The duchess completed her words with a worried glance toward Prince Edward.

"You are not here about my health, I think," Prince Edward said, directing his attention to me. His strength was depleted, but not his will or intellect. "What have you learned of Sir Giles's death?"

"'Twas indeed poison which struck him down," I said, and told him of the experiment with lambs which proved it so.

"The valet... Arnaud. 'Twas he which delivered the poison to Sir Giles?"

"So I believe. Your constables and bailiff cannot find him."

"And why else would he flee the palace, eh?"

"Why, indeed."

"What do you suggest? How are we to find the rogue? He holds the solution to this murder."

"Aye, he does," I agreed. "How long has Arnaud been in your employ, m'lord?"

The prince pulled upon his beard for a moment before replying. "Three years, thereabouts."

"Other grooms and valets in your service will know him, then."

"They will. What is your point?"

"Order your bailiff and constables to divide the city by parishes and send out grooms and valets to prowl the streets of each parish seeking Arnaud."

"I have given you warrant. Do as you wish," the prince said.

He had settled the matter. As he gestured dismissal I took in with concern the shadowed eyes and pallor of his face. I surely hoped my herbal concoction would bring some relief. I bowed to Prince Edward and his duchess, and backed to the door. I had no practice at departing from the presence of royalty, so hoped that I was retreating in the direction of the valet who guarded the privy chamber door rather than toward the wall. My aim was good. I found the opening and backed through it.

It was nearly dusk. There was too little daylight remaining to organize and carry out a search of the city. Arnaud would be safe from apprehension for a few more hours. But I could use the remainder of the day to advise the prince's constables and serjeants of what must be done on the morrow. They, in turn, could assign grooms and valets and pages for the hunt which could begin at dawn.

Prince Edward's chamberlain allocated me a sleeping chamber and said that Arthur would be accommodated with the palace grooms. He was nonplussed when I told him that I preferred Arthur to share the chamber he had appointed to me. I asked that he provide a pallet. Arthur is no fool. I have found it useful in past encounters with felons to have Arthur's opinion, which he is not hesitant to provide. And in seeking miscreants I have often found such men prone to violence when found out. Arthur is constructed like a tun set upon two beech stumps, and a frown from him will usually dissuade men from their intended villainy.

The only lamentable consequence of my request was Arthur's snoring. The man falls to sleep readily – as one who lays his head upon a pillow with a clear conscience – so his snores oft begin before my own slumber. Perhaps I have shared a chamber with Arthur often enough that I am becoming accustomed to his rasping and snorting, but the immunity is slow to acquire.

Moments after a groom produced a pallet, the bell sounded for supper. Prince Edward did not appear, although Lady Joan did. Perhaps he dined alone in his privy chamber upon something other than boiled rooster and did not wish for Dr. Blackwater to know.

Knights of the prince's household and their ladies at the high table supped upon roasted partridge, cormarye, and aloes of lamb, while we lesser folk contented ourselves with a porre of peas and wheaten bread with parsley butter.

The musicians whose entertainment was curtailed earlier in the day appeared, tables and benches were cleared away, and knights and ladies danced. The death of one of their own but a few hours before seemed no longer to darken their mood. Perhaps Sir Giles's demise brought joy rather than sorrow to most of the company.

Among the dancers was a vivacious, dark-haired damsel and her youthful swain. I wondered who she was, and if she was the lass who had followed me and Randall Patchett about the garden. There was no other maid dancing who might fit the description Arthur had provided. Seeing him leaning against a wall in conversation with other grooms, I made my way to him.

"Aye," he said, when I asked of the dancing lass. "She be the one."

Randall Patchett stood glumly by the wall a few paces distant. Perhaps the maid's interest had been directed toward him rather than me. This seemed a reasonable assumption. He is young, tall, and possesses a handsome visage, whereas I have now a few silver whiskers flecking my beard and possess a large nose over which I view the world.

"Amabil Cheyne," the squire answered when I asked of the maid.

"Cheyne? Sir Giles's daughter?"

"Aye, the same."

"With whom does she dance?"

"Sir Geoffrey Paget."

"She was observed this day following us in the garden, trying not to be seen. What interest has she in you and to whom you might speak?"

"Don't know," the squire shrugged. "She never paid me attention in the past."

"Did you once wish for her attention?"

"Once. Look at her. Most men would be pleased to win her attention. Until they received it."

"Why not then?"

"The knight who weds her will soon wish to be called to the king's service in France," Randall said with a wry grin. "She will be on her husband's back more than at his side."

"Her disposition does not match her face?"

"It does not."

"She does not seem much distressed at her father's death," I said.

"I think she would not feel sorrow for any man's death, unless he had been useful to her and would no longer be."

"Her father was no longer useful to her?"

"Oh, he'd provide a good dowry. She'll inherit his lands now, of course. Only child Sir Giles and Lady Maud had."

Such a legacy would be greater than any dowry the knight would have provided his daughter. Would a maid see her father murdered? Randall's description of Amabil was not flattering. What of Sir Geoffrey Paget? I asked the squire his opinion of the man.

"I've had little to do with him," Randall replied. "Gossip says that his father has gambled away much of the family wealth, so Sir Geoffrey was on the hunt for riches as well as a bride."

Here was no rare thing. Daughters who will inherit – and wealthy widows – are popular beyond their fleshly charms. The bloom may fade from a rose, but its fragrance lingers.

"Amabil was, or is, content with this?" I said.

"She is wise enough to know her worth. Sir Geoffrey may be the rooster, but she will rule the roost."

"You believe the fellow will permit this?"

"Aye. From what little I know of him I cannot see Sir Geoffrey standing up to Amabil."

Night darkened the hall windows. Valets lit candles and the musicians continued their entertainment, although the dancers were fewer.

Much had transpired this day. When I arose in the morning at the Priory of St. Bartholomew my vision for the future was that I would acquaint Prince Edward and his physician with the herbs that might ease the prince's ailment – herbs the physician should have already known – and after having done this Arthur and I would return to Bampton and our wives and families. Now I was assigned to ferret out a murderer, and could not escape the task, onerous as it might be, considering who had delegated the work to me.

Discovering a felon would be best accomplished well rested. I motioned to Arthur to follow, then took a lighted cresset from a shelf where they were kept ready for those who sought to illuminate their way to their beds, passed through a corridor which led to our chamber, and sought rest.

As always, Arthur was snoring soon after his head dented his pillow. On such occasions I find it a valuable use of time to consider any matters perplexing me while awaiting Morpheus to overcome Arthur's rumbling.

On the morrow I planned to send pages, grooms, valets, and Kennington's constables throughout the city seeking Arnaud. Would this be fruitless? Where would the man most likely seek refuge? Was he from London? Had he family members in the city? Would he go to them for aid? These questions should be answered before seekers went out helter-skelter seeking a fugitive where he might not be.

Chapter 6

Next morning I asked the assembled valets who had worked alongside Arnaud for information of his family and his home. Several knew the man well enough to know these things.

"Tonge was 'is name. Arnaud Tonge," one said. "Hailed from Faringdon Within."

Faringdon Within is within London's walls, near to the Aldersgate, as opposed to Faringdon Without, which lies to the west, beyond Newgate. At the time I did not know this geography, but I learned soon enough.

Armed with the knowledge of his name and home I sent the searchers, all of whom could recognize Arnaud Tonge if they saw him, to prowl the streets between St. Paul's Cathedral, Aldersgate, and Newgate. I sent them out in threes, so that if they found the valet and he was reluctant to accompany them back to Kennington Palace they would have enough strength to compel him to do so.

There was no reason for me or Arthur to join the search. I had likely laid eyes upon Arnaud as he poured Sir Giles's fatal wine, but had no recollection of the man and would not know him if I came face to face with him. He would surely have discarded Prince Edward's livery, so would appear garbed as any other man thronging London's streets. I told the seekers that I would await them by St. Magnus' Church, at the north end of London Bridge, when the noon Angelus Bell rang. If Arnaud was not found in the morning, we would return to the palace for our dinner, then resume the hunt in the afternoon.

Gentlemen and their ladies began to enter the hall as the searchers departed. There was to be hawking this day, I heard one say, in Kennington Park.

The valets who remained at the palace set out bread and meat and wine for the hunting party. It was consumed rapidly, the knights and their ladies being eager to go to their sport. Prince Edward did not join them. If William Blackwater had prepared and provided the herbs I suggested for the prince the physic had not yet improved his complexio.

Arthur and I departed the palace shortly after those I had sent to hunt for Arnaud in the streets to the north of St. Paul's. We elbowed our way through the hordes of men, horses, and carts all trying to cross London Bridge at the same time. May angels befriend any man who might stumble and fall upon the bridge. We were spewed out at the north end of London Bridge, and 'twas a relief to leave the stream of commerce and seek refuge beside the wall of St. Magnus' Church.

A few folk left the crowded street to enter the church, but most passed hurriedly by about their business, having no interest in two men standing apart, leaning against the church wall.

More than an hour after we took station at St. Magnus' Church I heard a commotion at the north end of the bridge, where a lane leads west along the river bank to Cold Harbour and the Steelyard. A group of ferrymen were pointing to the river, and as Arthur and I watched, one of these hoisted oars upon his shoulder and disappeared as he descended to the river. I assumed his boat was beached there.

It was. A few minutes later the man reappeared, the crowd parting to let him pass. Behind the fellow another man appeared, and behind him a third. These two carried between them a limp body.

"Fished some fellow from the river," Arthur said.

This was surely so, and I had an idea as to who the drowned man might be, for he wore black, the color of Prince Edward's livery, and I thought I caught a glimpse of the prince's badge, also black, with three white ostrich feathers embroidered upon it, sewn upon the tunic.

"Come," I said, and together we hurried across Bridge Street – easier to do now than an hour earlier, since the worst of the morning crush had passed – and pushed close to the corpse, now laid out upon the cobbles.

The men who drew the corpse from the river asked of each other and those who had gathered at the place if any knew who lay dead at their feet. No man did, which seemed to surprise them, as those who work upon the water are likely to know most of the others engaged in the business.

One after another shrugged in ignorance. I came close enough to identify the sodden, muddied clothing of the dead man. 'Twas Prince Edward's livery he wore, and no doubt of it. The ferrymen surely knew this also.

"The man is likely Arnaud Tonge," I said. "Valet to the Duke of Cornwall. See, he wears the prince's livery."

The ferrymen cast their eyes down to the corpse, then eyed one another as if seeking confirmation of my assertion. One spoke.

"What's to be done with 'im, then?"

"I will take the man to Kennington Palace. You need not trouble yourselves about him. Where was he when you found him? The tide is receding and the river's flow is strong."

"Seen a foot caught just there," one of the boatmen pointed, "stuck fast between the pilings."

The place indicated was on the upstream side of the bridge. Arnaud, if it was indeed he who lay upon the cobbles, had gone into the Thames somewhere to the west of the bridge, and the current had carried him to the place. Or he had gone into the water from the bridge, on the western side, and fetched up against the pilings as he entered the water. Was he dead or alive when this took place?

I saw no purse. This might mean that Arnaud had been slain for what it had contained, or it might be that he wore it under his tunic, as men in London oft do, so as to avoid losing it to a cut-purse. I examined the dead man's tunic, but found no lump of a purse hidden under it.

Early in the day carts loaded with grain and other victuals brought from the south of London had entered the city. Some had already unloaded their goods and were retracing their journey to the villages whence the provender came. I hailed one of these carters, offering the man six pence to convey me and a corpse to Kennington Palace. I told Arthur to remain at St. Magnus' Church to advise those who would have searched in vain that Arnaud had been found. So I thought.

"Hold! What is this?" a voice roared out as Arthur and two of the ferrymen loaded the corpse into the cart. The man who pushed his way through the gathered throng was clearly accustomed to exercising authority, and I saw a badge sewn upon his tunic. 'Twas a serjeant of London's sheriff who had come upon the scene. I was accustomed to my place in Bampton, where, as bailiff, my jurisdiction was supreme – but for Lord Gilbert. I had not considered that in London others had authority greater than my own.

Several voices spoke at once, informing the sheriff's man of what had occurred. My own was one of these. The serjeant shouted for all to be silent, then advanced to me. He had seen that others were deferring to my instructions, and demanded of me who was dead in the cart and where the corpse was to be taken.

I told him. And I told him that I had the authority of Prince Edward. The serjeant folded his arms skeptically. I invited the fellow to accompany me and the corpse to Kennington Palace and hear from the prince's mouth that what I said was true.

The serjeant was reluctant to do this. His warrant ended once we were across the bridge, and if what I had said of my duty to Prince Edward proved false he would have no authority in Southwark to detain me or seize the dead man and return us both to the sheriff and mayor of London.

As the serjeant pondered my offer, the first of the grooms and pages I had sent to seek Arnaud Tonge appeared. The two men and the lad all wore the prince's livery. I greeted the fellows and one replied, telling of their lack of success. Then his eyes settled upon the sodden corpse resting in the cart. 'Twas clear to him as he came near that the dead man was clothed in the same way he was, and wore Prince Edward's badge.

"Who's that?" he said.

"Come near. 'Tis Arnaud," I said.

The three pressed close to the cart. The perplexed serjeant watched, his brawny arms yet folded across his chest.

The older of the grooms bent over the side of the cart to view the dead man. "Ain't 'im," he said.

"What? This is not Arnaud?" I was now as perplexed as the serjeant. "He wears Prince Edward's livery, same as you. Has any other of the prince's servants gone missing in the past days?"

"Nay. But this man is not Arnaud. This fellow's hair and beard are brown. Arnaud was fair."

Perhaps the water had transformed his coloration, I thought. "What color were Arnaud's eyes?" I asked.

"Blue," the groom said.

I lifted an eyelid of the corpse. The iris was brown.

"Well?" the groom said.

"If Arnaud's eyes were blue and his hair fair, then you speak true. This is not Arnaud."

"Wonder who 'e could be," the groom thought aloud. "Wearin' the duke's livery, an' no doubt of that."

I also wondered who it was who lay dead in the cart. I began a closer inspection of the corpse and saw things I should have noted before, but did not, seeing only the livery and badge.

The dead man's hair and beard were matted and unkempt. Neither had seen a razor or comb for many days, or even weeks. I lifted a cold, wet hand. The fingernails were long, untrimmed, and filthy. Prince Edward would not have permitted such an appearance in one of his valets. He would not even have permitted a groom to be so slovenly.

The prince's servants are well fed. The corpse was scrawny. I lifted a sleeve and saw a bony wrist devoid of much flesh, and under the beard the dead man's neck was withered under sagging skin.

Before me lay a man who had acquired the livery and badge of a servant to Prince Edward. The only missing servant, if the groom spoke true, was Arnaud. It must be, then, that 'twas Arnaud's tunic and badge which had led me to believe this was Arnaud drawn from the Thames dead.

How did such a man get possession of Arnaud's tunic? Was it given to him? Did he slay the valet for the garment? Did he find it discarded? And for any of these questions, why, and how? And did his possession of the tunic lead to his death in the river?

Whatever the answers to these questions might be 'twas now certain that Arnaud could not be identified by Prince Edward's livery and badge. He would, if alive, be upon the streets garbed as any man. If he had not fled London. Had the valet been paid to poison Sir Giles's wine? I was sure of it. Had he been paid well enough that he could travel far from London? Had he already begun the journey?

The serjeant yet stood over the corpse, arms folded. He peered from me to the boatmen to the prince's newly arrived grooms to the corpse. His enthusiasm for taking control of the situation had waned. He foresaw, I think, a complication for his life this day which he would prefer to avoid. Better this corpse trouble some other man's life. Mine, perhaps.

"You act as the duke's agent in this business?" the serjeant said, then glanced to the prince's servants as if seeking confirmation.

They nodded.

"I'll release the dead man to you, then," he said, and without another word turned and strode around St. Magnus' Church and disappeared in the direction of Billingsgate.

Three more of the searchers appeared as the serjeant departed the scene. I was about to order the carter to set off for Southwark and Kennington Palace when they approached – hurriedly, I thought, as if they had information about Arnaud. They did.

The new arrivals glanced at the corpse in the cart and I explained as much of the matter as was known. One known thing was that we had not found Arnaud Tonge dead in the Thames.

"We found 'is brother's 'ouse," a valet announced when I had related to the fellows the events of the past hour and the mystery of the corpse clothed in Prince Edward's livery.

"Went about the streets near to St. Paul's askin' folk if any knew Arnaud. Found a man what knew Alan Tonge, 'is brother. The fellow said this Alan bragged about 'is brother bein' valet to the duke. Brother's 'ouse is on a lane just off the Shambles, across from Greyfriars Church."

"Did you question the man about his brother? Has he seen Arnaud in the past day?"

"Wasn't 'ome. Wife was there. She said Alan was off on 'is business somewhere. Didn't know where. She thought likely he'd gone to the villages north of London where 'e buys 'ides."

"This Alan Tonge is a skinner? Has he an appprentice?"

"Don't know," the valet replied. "Probably. Didn't ask."

"One of you who knows the way to the skinner's house, come with me. Arthur, you come also. The others, accompany this carter to Kennington Palace and see that the marshal pays him six pence for his trouble. Put the corpse upon a catafalque before the chapel altar and tell all that nothing is to be done to the dead man until I have examined him. He is not even to be washed for burial. Not yet."

The cart and its escort of Prince Edward's grooms and valets made for the bridge, and gawkers departed about their interrupted business. Meanwhile the valet who had volunteered to show us Alan Tonge's house led Arthur and me through teeming streets, past St. Paul's. When we came to the Shambles I bid the fellow halt. I wished to approach cautiously, unannounced, and observe the place for a while before seeking the skinner's wife or apprentice. I was suspicious of the woman's claim that her husband had departed to seek hides in villages away from the city. Every day animals are driven to London and slaughtered, their flesh feeding the citizens. Which means there are hundreds of skins available each day. Although, to be sure, skins of some creatures – beaver, otter, squirrel, rabbit, and fox, for example – are not plentiful in London and must be sought elsewhere. Perhaps Alan Tonge had a commission to make a robe of rabbit skins. 'Twas possible that he might tour the villages for men who could supply such skins.

I was shown the lane where Alan Tonge resided, and the house. It was substantial, the home of a prosperous burgher. Its upper story was built out over the narrow lane, as was that of the house opposite. The two dwellings came so close together that little sunlight passed between them to the lane.

From the south end of the lane, standing in the shadows of Greyfriars Church, we had a clear view of the skinner's house. Beside the structure was a narrow alley which led, I assumed, to a shop in the rear.

I watched as a baxter approached, calling out her goods and the price, and as she came to the skinner's house a lass of twelve or so years ran from the door and spoke to the woman. We were too far away to hear the conversation, but not so far that we could not count. The lass held out a sack and the baxter placed six pies in it. The maid placed coins in the woman's hand, and the transaction complete, the lass scurried into the house while the baxter resumed bawling out her trade.

"How many children did you see in the house when you spoke to the woman?" I asked the valet.

The man scratched his head, assembling his memories of the encounter. "Two, I think. That lass what just bought the pies, an' a little 'un."

"How old would you say the younger child was?"

The valet shrugged. "Seven... mayhap eight."

The pies were large. A lass of twelve years and a child of eight years would likely together eat but one. The mother might consume another, if near to starving. Why four more pies than required? Perhaps there were more children in the house than the valet had seen. But enough to eat four large pies filled with stockfish and turnips, as we had heard the vendor proclaiming? It was yet warm enough that pies unconsumed would soon go bad. And the baxter would surely walk this way again on the morrow when pies fresh from the baker might be had. Most such sellers have a regular route for their trade so customers may expect their approach. Something smelled about this business and it was not putrid pies.

If Arnaud Tonge, his brother Alan, and an apprentice were within the house, they would account for the pies I thought excessive for a woman and two children. The thought of crusty pies, filled with fish and turnips, caused my stomach to growl. No doubt the gentlefolk of Kennington Palace had returned from hawking and were at table in the hall, enjoying Prince Edward's hospitality.

We three could stand in the shadows of Greyfriars Church until the sun set and not know if men were hidden in the skinner's house. And when darkness came, the night would conceal any man who departed the place. If Arnaud was not within his brother's house, the longer I waited, the more time the fellow would have to escape. While those within the house were consuming their dinner would be a good time to set a scheme in play.

I told Arthur to go quietly through the alley to the rear of the house, where I assumed the skinner's workshop would be found. The only window visible which opened to the alley was of oiled skin, appropriate to the owner's business, so Arthur would not be seen passing through the alley, so long as his shadow did not pass over the window. I warned him of this, and told him I would give him sufficient time to position himself before any door which opened to the alley. The valet and I would present ourselves at the front door and demand of the matron license to speak to her husband's apprentice, if such a lad was within, and to search rooms if the woman protested that she was alone with her children. Prince Edward's badge upon the valet's tunic would act as incentive for the woman to do as asked. If men were within the house, heard my words, and attempted to flee through the alley, Arthur would be well placed to intercept them.

As I concluded these instructions I saw Arthur glance over my shoulder. I turned to see what had caught his eye. A weary and ancient runcie drew a cart upon which sat two men. This cart had entered the lane beyond Northumberland Inn and was perhaps a hundred paces distant from our location. Yet from that distance 'twas possible to see that one of the fellows upon the cart was not grown to manhood and wore no beard. Here might be a craftsman and his apprentice. I held out a hand to restrain Arthur, who was about to set off for the alley as I had bid him do.

As we watched, the horse and cart turned into the alley. Here was the skinner and either a son or apprentice. Likely the man's wife had spoken true. He had been out of the city seeking skins and had now returned. What, then, of the extra pies? Had the skinner's wife expected his return and prepared for it?

"Come," I said, and led the way from the church to the alley, thence to the rear of the house. There was indeed a shop attached there and beyond that a small barn. The horse and cart were halted before the barn, and the man and boy were lifting a bundle from the cart and carrying it into the shop. The runcie stood motionless but for an occasional flick of ears and tail, likely pleased that its labors were concluded.

The skinner appeared in his workshop door, saw the three of us approach, and stopped in his tracks. I saw dismay in his eyes and thought, "Ah, he sees Prince Edward's badge on the valet and fears his brother being found within his house." I failed to consider that a man going about his lawful business might be alarmed to meet three strange men at his door, one wearing the badge and livery of a great prince, another assembled like a cask of salted stockfish set upon two ship's masts.

"You are Alan Tonge?" I asked.

"Aye. Who be you?"

"I am Hugh de Singleton, bailiff to Lord Gilbert Talbot, but serving Prince Edward this day. Your brother is Arnaud Tonge, a valet to the prince, is he not?"

"Aye, Arnaud is me brother and serves the prince."

"Have you seen him in the past day or two?"

"Nay. I've been away seeking fox pelts. Sir John Relyk wishes a fur coat of me before winter arrives. An' Arnaud's duties keep him at Kennington or Berkhampstead... wherever the duke might be. Haven't seen Arnaud since" – the skinner pulled at his beard – "Candlemas."

Alan Tonge was claiming not to have seen his brother for eight months. This did not mean that Arnaud might not be within his house. The man's wife would have admitted her brother-in-law even if her husband had been away.

"Why do you ask of Arnaud?" the man said, glancing at Prince Edward's badge upon the valet's tunic. "Do you seek him? Is he not at Kennington? Last I knew, the prince was in residence there."

I decided to tell Alan as little about his brother's disappearance as possible.

"Your brother left Kennington Palace sometime during the prince's dinner yesterday. He has not been seen since. Prince Edward is concerned for his welfare and has sent us and others to search for him. Perhaps he came here while you were away?"

"Not likely, but mayhap. Why'd he leave the duke's employ?"

"If we find him, perhaps he will tell us."

"Mary will know if Arnaud's been here. Come."

The skinner waved us into his shop, which smelled of hides and rancid flesh and the urine used in tanning. The youth stood aside to allow us to pass, then walked to the cart for the last bundle of skins.

"Ah. Thought I 'eard voices," Alan's wife called through from the passage leading into the shop from their living quarters. "So you're 'ome. Did you – oh" The woman then saw us behind her husband as she came into the doorway and fell silent. "Who's this?" she finally said.

"Men in Prince Edward's employ," the skinner said. "Arnaud's gone missing and the prince wishes 'im found."

"Men came this morning seeking Arnaud," Mary said. "Told 'em you was away an' Arnaud's not been 'ere. They wore the prince's badge, as that fellow does."

"A short time ago a lass from this house bought six pies from a baxter," I said. "How many of you are here present to consume six pies?"

I thought to catch the woman in some falsehood, but rather 'twas me caught out as Mary enumerated the inhabitants of her house. So I thought.

"Well, there's me an' the children. Alan's elderly father an' mother, what lives up the stairs, an' I had Millie buy two more 'cos I thought Alan an' John might return today, an' did they do so they'd be hungry."

"As I am," Alan added.

I could see no point in delving more deeply into Tonge family matters. Either Arnaud had not visited the house since yesterday or Alan and Mary were skilled players. And as for the many pies brought to the house this day, I had heard, as Mary related the inhabitants, the scraping of a chair upon the floor of the upper story just over my head. Someone was there. Who, and how many pies they might consume, I would trust the woman to know.

I told the skinner that if he learned anything of his brother's whereabouts he should send his apprentice to Kennington Palace with the news. He promised to do so, and seemed genuinely worried about what might have become of Arnaud.

Chapter 7

Arthur, the valet, and I made our way through London's crowded streets, the journey to London Bridge being somewhat entertaining when, near to the stocks market, a pig, perhaps aware of its destination, ran helter-skelter through Lombard Street scattering pedestrians like dandelion seeds in a gale.

'Twas well past time for dinner when we reached Kennington Palace. The other searchers, I discovered, had returned at the chiming of the noon Angelus Bells throughout the city, and now, with full bellies, awaited me and further instructions. They would have to wait a while longer. I had no thought of what I should do next to find Arnaud Tonge.

The corpse hauled from the Thames was before the chapel altar. Perhaps an examination of the dead man and his garments would provoke a new theory. I did not relish the thought of such a study on an empty stomach. Of course, there is little pleasure either in enquiring of the dead on a full stomach.

A table was laid for us near to the screens passage and we ate our fill of eels in bruit and crispels. I was in no hurry to finish my meal, for after I must inspect the corpse. 'Tis a delight when a man's duty brings him pleasure. My duties, as surgeon and bailiff and now as constable to Prince Edward, bring me woe as often as joy. Although when I succeed in patching an injured man whole I feel much satisfaction.

There are few windows, and therefore little light, in Prince Edward's chapel. Candles and cressets would not provide illumination enough for a thorough examination of the man. The dead – Sir Giles and the drowned stranger – were laid out upon biers side by side. The knight would have disdained the presence of his unkempt companion in life. In death these distinctions evaporate. A corpse is a corpse, whether gentleman or commoner.

I directed that a table be set outside the door to the kitchen garden and the drowned man placed upon it. I had entertained the thought that the tunic and badge upon the dead man were counterfeit. Not so. The tunic was of finest wool, and the embroidered badge matched those worn by others in Prince Edward's service. The chauces were another matter. They may at one time have been of quality, but were no longer. At the ankles they were frayed and the seat was worn thin.

Beneath the tunic and chauces the dead man wore a filthy kirtle and braes, and as I watched, fleas abandoned the folds of these garments, escaping the sunlight and their cooling host.

The corpse now lay naked before me. I saw no indication of violence on the emaciated form, but ran my fingers through the man's thinning hair to learn if he had suffered a blow to his skull. I found lice, but no bruises. If the fellow had drowned, there would be no sign of the cause but for water in the man's lungs. Folk who are slain, then pitched into a river, will not inhale the water, having their breath stopped before they can fill their lungs.

Twice before I had sought the cause of death of a man plucked from a stream. Arthur had assisted in one of these examinations, so guessed my request before I made it.

"You want me to press upon 'is chest, see if water flows from 'is mouth?"

"Aye."

It did, in copious amounts. The man had indeed drowned, but was it mischance or felony which put him in the Thames? And where had he come by Prince Edward's livery and badge?

One of the prince's constables had accompanied me to the examination. I released the corpse to him. The man would be taken, no doubt, to the nearest churchyard and buried without fanfare. I doubted his bearers would even pause in the lychgate for the priest to pray over him.

Did the man find Prince Edward's livery and badge discarded, or did he steal the garments? If he was a thief, he must have overpowered Arnaud. I thought that unlikely. His wizened frame would have been too frail to subdue a robust, well-fed man. And the livery must have belonged to Arnaud. No other of Prince Edward's servants or their garb had gone missing.

What if he had happened upon Arnaud in some inn, where the valet drank too much wine celebrating his newly fattened purse? Even a feeble man might vanquish a fellow in his cups.

Prince Edward did seemed not to enjoy his supper that evening. Perhaps he would have enjoyed it even less had he known of the second corpse now resting in his chapel. He learned of it soon enough. After the meal I followed him and Lady Joan to his privy chamber and told him of the day's events. He nodded but had no comments, nor had Lady Joan.

There was music and dancing again that evening in Kennington Palace hall. My Kate would have enjoyed the spectacle and delighted in the gowns the ladies wore. She would also have delighted in the dancing, I think, but not in the competence of her partner.

The music and swirling dancers became an abstraction as I considered what I had learned this day, or rather, what I had not learned.

Had I discovered anything at all that could lead to Sir Giles's murderer? I thought not. But how to know? Until the felon was found I would not know what information led to the guilty and what did not.

Here was a conundrum. I sought knowledge. Some discoveries would lead to the felon. Others would not, and may even mislead. How to know beforehand what would assist and what would impede the investigation of Sir Giles's death? I may waste time enquiring of matters which would bear no fruit, and fail to seek understanding that would. There were things which I knew not, and did not need to know. There were other matters which I needed to know of, but how might I understand which was which? What knowledge must I seek, and what might I discard? I did not yet know what I needed to know.

Was it important to find Arnaud Tonge? He must, I thought, be found if he lived. But what if, when he was discovered, the find proved of no value in identifying a murderer? I would know that only when I found the man. I had to learn many unimportant things before I could discover the few important matters. The path before me seemed strewn with obstacles, but a path with few obstructions may not lead to anyplace important.

Early next morn, as Arthur and I broke our fast with wheaten loaves and ale, Prince Edward's chaimberlain found me with news that the prince wished to speak to me. I hurriedly finished my ale and climbed the steps to the great chamber and beyond to the privy chamber. A man must not keep his future sovereign waiting.

The valets attending the doors to the privy chamber had been told to expect my arrival. One opened the door and stepped aside. The other announced my arrival to the prince as I drew near.

Prince Edward sat alone, and I immediately discerned why he was solitary and also that the herbs I had advised had not yet been effective. Perhaps they never would be. A fire blazed upon the hearth to counter the cool morning air entering the chamber through an open window. The need for ventilation was acute. The prince had been passing foul wind which had made the privy chamber objectionable even to him.

I believe he saw my nostrils twitch in protest, although I certainly would not speak of the matter. One must not tell the Duke of Cornwall that he stinks. To do so would be unnecessary. To his chagrin, the prince knew this. So the issue was not addressed.

"The day before yesterday," he began, "I made you my constable and charged you to discover what caused the death of Sir Giles Cheyne. What have you learned?"

I was compelled to admit that I had found more questions than answers since the previous day. I told the prince again of the drowned man garbed in his livery, wearing his badge, and of discovering Arnaud Tonge's brother.

"This brother knew nothing of Arnaud's whereabouts?"

"Nay. The man had just returned from purchasing fox skins to make a fur coat on commission."

"So he said," the prince remarked. "Who is this coat to be for?"

"Sir John Relyk."

"Hmmm. Aye, Sir John would wear a new coat, I think. Likes his garments new and of the latest fashion, does Sir John."

"Where does Sir John reside?" I asked.

"His manor is Coulsdon."

My blank expression told the prince that I was unfamiliar with the place.

"Ten or so miles to the south. That you ask this tells me you may doubt the skinner's word. Will you go to Sir John and learn if this commission is false?"

"Bailiffs are hired and paid to be mistrustful of others. But 'til now I had not thought to doubt the skinner."

"Believe only what can be proven true, eh? A safe policy for princes as well.

"I have a tunic for you," the prince continued. "So long as you are in my service you should don garb which proves it so, else men may resist your authority." He pointed to a bench where a black tunic lay neatly folded.

I departed the privy chamber with the tunic and the thought that I had perhaps been too eager to believe the skinner and his wife when they claimed not to have seen Arnaud for many months. Someone had scraped a chair or bench across the floor of the upper story of the skinner's house while I was within the place. Why did I not then ascend the stairs to learn if indeed the skinner's elderly parents did share the upper floor? And even if 'twas so that Alan's aged parents shared the dwelling, might there not have been a third person there?

The beasts Arthur and I had ridden from Bampton to London were stabled in the Kennington Palace marshalsea. I went directly there and told a stable groom that I would need the palfreys saddled and ready for travel immediately after dinner, then went to the chamber assigned me, took off my cotehardie, and donned the prince's tunic. I felt already the authority the garment represented. 'Tis no wonder that knights in maintenance feel unconstrained in their dealings with common folk.

At dinner this day I watched as Prince Edward and others at the high table consumed ravioles, longworts of pork, and cyueles. The prince seemed pleased with his dinner. I saw no boiled rooster flesh.

I and those who dined near to me were served a porre of peas and ravioles. Those who dined at the foot of the long tables, however, contented themselves with beans yfryed and barley loaves. Arthur was one of these, and I glanced his way once. His fare did not seem to dismay him.

Coulsdon, the prince had said, was nearly ten miles south, and the days were growing shorter. If Arthur and I wished to visit the place, question Sir John, and return before the twelfth hour we must make haste. But I could not leave the hall while Prince Edward was at his meal. When the prince stood from the remains of his meal, all in the hall stood also. I caught Arthur's eye and indicated to him that we would depart. He crammed the remains of a barley loaf into his mouth, took a final swig of ale, and followed.

The marshalsea had our palfreys ready, and knew the roads we must travel to find Coulsdon. We urged our mounts and two hours later we saw the spire of the village church rise above a forest where men were pannaging pigs, and fields under the plough where men readied the soil for planting rye. In their tofts other men of the village were occupied threshing wheat.

Seeking the lord of such a manor is a simple matter. Identify the grandest house and rap upon the door. Occasionally the village bailiff will possess a fine house. This will depend upon how much coin the lord has permitted his bailiff to extort from manor tenants and villeins. What I took to be the bailiff's house in Coulsdon was pleasant but not grand. There was no mistaking Sir John Relyk's residence. Other than the church 'twas the only stone building within the village.

A servant answered my knock upon the manor house door, saw my badge, and tugged a forelock while asking how he might serve me. I asked for Sir John and was invited to await him in the hall. The servant trotted off to locate the knight.

The man who soon appeared was tall, wore a neatly trimmed beard tinged with red and speckled with silver whiskers, and had not suffered hunger for many years. Here was a knight who would be of small benefit in battle against the French. Or against the Scots or Welsh, for that matter. Armed with a knife, however, I doubted not that he could acquit himself well in combat against a haunch of venison.

Sir John peered quizzically at me. Perhaps he had recently been at Kennington Palace and did not recognize me as being in service to Prince Edward. But the badge told him this was so.

"Good day... how may I serve the prince?" he began.

"I am Hugh de Singleton, bailiff to Lord Gilbert Talbot in Bampton, and constable to Prince Edward in the matter of a man slain in Kennington great hall."

"A man slain? In the hall? Who?" Sir John asked. "How?"

I explained as much of the matter as the knight needed to know, then came to the reason for my visit.

"The man I seek, who likely delivered the poison to Sir Giles, has a brother who lives in a lane just off the Shambles, near to Greyfriars Church. Alan Tonge by name. A skinner by trade. He told me that on your commission he was collecting fox skins to make for you a winter coat. Is this so?"

"Hmmm. Aye and nay. I did commission a fox fur coat from the man. Would you care to see it? 'Tis a fine garment and will warm me well this winter."

"The coat is already delivered?"

"Aye. A few days after Lammastide. Alan Tonge did gather skins for my coat, but if he does so now 'tis for some other man's coat, not mine."

Alan Tonge had departed London with a cart and returned with two packs of skins. Some of these were fox. So he said. Did he leave the city with an empty cart, or was a man hidden in it? I saw the bundles carried from the cart yesterday, when he returned to London. What, I wondered, was in those bundles? Fox skins? Not for Sir John Relyk. Why would the skinner lie about such a matter? Probably because he knew Sir John resided in Coulsdon and I was not likely to travel that far to learn of something so innocuous as the purchase of a fur coat. And also because there was some truth about his travel from London which he did not want known. I resolved to know it.

But not this day. Sir John bid us linger for a cup of ale, and would have had us refresh ourselves with a hastily laid on meal – so influential is Prince Edward's livery – but I protested that we must be away so as to reach Kennington before darkness and thieves descended upon the road.

Chapter 8

Next morning, as Prince Edward's grooms and valets broke their fast, I selected six of the stoutest to accompany Arthur and me to the skinner's house.

London Bridge was again clogged with folk desiring to cross the Thames and enter the city. Woe betide any man who at that hour wished to leave London rather than enter. However, seven men wearing Prince Edward's badges, six of them robust fellows – and Arthur – had little trouble opening a path across the bridge, dividing the throng. Men garbed in some lord's livery are a common sight upon London's streets, but seven men wearing Prince Edward's livery and apparently upon some business of importance to the prince will gather attention and raised eyebrows. Although few men wished to be caught openly staring as we passed.

Again I halted our group at Greyfriars Church and assigned duties to each. I told two men to pass behind the church, so that their livery would not be seen from the skinner's house, and set themselves at the north end of the lane to block any man who might escape that way. Two others I assigned to wait where we stood, for the same purpose.

Another man I sent with Arthur, to creep through the alley to the rear of the house. A place with which Arthur was now familiar. The last of the fellows I required to accompany me to Alan Tonge's door.

The skinner's wife answered my knocking and stepped back, her mouth open, when she saw me. Perhaps she had not expected to see me again. Or perhaps men garbed in Prince Edward's livery startled her. When such men in service to a great lord take notice of a man or woman of the commons 'tis usually because that man or woman has drawn attention they would prefer to avoid.

Mary composed herself and greeted me. "I give you good day, Master... Hugh. You seek Alan? He is at his work. Shall I fetch 'im?"

"Aye. I'll not take him from his labor a long while."

The woman so forgot herself that she offered no hospitality but left us standing at the threshold. She disappeared into a passageway and I heard her call to her husband. His response was curt. The woman spoke again, this time in a voice so soft I could not hear.

Alan appeared a moment later, wiping his hands upon a leather apron. "How may I serve you?" the man said. His manner suggested that he could not decide whether he should be worried that he had attracted my attention for a second day, or exasperated that he was interrupted while at his trade. "Have you found Arnaud?" he continued before I could reply. The man did not seem hopeful.

"Nay. I have discovered a few things since we last spoke, but your brother's whereabouts is not one of them." Prince Edward's badge made me bold. "Why did you lie to me?" I said with as grim a tone as I could muster. I did not specify the lie in question. I thought the skinner might, if he had prevaricated about matters other than Sir John's fox coat, incriminate himself regarding them. So he did.

I watched Alan's adam's apple bounce as he considered a response. Perhaps he had spoken numerous falsehoods and was wondering which I might have found out. Or mayhap the skinner was alarmed that Prince Edward's man had accused him of being untruthful. Such an accusation would frighten even an honest man, which Alan Tonge was not.

Tonge swallowed deeply and protested my accusation. "Nay, I spoke truth."

"Not all of your words were truthful. This I know. Will you tell me which were deceitful and which were honest, or must you meet with Prince Edward's serjeants?"

I needed to say no more. Even a man with little imagination would understand the implication.

"I did not return from my journey with fox skins for Sir John Relyk's coat."

I said nothing. Alan would not know if this was the lie I had discovered if there was another falsehood from his lips.

"Rabbit skins, and a few of otter," the man said. "Show 'em to you, if you doubt."

"Why speak falsely of your business?" I said.

Alan shrugged. This was no good answer.

"Why should I care if you traveled seeking fox skins or rabbit or otter – or squirrel for that matter?"

The fellow shrugged again. A reason came to me.

"The skins of lesser creatures are easier to come by than fox," I said. "Such skins may be had but a few miles from London's walls. But fox... such a wily creature is not easily trapped. You might be required to visit many villages before you could collect enough skins for a gentleman's coat, whereas you could purchase rabbit skins aplenty and return the same day to sleep in your own bed."

The skinner did not dispute this assertion, but chewed upon his lower lip and glanced over my shoulder as if seeking some diversion to distract me from my charge.

"Your wife said that your parents abide in this house also, in a chamber above."

"Aye."

"I will see it."

Did Alan hesitate before stepping back and inviting me to enter, or did my imagination see reluctance where none was?

"This way," the man said and led me and the valet to the stairs opposite his door. I saw Mary peer from around the opening to her kitchen as I crossed the room. She hesitated for a moment, then followed.

'Twas as the woman had said. Two aged folk occupied this upper chamber. A man lay upon a bed, his frail form barely lifting the bedclothes which covered him. I wondered if such a feeble-appearing fellow yet lived. His covering rose and fell in answer.

A crone sat upon a bench beside the bed. Her grey locks were long and tangled, although some time not long past someone, likely Mary, had attempted to arrange the woman's hair under a wimple.

The skinner's lass had purchased six pies. Mary might consume one, her children another, and she had purchased two, she said, in the expectation that her husband and his apprentice might return that day and be hungry. This left two pies for the aged parents.

I studied the pair again. I doubted that between them they could eat one of the pies. This left a pie unaccounted for. Was it divided and consumed? Did it rest in a cupboard to be consumed this day?

"What villages did you visit seeking skins, and what men sold such to you? Are the suppliers men with whom you have dealt before?"

The skinner's throat constricted again and he swallowed deeply.

"Poachers, eh?" I said. "Prince Edward has little interest in tenants who have taken their lord's rabbits. But he will take interest in a man who will not answer my questions." The time had come to impress upon Alan Tonge the grim nature of my business. "Prince Edward seeks your brother because a knight of his household was slain two days past. The prince thought much of this knight, and has required of me that I find the felon who slew him."

"Thought you was seekin' Arnaud," Alan said.

"I am."

Silence followed. Mary's mouth opened and she exchanged a glance with her husband.

"Does the prince believe whoso murdered the knight slew Arnaud also?" the skinner said.

"Nay."

"Then Arnaud must know who did murder and has fled Kennington Palace to escape the man," Alan concluded.

"Not quite," I replied.

All this time I was becoming certain that the skinner had hidden his brother in the cart, departed the city, and visited villages where he had in the past purchased skins so as to justify the journey. I thought it likely that Arnaud had disappeared to some northern town, where under a new name he would invest the profit of his felony to set himself up in some new trade.

"But 'tis true Arnaud knows who did murder."

Alan and Mary exchanged puzzled glances.

"But he..." Mary began to speak, but fell silent when her husband glared at her.

"He what?" I said.

The silence which followed was interrupted by the elderly man's gentle snore. I looked from Alan to Mary, awaiting a reply.

I received none, so repeated the question. This was no more successful.

Perhaps the woman could not resist glancing above her shoulder. Guilt does strange things to folk unaccustomed to speaking falsehood, or attempting dissimulation. Above Mary's head was a plastered ceiling which featured a small opening covered by two sawn boards. The aperture allowed entrance to the attic. The boards were in place. There was no sign that they had been recently moved. Nevertheless I decided to view this attic. I did not expect to find Arnaud there, being convinced that if the valet had sought his brother he had been taken to some village to the north of London.

"No doubt you have a ladder to gain entrance to your attic," I said to Alan.

"Broken," the skinner replied.

"Fetch it. We will make do."

Alan spoke true. One rung was cracked, but this did not prevent the ladder from being used as intended. I inspected the ladder to be sure only one rung was suspect before trusting myself to it and thought then that the split in the lowest rung seemed new, the broken wood not darkened with age.

The attic door was near to the center of the chamber, so the boards closing it had to be pushed aside by the ladder itself. No dormer with a skin window illuminated the attic. I demanded a cresset of the skinner, and when he brought it I cautiously climbed to the attic, one hand to the ladder, the other holding the lighted cresset.

The roof had been recently renewed. The thatch was clean. Vermin had made their home there, for in the flame of the cresset I saw droppings. I also saw something else upon the dusty boards which caught my eye.

A path had been recently swept through the dust, leaving a track upon a joist the width of my hand. I studied this dust-free mark and in the close light of the cresset saw yet another anomaly. I could not be certain, for the flame of a single cresset did not provide enough light, but it seemed to me crumbs lay upon the wattles of the attic floor and joists. I gathered a few of these tiny specks and retreated back down the ladder. The decline was precarious, for

I held cresset in one hand and the particles between thumb and forefinger of the other.

I handed the cresset to the valet who had been holding the ladder steady, walked to the window, and inspected my find. The window was of oiled skin, but split thin and smooth and well-oiled so that nearly as much light passed through as if it had been glass.

There was no doubt. I held crumbs in the palm of my hand. They had not been deposited in the attic long before, else vermin surely would have found the morsels and consumed them. Who would consume a loaf or pastry in an attic? Or a pie?

Alan Tonge and his wife stood transfixed, mouths open, hands opening and closing involuntarily.

"Not a very pleasant place to eat a pie," I offered. Neither the skinner nor his wife replied. I glanced to the dark square in the chamber ceiling. "Where is he?" I said.

The voice that answered this question surprised me. The aged man in the bed had awakened. He squinted with milky, red-rimmed eyes at the opening in the ceiling and said, "Why's Arnaud sleepin' up there?" in a voice so weak I could barely make out the words. "Tell 'im to come down."

"A good question," I said. "Why did you hide Arnaud in your attic, and where is he now?"

The skinner stammered for a moment, as if collecting his thoughts and arranging them in some order that I might believe. "Said 'e'd been in a fight with another of Prince Edward's valets, a favorite of Lady Joan's. The man threatened to slay Arnaud, an' 'e feared the fellow would do it. An' bein' a toady to the prince's lady, Arnaud thought the man would escape the noose if he did slay 'im."

"So he fled the palace to save his life? Is that what he told you?"

"Aye. Feared the rogue would seek 'im out, so come to me for aid."

"Where did you take him?"

"Not far. Said 'e wished only to be past the city walls a few miles. Said the knave would not follow, even did he discover where Arnaud had fled. You going to tell the prince of this?"

"What of his badge and livery?"

"Oh, couldn't be seen in that. I gave 'im chauces and a cotehardie of my own."

"What of Prince Edward's livery? What became of that?"

"I waited 'til I heard curfew ring from St. Mary le Bow, an' took the tunic to St. Paul's, where poor folk do gather in the night. Nights become cold, and an extra tunic will warm a man."

"Why did you not tell me this yesterday?"

"Thought you was the mate of the valet what sought to slay Arnaud."

"It is true that when Arnaud is found he will likely soon after die," I said. "But no valet seeks him to slay him. In Prince Edward's hall three days past a knight of the prince's household, a man he held in much esteem, was poisoned. 'Tis sure that Arnaud delivered the poison in the knight's wine as he sat at table."

"But why would Arnaud do such a thing?"

"Why did you hide him in your attic and then hire a horse and cart to carry him from the city?" I asked.

"He's me brother, an' 'e paid me… Ah, some man paid Arnaud to slay the knight?"

"Likely. Arnaud had no reason we know of to dislike the knight, but others did. How much did Arnaud pay you to take him from the city?"

"Twenty pence."

"Did you not ask yourself where your brother found twenty pence and why he was willing to part with such a sum?"

Alan shrugged. "A man who fears for 'is life will pay much to save it."

I could not argue with the skinner's point.

"You took your brother beyond the city walls, you said. Where? And did Arnaud say where he intended to go from there?"

"Took 'im to Hornsey."

I had not heard of the place, and no wonder. When I did visit the hamlet I found half of the houses fallen in, the population much reduced. The village was but a few miles to the north of Aldersgate so those who had survived the plague found it easy to move to London. Plague in the city had reduced the supply of laborers, so a man with a strong back found himself much in demand, and landlords had few folk eager to lease their houses, so lowered the rents to attract custom.

"How far north is that?" I asked. "May a man travel there and return the same day?"

"Aye. 'Tis but eight or nine miles."

"But you did not?"

"Nay. I sought skins, as I said. That was true enough."

The morning was far gone. To return to Kennington Palace, acquire horses, then set off through London streets to Aldersgate and the road north would consume another hour or two. I might gain Hornsey before dark, but a return to London before the sun set was impossible. I would travel there on the morrow.

But what if in the intervening hours Alan Tonge took it upon himself to hurry to Hornsey, find his brother, and warn him of my search – if Arnaud had not yet fled farther north? I must not permit this. I told Alan that one of Prince Edward's grooms would remain on guard while we others returned to the palace. His duty would be to see that no man, or woman, left the house 'til I returned next morn on the way north to Hornsey. I chose Maurice to stay. He is constructed much like Arthur and seemed content with the duty given him.

We broke our fast on the morrow with wheaten loaves fresh from the palace oven, and ale. The marshal had our beasts ready, and we set off for London Bridge before the second hour. Arthur and two of Prince Edward's grooms accompanied me, one of the grooms leading a palfrey for Maurice.

A few miles north of Aldersgate the road divided. A stone at this junction pointed the way to London, but made no mention of Hornsey or villages to the north, as if to say that folk leaving the city had no need to know their way. Only those bound for London needed guidance.

I chose the dexter road. This was a mistake, but we discovered soon enough that little time was lost before returning to the proper road. We came upon a village but a mile from the junction. 'Twas too soon to be already Hornsey. I saw a man patching the daub of his house, preparing for winter, and asked what place this was and how far to Hornsey.

"This be Stroud Green," the man said, tugging a forelock, "but you'll not get to Hornsey followin' this road. Return the way you come, an' take the other way. Hornsey be three miles, thereabouts, from where the road from London do split."

I thanked the fellow, who in deference to my tunic and badge tugged again upon a forelock. Little more than an hour later, upon the right road, we came to Hornsey.

As we approached the church – dedicated to St. Mary, I later learned – I saw a small band of men draw near from the opposite direction. Two of these carried some object between them and as we closed the distance between our parties I saw that they bore a pallet with a black-shrouded corpse. Two others carried spades over their shoulders. They were bound for the lychgate and churchyard.

The village priest and his clerk led the small procession. I thought to wait until the corpse was interred, then ask the priest of any new face in the village. A priest would know of any recent arrival in his parish.

The priest, his clerk, four others, and the corpse halted under the lychgate. No women. I wondered at that. Would a dead man have no female relatives to mourn his death and accompany his corpse to the churchyard? And why so few men attending the dead man? I assumed the form under the shroud was male as only men attended the corpse. A man known to villagers would attract more than four mourners, even if the spectre of plague had ravaged the place. Most folk, on the other hand, would see no need to march behind the corpse of a man they knew not.

We stood a respectful distance from the lychgate, caps in hand, while the priest prayed over the corpse. When he was finished, and the bearers were about to lift the pallet, I spoke.

"Who has died in Hornsey?"

The priest turned to me. His companions stared at me, unmoving.

"We don't know," the priest said.

"A man unknown to you has died in this village?" I asked.

"Unknown, aye, but died not in the village."

It was my turn to be surprised. "If he did not perish in Hornsey why do you bury him in your churchyard?"

"A man must be interred somewhere. St. Mary's Churchyard is the closest hallowed ground."

"Closest to what?"

"Where Rowland found him lying dead," the priest said and looked to one of the men who bore the pallet.

"You are Rowland?" I asked.

"Aye. Who be you?"

The priest and his companions had surely taken note of my livery and badge, but they might not have recognized the badge as that of Prince Edward. I enlightened them. A tugging of forelocks ensued, but for the priest, who made a slight bow of his head.

"Is the man a stranger? You said you do not know his name, but has he been seen in Hornsey?"

"Rohese said she seen 'im yesterday."

"Who is Rohese?" I asked.

"She's our ale wife. Said this fellow sat near 'alf a day in 'er 'ouse, drinkin' ale. Waitin' for someone, she thought."

"Where did you find the dead man?"

"In a ditch, 'bout three 'undred or so paces to the north, aside the road to Enfield."

Under the shroud was a man unknown to the inhabitants of Hornsey. I wondered if he might be known to Prince Edward's grooms who stood at my shoulder.

"Draw the shroud from the man's face," I said to the priest. He did so.

I turned to the grooms and asked if they recognized the dead man.

They did. "That's Arnaud," they agreed. "Had a wart on 'is chin, did Arnaud," one said. "See there... just as that fellow has."

"You have no doubt?" I asked.

The grooms looked to each other and shook their heads. "That be Arnaud," one said. "No doubts."

"How did the man die?" I asked Rowland.

"Stabbed. A thrust through 'is 'eart."

As if to confirm the man's words the priest drew back the shroud further so that Arnaud's torso was visible. I saw a dark stain circling a slash in his cotehardie. Blood.

I looked to his belt and saw attached to it a leather purse. Empty. Not surprising. Who would bury a dead man's coins?

The priest watched as I inspected the purse and perceived my thoughts.

"As we found him. Slain for his money, no doubt."

If so, the felon may have known that Arnaud possessed a heavy purse. Surely Arnaud would not have slain Sir Giles for but a few pence. To risk both a lucrative position and a noose, a man would likely demand many shillings. Perhaps some Hornsey villager had learned of Arnaud's wealth. But why take a man's coins and leave his purse? If Arnaud had been paid as well as I suspected no man could carry off the coins in his hands. Perhaps the felon transferred the coins to his own purse rather than cut Arnaud's free. But why do so? He had a dagger in hand. He had used it to slay the valet. 'Twould take less time to slash Arnaud's purse free than fill one purse with the contents of another.

The ale wife had told the priest that the day before, Arnaud had sat for half a day drinking her ale. She had thought he awaited the arrival of some other man. I decided to visit the woman.

"Where does Rohese keep her alehouse?" I asked.

"Third house this side of the well. She has fresh-brewed ale this day, and has raised a basket upon a pole. You will find her readily enough."

We left the priest and his assistants to bury Arnaud, and led our beasts toward the village green and well. 'Twas as the priest said. The ale wife's house was easily identified by the pole and basket, and the folk who came and went with ewers of ale.

The door of the house stood open for the frequent customers. I entered the room with Arthur and a groom behind me. Two other grooms remained in the street with our palfreys. Our party darkened the doorway and a woman within looked up to see what new customers she had. When she saw that we were strangers her eyes widened and her face registered alarm. Perhaps her response was due to the livery that two of us wore. Men who are garbed as we were have been known to seize what they will.

"You are Rohese?" I said.

The woman nodded.

"The priest has told me that you served a man yesterday who is now being interred in the churchyard. Did the man speak to you? The priest said you thought he awaited some other man."

"He said naught but 'More ale' when 'e'd finished a cup. You a friend of 'is?"

"Nay. But we knew the man. How long did he remain here?"

"He came through the door 'bout noon, an' remained 'til ninth hour."

"He drank for three hours? Was he drunk when he left?"

The woman smiled. "Aye. Staggered a bit. Don't water me ale as do some."

A thought had been nagging me. "Did any other man unknown to you ask for ale yesterday?"

"Nay," the woman said. "Travelers oft stop for ale when they see me basket up, this bein' the road to London, but none yesterday."

"On the day before?" I asked.

"Thursday?" She frowned, thinking back. "Two strangers stopped for refreshment Thursday. Gentlemen, they was."

"Going to London, or leaving?"

"Don't know. Didn't see 'em arrive or leave. I had other customers, y'see."

"How old were these gentlemen?" I asked.

"Oh, not old. Barely more than lads."

"Did they wear livery? Badges of the sort that would proclaim who they served?"

"Nay... nothin' like your garb."

"Describe for me what they did wear, and their appearance."

"Tall, they was, an' slender, as are young gentlemen before time at the trencher increases their girth. One was dark, the other fair. The fair-haired one wore a russet cotehardie an' blue cap. T'other wore a grey cotehardie an' greenish cap. Both of 'em wore parti-colored chauces."

Here was a feminine eye at work. I doubt a man would have recalled so clearly the apparel of other men he had no reason to remember.

But the ale wife spoke true. Many travelers would pass through Hornsey on the way to or from London. That two did so two days before Arnaud Tonge was found slain was not likely remarkable. An accumulation of unremarkable events may, however, prove to be of cumulative significance.

I had one more question for the woman.

"Did men of the village enter here to consume your ale whilst the man now dead was here?"

"Aye. Two was 'ere for a cup, an' Isobel Legget came to fill her ewer."

"Did any of these three speak to the man? His name was Arnaud."

"Not that I heard. Kept to 'isself. Sat just there" – the woman pointed to a stained and scarred bench against the wall – "an' said naught. But to ask for more ale."

"Did he open his purse to pay while other men were here to observe?"

"Ah… I know what you're thinkin'. He did, but John an' Richard ain't men who'd slay another for 'is purse."

"Someone surely did. His purse was empty when he was found."

Was it? So the priest had said. But the priest had not found the corpse. Could he trust the word of the man who did?

"Purse wasn't fat when he lived," the woman said.

I must have raised my eyebrows in disbelief, for Rohese continued and explained.

"He dumped 'is coins on the table to sort 'em out when 'e bought 'is last cup. He'd maybe two pennies an' 'alf a dozen farthings an' a ha'penny."

"That was all?"

"All that was in 'is purse. Turned it upside down on the table. Give me two farthings an' put t'other coins back in 'is purse."

If Arnaud Tonge had brought poisoned wine to Sir Giles, why would he do so but for ample payment? Randall Patchett had said nothing about Sir Giles earning Arnaud's enmity, so why would the valet desire the knight dead? But if some man paid Arnaud to do this evil, where were the coins? Not in his purse. What man would do murder in Prince Edward's hall for so few pence? Was he perchance paid a few coins to seal the wicked bargain with the promise of complete payment when Sir Giles was carried to his grave? Was that what he had waited for at Rohese's alehouse a day before? If so, the payment he received was not what he had expected.

I must speak to Rowland. I bid the ale wife "Good day" and hurried from the place. Perhaps the priest had not yet concluded Arnaud's funeral mass and I might find Rowland yet at the church. I did.

Chapter 9

Two men were at work with spades filling Arnaud's grave, and the priest, his clerk, and two others were departing the churchyard when we came in view of the lychgate. The shroud that had covered Arnaud Tonge when he lay upon the pallet was folded across the clerk's arm. I recognized one of those walking with the priest as the man who had found Arnaud dead.

The priest saw us approach, noted that we seemed hurried, and turned to us. His clerk and the man accompanying him did likewise.

"May I do more service for Prince Edward's constable?" the priest said when I came near.

"You may, but 'tis Rowland's service I seek." The man tugged a forelock and awaited my request.

"I wish to be shown the place where you found the man who has just been buried. You come also," I said to the priest, "if you saw the corpse where Rowland found it, before it was moved."

"I did," the priest replied, "as did John." He glanced to his clerk. "We will show you the place. 'Tis not far."

It wasn't. We passed Rohese's alehouse and the village well, then no more than three hundred paces north of the village manor house we came to a place where Rowland pointed out a patch of brown, flattened grass at the side of the road.

"Just there he lay," the man said.

I stood five or so paces from the oval of compressed vegetation and studied the surrounding area. Stones here are sparse, so the folk of Hornsey had built but few walls about their fields. A meadow to the west had been walled, but where the corpse lay, a man could approach, or depart, along the road to or from the north or south, or could walk freely across the stubble of a harvested oat field. The stubble had recently been cut close to augment winter fodder. I saw in the field the occasional footprint, but nothing which might speak to the approach of a murderer across the field.

The road was another matter. Many men had come to the place since Rowland had discovered the corpse. Fresh footprints and hoofprints in the road gave evidence of this. But the footprints did not entirely obliterate two parallel grooves in the mud of the road. These furrows occasionally disappeared into the grass of the verge, and ended two paces from where Arnaud's corpse had lain.

I had not noticed these marks when approaching the place, but when my eye fell upon them I began to walk toward the village following the grooves, my face cast down to the road. Arthur followed, sensing that I had discovered some important thing, and voiced what I had already assumed.

"Some man's been dragged along the road. Them's heel marks, or mayhap 'is toes bein' dragged."

Because many men and a few horses had traveled the road this day the furrows were not continuous. But they were never completely obscured for more than a few paces. I continued toward the village, watching for the twin grooves as they appeared and were then hidden. Rowland, the priest, and the clerk followed, and I heard Arthur behind me explaining to them my curious interest in the road.

The marks came to an end in the road before the manor house. I searched the road and the verge for ten or more paces in both directions, but saw no further sign that a man, if 'twas indeed a man's feet which had carved the furrows in the road, had been dragged from beyond the manor house.

I returned to the place where the twin grooves ended – or began, as I thought – and cast about in the drying mud of the road for any sign of what might have begun here and ended with a corpse aside the road three hundred paces distant.

Had the road been dry I might have seen the stain sooner. But then of course the man who stabbed Arnaud Tonge in the road would likely have seen the blood soaking into the dirt and covered it or swept it away.

The dirt was dark with damp, but a slightly darker circle caught my eye. I squatted for a closer look, and at that moment the sun, which had been obscured by clouds much of the day, broke through and illuminated the road before me.

Blood when no longer fresh loses its red hue and becomes brown. But in less than a day since blood was spilt upon this road there was yet some red tint to the brown of the stain melding with the brown of the mud. Without the brilliance of the sun I would not have seen this, I think.

Would a man be stabbed to his death in the middle of the road before a village manor house? Not in the light of day. But in the dark of night? Surely. Men love darkness rather than light when their deeds are evil.

Arnaud Tonge had left the alehouse – having met no man there, if that was ever his intent – at the ninth hour. Sometime after the twelfth hour he had stood in the street before the manor house where some other then slew him.

Arnaud's corpse had not been hidden. Any man upon the road next morning would see it. Why, then, drag the body from the place of murder? It must be that the felon was unconcerned that Arnaud would be found dead, but did not want him found where he had died, within the village, before the manor house.

Did this mean that some inhabitant of the Hornsey manor house had slain Arnaud? Why would such a thing happen? Was Arnaud known to some man of this place? The priest had said he was not, but would a village priest know who was known or unknown to all the folk of his parish?

"Who is lord of Hornsey Manor?" I asked the priest.

"Sir Thomas Jocelyn," he replied.

"Come with me. Perhaps he or some person of his household saw or heard something in the night."

"You believe the felony was done here?"

I pointed to the nearly invisible dark patch at my feet. "Here is a bloodstain in the road. And a few paces from the stain the furrows in the mud of the road begin, ending where Rowland found the corpse. Would a man slay another here, in the road, in the day, when many folk might be about to see what he did and then watch him drag his victim from the village?"

"Unlikely," the priest said. "So you believe the man we have buried must have been slain here, in the night? It seems reasonable to assume so. Come. We will seek Sir Thomas."

A servant answered the priest's rapping upon the manor house door and in response to his question replied that Sir Thomas was expected soon for his dinner, after seeing to matters upon his demesne in the morning.

The servant seemed perplexed about his duty. He knew the priest, and the clerk, and these should be invited to the hall to await his master. The two tenants he would also know, but should they too be brought into the hall? And I saw him glance several times at my badge and livery. Did he know whose these were, and whom I served? If he did, he would not leave me or those accompanying me to stand before the house. The badge, even if unknown to the man, indicated that I served some great man. The servant solved his problem by inviting all of us into the hall, leaving his master to sort out custom.

The smell of fried stockfish caused my stomach to growl and reminded me that I and my companions would not have our dinner at Kennington Palace this day. 'Tis a privilege to serve a great prince.

Perhaps the aroma of his dinner had wafted to wherever Sir Thomas was at his business, for we had waited only a short time when a stout young man, finely garbed in a blue velvet cotehardie, strode into the hall in the manner of one who knows and is confident of his exalted place. Exalted in Hornsey. Was he this day enjoying dinner at Kennington Palace he might not even be seated at the high table.

The priest and I and our companions had awaited the knight pressed against the wall of his hall while grooms set up trestles, tables, and benches. The servant who had greeted us at his door spoke to Sir Thomas and pointed to us. The knight turned to us and stared for a moment, then stalked to our place. His eyes were fixed upon my badge. He knew, if perchance others did not, who I served.

The priest bowed to Sir Thomas and gave every indication that he recognized in the knight a superior. No doubt, as with most of his position, he served his parish at the sufferance of the lord of Hornsey Manor.

The knight did not acknowledge the priest's bow but came straight to me.

"I give you good day," he said. "Jaket has said you wish to speak to me. How may I serve Prince Edward?"

"Murder was done in the road before this house not many hours past," I said. "Likely in the night. Did you hear any sounds of violence during the hours of darkness, or have any of those in your service spoken of hearing discord in the night?"

"Murder? In Hornsey? Surely not. A man was found dead this morning, I am told, along the road to Enfield." Sir Thomas turned to the priest. "Did any man know who it was found dead?"

"Aye. He was unknown to us of the village, but these fellows knew him. He was slain. Pierced through the heart."

"You knew the fellow?" Sir Thomas said to me.

"Aye. Arnaud Tonge. A valet in service to Prince Edward."

"Ah. The prince is loyal to his retainers so has sent you to seek who has slain this Arnaud."

"Nay. Prince Edward does not yet know of Arnaud Tonge's death. I did not know of it 'til an hour or so past. But I did come here at the prince's charge, seeking Arnaud."

"Did the fellow take goods from the prince? Silver spoons or cups or the like? Is that why he left the prince's service and you have been sent after him? Perhaps some man knew he possessed stolen goods and he was slain for them?"

"Nay. He took nothing from Prince Edward, but he was a felon."

Sir Thomas scowled in response to my words. Why did the knight think that Arnaud had left Prince Edward's service? Because he traveled from London? He might be on his way to another of the prince's properties. Perhaps Berkhampstead.

"A felon? How so, if he took nothing of the prince's chattels?"

"A knight of the prince's household was poisoned. Arnaud served the tainted wine which sent the man to his grave, then fled the palace. He surely was persuaded by some other to do this, as no man can suggest a reason for animosity between the valet and the slain knight."

"Persuaded? How so?"

"Arnaud was likely paid, and paid well, to do this murder."

"Ah… perhaps some man knew of his new wealth," Sir Thomas said, "and followed him from London to seize it from him."

"Mayhap. But why would he linger here, in Hornsey? He was brought to this place two days past. The village is not so far from London. A man facing a noose if he is found would, I think, put more miles between himself and his pursuers, and be in a hurry to do so."

A bell rang, indicating to Sir Thomas that his dinner was served. The knight shrugged and spoke. "I heard nothing in the night. And none of my servants has spoken of any untoward sound which might have awakened them. If the fellow was slain before my house he did not cry out. Not loud enough to be heard anyway. I give you good day," Sir Thomas said abruptly, and turned away to take his meal. I was dismissed.

There was no offer from the knight to share his dinner, nor is there in Hornsey an inn where a man might find bread and perhaps a pottage of eels. This cheerless thought evidently came to the priest as it did to me, for as we stepped from the manor house threshold he spoke.

"My cook is not expecting guests, but there will be loaves and pottage enough to share. You will be hungry before you can return to Kennington Palace for your supper, so take a meal with me before you return to London."

The priest – Father Patrick – fed us decently considering that he was a poor parish priest serving a village much reduced by plague and by folk who had survived abandoning the place for London.

Father Patrick's cook had prepared a pottage of peas and beans for the priest and his clerk for their dinner. The kettle held barely enough for three. The priest offered to share the meal, but his heart was not in the suggestion and portions reduced to serve seven rather than three would be paltry indeed. I told the priest that we would be content with loaves and ale. Arthur assumed a wounded expression. The loaves were fresh that day and plentiful enough that each man had his own. Arthur was much relieved.

"Sir Thomas is a young man," I said to the priest between bites of maslin loaf.

"Aye. His father died two years past. Sir William was a good lord to the village."

"You say so as if there is a contrast between father and son," I said.

"As you say, Sir Thomas is young."

The priest would say no more of the lord of Hornsey, likely aware that words spoken in private will not always remain concealed. And while Hornsey was a small parish, its tithes stunted since plague came, 'twas a position, and better than no parish at all.

"Is Sir Thomas wed?" I asked. I had little interest in the answer, but simply thought to make conversation 'til I had consumed my loaf.

"Aye," the priest answered. I expected that he might name the lady or make some comment regarding her great virtue. All ladies are virtuous, so 'tis claimed. But Father Patrick said no more of the Lady Jocelyn. Rather, he changed the subject. I wondered why.

"The sky is darkening," he said with a glance to the skin-covered window of his vicarage. He was correct. The oiled skin had been a bright yellow when we began the meal, but was now a gloomy grey. "I fear you will see rain before you return to London."

I walked to his door, opened it, and peered out. The priest spoke true. Dark clouds rolling from the north appeared heavy with rain. Was the priest concerned for my comfort, or did he wish to be rid of a man asking questions he did not wish to answer? Whatever the reason, his observation was accurate. If I did not want to be soaked through I must set off for Kennington Palace immediately.

I thanked the priest for his hospitality. We released our palfreys, which had been tied to a rail before the vicarage, and set off at a canter. But rain caught our party while we were yet several miles from Aldersgate. The road became a mire and London's streets were no better, so by the time we came to Kennington Palace men and beasts were sodden and spattered with mud. I had much to tell Prince Edward, but was not fit to enter his presence until I had washed the mire from face and hands, and donned a dry tunic and chauces. Grooms were making the hall ready for supper, erecting tables and benches, as I climbed the stairs to the prince's privy chamber.

Valets at the privy chamber door recognized me and knew my purpose before I could speak.

"Prince Edward is in conversation with Sir Robert Hardwicke and Archbishop Whittlesay," one of the valets said.

"I will return another time," I replied.

"Nay," the valet said. "We have been given instructions that when you return you are to be announced."

Here was more evidence of the regard Prince Edward felt for Sir Giles Cheyne. The prince was so eager for news of the search for Sir Giles's slayer that he would interrupt discourse with the archbishop to learn of my progress, or lack of it.

The valet opened one of the doors, apologized to the prince, and told him of my presence in the great chamber. I heard, "Send him in," and the valet turned to me, held an arm to the open door, and bade me enter.

I had never before seen Sir Robert Hardwicke or the archbishop, nor they me. I bowed to the prince, then the archbishop, and lastly to the knight. I am learning the priorities of gentlefolk and the court.

The two men who sat before Prince Edward were a contrast to each other. Sir Robert was a hale fellow with ruddy cheeks, his frame nearly as sturdy as Arthur's. The archbishop was frail, his skin as fragile as ancient parchment, the cords of his neck standing out from a lack of flesh. His hands, folded in his lap, were bony, and purple veins were prominent upon them.

The knight gazed at me curiously, the archbishop with displeasure. Both, I suspect, wondered why a man of my rank – which I suppose neither knew of a certainty, but assumed to be beneath them – was allowed to insert himself into their parley with Prince Edward.

The prince did little to illuminate them. "Ah, Master Hugh. Have you news?" Then, to the knight and prelate he said, "Master Hugh is in my service, seeking a felon. I must speak privily to him. I will see you shortly, at supper."

And with these words he dismissed his companions, watched as they bowed their way from the privy chamber, then bid me take the knight's chair.

The windows of the privy chamber were closed against the rain and chill, but no foul odor permeated the room this day. Perhaps, I thought, the physics I had suggested were reducing the prince's repulsive wind. I did not wish to be obvious as I sniffed the air for an offensive scent, but perhaps Prince Edward has become accustomed to folk testing the atmosphere when they enter his presence.

"The herbs you suggested," he began, "have been effective. Folk no longer seek to escape my presence. Of course, Dr. Blackwater claims 'tis due to his diet of boiled roosters."

"Perhaps," I said, "the physician may rightly claim a part of the success."

"We shall see. I have told Blackwater and my cook I will now consume the same fare as others who dine at my table. I will not see upon my trencher one more boiled rooster. If my malady continues to improve we will know 'twas your herbs which have eased my affliction. If the illness returns as before, well, then I shall return to gnawing upon boiled roosters.

"Now, to the matter of Sir Giles. What have you learned this day?"

"Many things, but most important is that Arnaud Tonge is dead. He was buried this day in the Hornsey churchyard."

"Did you slay him? Did the man put up a fight when you found him?"

I explained to the prince the events of the day. He listened with chin resting upon a fist, occasionally breaking into my report with a question.

"Some man knew he carried a heavy purse, then," Prince Edward said to summarize my account, "and slew him for the coins. You agree?"

I did not immediately reply.

"You do not agree?"

"The ale wife said Arnaud appeared to her to be waiting for someone. Who? And when he paid for his ale his purse held few coins. He would not have risked the scaffold for so little gain, I think."

"What is your theory, then, if he was not slain for his money? Did he hide his gains away, so that men would not see his fat purse and slay him for its contents?"

"I thought much upon this while we rode back to London. Mayhap Arnaud awaited some man in Hornsey for the completion of his payment. 'Tis possible he was given but a portion of his due, and was promised the remainder when the deed was done and Sir Giles lay dead."

"Ah," Prince Edward exclaimed. "I see your drift. Whoso hired him to poison Sir Giles's wine had him slain. This would solve two problems for the man who wished Sir Giles dead. He would not need to complete payment, and Arnaud being dead could not tell who had employed him, even if my serjeants relieved him of his fingernails."

"Aye, just so."

"So the man who paid to have Sir Giles slain has succeeded and will escape the consequences of his felony?" This was said as a question, but I believe the prince was resigned to the failure of my warrant.

"Perhaps not," I replied.

"What? You have suspicions?"

"I am Lord Gilbert Talbot's bailiff. Bailiffs always have suspicions. If they do not, they will soon lose their post."

"Tell me of your suspicions. Can you name a man?"

"Nay. Not yet. But I can tell you I do not suspect some man of Hornsey. No man of the village would slay him for the few coins in his purse."

"If you can name no man you believe guilty, what is the foundation for your suspicion?"

"I know there are men, some under your roof, who despised Sir Giles. Any of them could have seen Arnaud at his assigned tasks at dinner, keeping wine cups filled. One of these men is perhaps guilty of the felony. And I am troubled about Arnaud's death."

"How so?"

"He was upon the road in Hornsey, sometime after darkness fell, standing before the manor house. What was he doing there at such a time? And where had he spent the previous night? The village has no inn.

"The lord of Hornsey manor said he heard no man cry out in the night, nor did any of his servants. Would a man allow himself to be attacked and a blade shoved between his ribs yet not shout for aid, or fight against his assailant and create a tumult?"

"I take your point," Prince Edward agreed. "Who is lord of Hornsey?"

"Sir Thomas Jocelyn."

"I don't know the man. Heard his name. His father was at Poitiers. Sir Thomas was too young, I think. So what do you intend, if you are unwilling to allow Arnaud's death to end this business?"

"I will return to Hornsey. There are other houses along the road, tenants of the manor. Some are decayed and empty, but I saw several which are occupied. Perhaps some villager heard what Sir Thomas did not. Or claims he did not."

"Even so," the prince said skeptically, "how would that help you discover who hired my valet to slay Sir Giles?"

"I cannot say. But unless I ask, 'tis certain I will learn nothing. If I do ask, mayhap the same will be so. But mayhap not."

Chapter 10

The road next day was yet muddy, but the rain had ceased and the sky had become bright blue. I took with me to Hornsey only Arthur, seeing no need for extra men in case a felon might contest his arrest. Arnaud Tonge was dead. Who would there be in Hornsey to apprehend? His slayer? If, against my judgment, I found such a man there, his seizure would be a matter for Sir Thomas and his bailiff.

The Aldersgate was busy that morning with folk entering and leaving the city. Most entering, few leaving, which is likely why I noticed four well-garbed gentlemen upon noble steeds who passed through the gate fifty or so paces behind Arthur and me. One of these wore a bright blue cotehardie, which was the more noticeable because his companions were less flamboyantly dressed.

The sloppy road had begun to dry beneath the weak October sun when we entered Hornsey. Father Patrick and his clerk were leaving the church porch as we rode past after mass and I saw his mouth open in surprise. He did not likely expect to see me again and surely wondered why I had returned to his parish. I saw no reason to stop and enlighten him, but I did wave a greeting. His conversation the previous day had told me that he was chary of speaking that which might be construed as critical of Sir Thomas, and if that was so he might also be eager to do or say that which would please the lord of Hornsey.

Sir Thomas had heard no sound of a man slain before his house in the night. I was suspicious of this claim and consequently skeptical of what the knight might think or do regarding other matters. Matters of which the priest might tell him.

An occupied house, in decent repair, was located about twenty paces from the place in the road where yesterday I had seen the twin grooves stop and the dark stain in the dirt. A stain now washed away after the rain.

There was no rail to tie our palfreys to before the house. Few tenants entertain guests who arrive at their door mounted, so I charged Arthur with attending the palfreys while I rapped upon the tenant's door.

No one answered. I knocked upon it a second time. I was certain that someone was within, for the smoke of a fire curled from the vent at the peak of the roof. Likely the wife had set a kettle of pottage to her fire for the family dinner. Would she leave it for some other duty? Perhaps.

I was ready to pound upon the door a third time when it suddenly opened, its hinges squeaking. This tenant was prosperous enough that his door was suspended from iron hinges rather than the leather poorer folk used.

A man stood in the open door. Behind him, in the dim, smoky interior of the house, I saw a woman. She was wringing her hands upon her apron, which seemed an odd reaction to an uninvited guest. I do not usually cause folk distress. Unless they know me to be seeking from them intelligence they would prefer not to disclose. It seems a part of my office that I must often speak to folk who would rather avoid the conversation.

The man at the open door did not speak. He looked me up and down, his eyes rested upon Prince Edward's badge, and his expression, which had been a scowl, softened. I believe he did not know then who I served but that it was some great man. He did soon. I told him.

"What does Prince Edward's constable want w'me?" the man said.

"A few nights past a man was slain on the road close by your house," I began.

"Heard talk of it," the fellow replied.

"That's all? You heard nothing in the night? No sounds of struggle or mayhem?"

"Nay."

"Is it likely," I said, "that a man would feel a blade slipped between his ribs and into his heart and yet not cry out?"

The tenant pursed his lips and shrugged. "Mayhap 'e did, but not so loud as to rouse me or me wife from sleep. A man can 'ear a noise in the night an' think it naught but a dream."

"You have children?" I asked. I was convinced that something was not as it should be. Perhaps a child might speak more truthfully, although why this man would not I could not guess. I represented trouble at his door, which perhaps he wished to avoid. So I thought.

"Three," he said.

"How old are they?"

I saw puzzlement in the man's face, but he would not deny this information to Prince Edward's man. "Oldest is ten years. Youngest but a babe."

"I wish to speak to the oldest. Lass or lad?"

"A lass. But why –"

"Bring her to me. Immediately."

I saw the woman turn and speak a name into the murky interior of the house. The structure had but two windows and even upon a bright day was gloomy within. A moment later a lass appeared wearing a ragged cotehardie which had likely belonged to her mother before being cut down for her.

The child looked from her parents to me with apprehension. I surmised she had heard my words, and was old enough to understand that she was about to be questioned regarding some evil which had come to her village. The lass saw my badge, understood that it represented the great man I served, and curtsied. Her training had not been lacking.

"Do you sleep in the loft?" I asked the girl, and looked above her head.

"Aye. Me an' me sister."

"Three nights past," I said softly, "think back – were you awakened in the night? Did you hear the sounds men make when they fight?"

The lass looked to her mother, then her father, as if seeking permission to answer. The father, not noticing my glance in his direction, shook his head. The movement was slight, nearly imperceptible. But bailiffs are paid to perceive that which others may miss, else they do not long keep their post. The child had heard something in the night, the father knew it, and had likely heard the same conflict himself. Why would he not admit this? Or allow his daughter to tell of it? The child did not reply.

"I am here for Prince Edward," I reminded the tenant. "He will be displeased with you when he learns that you have spoken false to me."

"The prince ain't 'ere, is 'e?" the man said. "Just you."

"Indeed he is not. But his reach is long. Do you not fear this?"

"I fear some things an' some men. Them what is close by, but not men far away."

Fear. Here was why neither the man nor his wife would speak, nor permit the child to do so. Who in Hornsey would such a man fear with a dread so great he would risk angering Prince Edward's constable? There was but one man in the village likely to have such power over this tenant: his lord, Sir Thomas Jocelyn.

I had not been asked to enter the dwelling. Our conversation had taken place over the threshold. I turned to Arthur, told him to wait for my return, then invited myself into the house. The man did not resist. He and his wife backed away, I followed, and closed the door behind me.

"How long after you heard the noise of a man slain in the night did Sir Thomas come to you?"

Whether or not Sir Thomas, or one of his servants, had approached this tenant in the night or early next morning I did not know. But I was certain that the man had been warned to swear, if asked, that he had heard nothing which awakened him. I could devise no reason for such instruction, but just because I did not understand why the fellow had been told to keep silent did not mean that some man did not have reason to demand he hold his tongue.

The tenant glanced to his wife, seeking reassurance. He found little. The woman's eyes watered and she went to twisting her apron again. If the man did not fear a duke's wrath, his wife evidently did. The lass peered open-mouthed at one parent, then the other.

"Sir Thomas never come 'ere," the tenant said.

"A groom then, or perhaps his bailiff. Someone told you to keep silent. Who? I will have the information from you, or I will place you under arrest and take you to Prince Edward. If you will not speak to me, you will tell what you know to the prince. His serjeants have mastered methods to make men speak of what they would rather not."

The man unconsciously shrank from me as he considered the procedures which might be used to loosen his tongue. I dislike threatening honest men, and but for his instructions to deceive, the fellow was likely as honest as most. Fear had caused him to lie. A greater fear might bring truth from him.

The tenant's shoulders dropped. "'Twas Henry what told us we must hold our tongues."

"Who is Henry?"

"Sir Thomas's bailiff."

"When did he command this? The same night the man was slain?"

"Aye."

"Did he supply a reason for requiring your silence?"

"Said as some fellow had tried to enter Sir Thomas's house in the night. Sir Thomas 'eard 'im an' drove 'im away. Called for Henry an' some grooms, an' they sought the man what tried to do hamsoken. Found 'im hidin' behind Sir Thomas's barn, so Henry did say. Took to 'is 'eels, but John is fleet."

"John?"

"John Dessex, Sir Thomas's squire."

"So this squire chased a man, caught him, and dispatched him in the road before your house. Is that how it was?"

"Guess so," the man shrugged.

"And you heard this conflict? What was said? Men seeking to harm one another, or to escape harm, are not generally silent when they come to blows."

"Asleep, wasn't I? I got woke up, but all I 'eard was men shoutin' at one another. Couldn't tell what they was sayin'."

"I 'eard," the lass said. She sensed that her father was in some difficulty and thought to reduce his trouble by answering questions when he could not. Or would not. "One man said, 'Here's what's owed you.' An' then there was the sound of a man 'owlin' like 'e was 'urt. But not for long. All was quiet in just a moment."

I turned to the lass's father. "You heard none of these words? Only the wounded man crying out?"

"Aye. 'Twas 'is yelp what woke me."

"The man found slain was pierced in the heart," I said. "Does it not seem strange that if he was chased and caught he was not stabbed in the back?"

There was little more to learn from this tenant. A man was slain before his door, he admitted, but did he know why? 'Twas not likely. Only what he was told. If I continued to threaten him with a meeting with Prince Edward's serjeants he might conjure some false explanation to satisfy me – faulty explanation which could lead me astray rather than to a felon who did murder and another who employed a murderer.

If the grandest house in a village belongs to the lord, the second best house will likely be the habitation of the bailiff. This is so in Bampton, where Galen House is rivaled only by Father Thomas's vicarage. The house in Hornsey which fitted this description was adjacent to the priest's house. I bade the reluctant tenant "Good day," collected Arthur and our palfreys, and together we led the beasts the short way to what I assumed was the bailiff's dwelling. It was.

Hornsey's bailiff, the man's wife said, was somewhere about the village carrying out his duties. What these obligations were upon a Sunday, and where they took him, she knew not. So she said.

"Will he return for his dinner?" I asked. The scent of a steaming pottage told me that he would, and soon.

The woman glanced over her shoulder to her kitchen, realized that the fragrance of a pease pottage had come to my nostrils, and agreed that her husband would soon appear.

It was past the fifth hour when I rapped upon the bailiff's door, so I knew I would not need to wait long for his return. The agreeable smell of the man's dinner, however, made the time pass slowly. The woman had invited me to await her husband's appearance in the hall. My stomach would have made less protest had I returned to Arthur and the palfreys outside her door.

I peered about the bailiff's hall while seated upon a bench

opposite the entry door. Beside this bench was a fine cupboard, and within it I saw three pieces of plate displayed, along with a half-dozen silver spoons, a supply of pewter utensils, and eight pewter cups. One of the hall windows was of glass, although this glass was of the meaner sort, each diamond pane having much distortion. This was the home of a prosperous man, and his wealth was surely due to pleasing Sir Thomas, and before him Sir William. If the bailiff's lord required of him that he dissemble when asked of murder in the street I had no doubt he would do so. Truth might cost him his position, his house, and his income. How, then, was I to learn from the bailiff what Sir Thomas Jocelyn did not want me to know? And why was I not to know it?

Henry Attewood is a small man, with a chin always pointed out as if daring some other to strike a blow at it. He reminded me, when I first saw him, of a small dog seeking to antagonize an alaunt. Not that I consider myself such a mighty foe, but the bailiff seemed poised to challenge me before I said a word. Perhaps he was warned that I would seek him. And what I would ask of him.

The bailiff entered his house through a kitchen door. I heard him greet his wife and ask of his dinner. The woman then spoke softly, advising him, I am sure, of my presence in his hall. A moment later he appeared, chin thrust forward, scowl upon his brow. He offered no greeting.

I introduced myself and decided that mentioning the names of the men I served might persuade the bailiff to be helpful. My first impression of the man was that he had little interest in assisting any man at any time for any purpose.

So I announced to the fellow that I, like him, was a bailiff, and made the point that I served a greater lord than he. Lord Gilbert Talbot far outranks a mere knight. Henry Attewood's demeanor moderated even more when I touched a finger to Prince Edward's badge and disclosed that I was in Hornsey upon the prince's business. Unlike the tenant I had spoken to an hour earlier the bailiff had wit enough to understand the precarious footing he would be upon were he uncooperative. I did not assume, however, that all he said would be truth. It wasn't.

"I have just come from speaking to a tenant of Hornsey Manor. The man resides just across the road from Sir Thomas. I asked the fellow questions he was reluctant to answer."

"What questions?"

"About a man slain in the road before his house. The dead man was Arnaud Tonge, valet to Prince Edward. The tenant told me that you commanded his silence. Why so?"

"Wasn't a command," the bailiff said.

"What, then?"

"More like a request."

"From you? Every tenant and villein in the realm knows that a bailiff's request is a command. Why would you, the man whose duty it is to seek out felons here, request silence of a man who had knowledge of a murder?"

"Why did the prince's valet attempt to enter Sir Thomas's house in the night?" the bailiff asked.

I had thought the claim that Arnaud was caught in the act of hamsoken was a subterfuge, but the bailiff's question seemed genuine. Whatever the truth of the matter, he seemed convinced of what he had been told of Arnaud's actions in the night. The bailiff would not have been present when – if – Arnaud had attempted to enter the manor house in the night. He would have been sleeping in his own bed until awakened to search for Arnaud.

"I am told the man was seen about the village the day before, and spent time at the alehouse," I said.

"It wasn't me seen 'im," Attewood answered quickly.

"You had no knowledge of any strange man in Hornsey three days past until he tried to enter Sir Thomas's house?"

"That's right."

"If you knew nothing of the man, why charge that tenant with silence about his death? Why should you care if any other man was told of the slaying?"

The bailiff pursed his lips and shrugged. "Don't care, myself... I was told to require Watkin's silence, and any other's who may have heard the struggle in the night."

"Watkin is the tenant before whose house the man was slain?"

"Aye."

Only one man in Hornsey had the authority to order others to silence regarding a death in the village.

"Did Sir Thomas give you reason for his command that the death of Arnaud Tonge be hid?"

"Said the man was caught in the act of hamsoken and he had the right of infangenthef."

"So why then demand silence? Everyone in Hornsey would know Sir Thomas had the authority to do away with a thief caught in the act of his felony. To what purpose would he not want it known?"

"Don't know. Best ask him."

I thought that a good idea. I left the bailiff to his pease pottage and, my stomach growling, Arthur and I retraced our steps to Sir Thomas's manor house. We interrupted his dinner. The knight was not pleased to be drawn from his table a second day in a row, nor was his disposition improved by my questions.

"Yesterday," I began, "you told me that you heard no struggle in the night when Prince Edward's valet was slain in the road before your door. Others said the same at first, but have since collected their thoughts and are now persuaded that they did hear conflict in the night."

The stocky young knight shrugged. "Some men," he said, "can be persuaded to speak what is not true if goaded to do so."

"And persuaded to keep silent about what is, if commanded. The valet was slain before your door. This I know. Do not deny it. What puzzles me is why he was in such a place after curfew, why you claim not to have heard a murder which other folk did hear, and why you demanded of your tenants that they say nothing truthful of the matter."

"The man did hamsoken," Sir Thomas sighed with exasperation. "He was in the duke's employ. It would, I thought, displease the prince if he learned that his servant was slain upon my demesne."

"Slain by your squire, I was told."

"Aye."

"As he ran from the village."

"Tried to. John caught him. I have right of infangenthef."

"If your squire chased the valet down and slew him, why was the man stabbed in the heart? Seems to me he'd be wounded in the back. Where is your squire? Consuming his dinner, I'd guess. Fetch him."

The knight turned to a groom standing behind him and relayed my request. While I awaited the squire's appearance I considered Sir Thomas's words. He claimed to have ordered all of his manor to keep silent about Arnaud's death because he feared Prince Edward's wrath if the duke knew that his valet was slain in Hornsey. Did Sir Thomas know that Arnaud was a valet to the prince that night, when he was slain? How so? I had not told him of Arnaud's service to Prince Edward 'til the valet was buried, and when I did, it was because Sir Thomas claimed ignorance of the dead man and his murder.

I did not point out to Sir Thomas the discrepancy in his words on different days. Perhaps he would assume that I did not notice the variance. I have discovered in past dealings with miscreants that such men are less likely to be cautious of what they do and say if they believe me ignorant of their errors and villainies. This ignorance is often genuine.

Was Sir Thomas a villain? He was a liar, this I knew. But why?

Sir Thomas's squire appeared as these thoughts passed through my mind. The lad gave the appearance of possessing a quick pair of heels. He was of my height, and as slender as I was before Kate's cookery added somewhat to my girth. He looked to Sir Thomas as he stepped toward me and an unspoken message passed between them.

"I am told that you are quick on your feet," I began. "Quick enough to chase down and pierce a man three nights past."

The lad chewed upon his lip but did not speak. My words were not a question to which he must reply.

"What did the man say when you caught him? Did he speak? Did you slay him because he turned on you?"

"Aye," the squire said. "When he knew I'd caught him he drew his dagger."

"What did he say? Anything?"

"Nay. Spoke not a word. But in the moonlight I saw his dagger flash as he thrust at me. He was not skilled. I parried the thrust and brought my own dagger against him."

"Did he then cry out? Did he then speak?"

"He said, 'I am slain,' or some such words, and tried to flee, but he stumbled only a few paces before he fell."

"And he cried out for the pain of his wound?"

"Aye, he did so."

"Who dragged the man from where he fell to where he was found next morn?"

"Henry and I did."

"Sir Thomas told you to do this?"

"Aye."

I turned back to the knight. "Why place a dead man in a ditch so far from where he died?"

"I told you, didn't I?" Sir Thomas said in an exasperated tone of voice. "I didn't want Prince Edward to hold me answerable for the death of his valet. If he was found far away from the village the prince might assume 'twas some highwayman who slew him."

Again the knight had contradicted himself. If I could discover why, I might learn why he, or some other man, had wished Arnaud Tonge dead. And why Arnaud had tried to enter the manor house in the night. If he had.

"You may tell the prince what you will of this sorry business," Sir Thomas continued. "But I have spoken truth. If Prince Edward does not believe it so, I can but say to him what I have already said to you. Now my dinner awaits and grows cold. I bid you good day."

The knight turned away, disappeared through a doorway to his hall, and a groom and squire followed. One groom remained, to show me the door. As if I would not find it. More likely he was assigned to ensure my departure.

Chapter 11

I departed the manor house willingly. I had this day learned what I had previously suspected. Sir Thomas Jocelyn was a liar, and would exercise his power over the folk of Hornsey to prevent truth from being known.

If the knight had reason to slay or silence Arnaud Tonge, did this mean he had some association with the man who had hired Arnaud to poison Sir Giles's wine? If I followed this thought, would the path lead me closer to the man who wished Sir Giles dead, or further away? There was no way to know this but to follow the track and see where it led. If I lived long enough to do so.

Hornsey had no inn, but a cup or two at the alehouse would relieve our hunger while we traveled to London and I considered on the way what next I might do in Prince Edward's service. The basket remained atop the pole before the ale wife's house, but the ale Rohese served was no longer fresh. 'Twas not yet gone stale, but in honesty she should have no longer displayed the basket. Was there anyone in Hornsey who could be trusted? Surely. I have become jaded. 'Tis, I fear, a feature of my position. Bailiff, I mean, not surgeon.

Arthur and I drank two cups each of ale, and I left a penny on the table – although we'd not come near to consuming a gallon. We mounted our palfreys, stopped where the road crossed a small brook for the animals to drink, then set off for London and a decent supper.

We were near to the junction where the road from London divided, at a place where a wood came within a hundred paces of the west side of the road, when I heard a sound of dry, dead branches upon a forest floor being trampled and broken underfoot. A heartbeat later, as I turned to see whence came this crashing and splintering, a mounted man appeared from the wood, followed by another. Before I could collect my wits, two more riders emerged from the wood, spurring their horses across a meadow, directly toward Arthur and me.

Arthur heard, and saw, the approaching horsemen and realized, as I did, that they meant us harm. I spurred my palfrey and shouted for Arthur to do likewise. He needed no further encouragement. Our beasts galloped furiously at our command, perhaps sensing danger, although the peril was not to them but to their riders.

Within fifty paces I could see that we had no chance of escaping the horsemen charging after us. Their animals were powerful and swift; they would soon be upon us. I glanced over my shoulder to calculate how quickly our pursuers would overtake us and saw that one of these, now waving a sword above his head, was garbed in a bright blue cotehardie.

This recognition registered in my mind, but the consideration of it took second place to thoughts of escape from the men and beasts thundering after Arthur and me. The road turned sharply and as we entered the bend I saw that two of our pursuers had departed the thoroughfare and guided their horses through the adjacent field, following the hypotenuse of the triangle created by the acute curve in the road, so as to cut off our escape.

This field was newly plowed ready for the autumn planting of wheat or rye and so made soft footing for galloping horses. I was about to call to Arthur that we must halt and fight even though the odds against us were terrible – two daggers opposing four swords – when I heard a shouted curse and glanced to the horsemen who were racing across the plowed field.

One of the beasts had stumbled and pitched its rider headlong into the soft earth. I heard him yelp as his shoulder made contact with the soil. The field was soft enough, I think, that his hurt was not severe. But as I watched, the other of the pursuers who had ridden across the field yanked back upon his reins in order to avoid his companion. He was not successful.

Another curse resounded as the second horse and rider struck the fallen man, and this rider joined his companion on the ground. The second man's horse fell upon its rider, crushing him to the earth. I saw the frightened steed kick wildly as it tried to regain its feet. One of these blows struck the first fallen rider squarely in his gut as he tried to stand, and he flew through the air to make a second impact against the plowed field. This time he lay motionless where he fell.

Two of our pursuers now lay crumpled upon the plowed field. We are to do good to those who use us ill, so the Lord Christ commanded, but I felt no sympathy for the men who lay bruised behind my galloping palfrey and I did not stop to learn if either of the fallen men required my surgical skills. Besides, I had none of my instruments with me. Later that night, as Arthur snored, I thought upon Jesus' charge that Christian folk must do good to those who would do evil to them. What had these pursuers intended? Likely they meant to slay me and Arthur. Men do not gallop after other men, waving swords above their heads, if they wish only discourse. No man can return good for evil if the evil has ended his life.

With their companions groaning in the field, the two horsemen who had remained upon the road behind us lost heart for the chase and reined in their beasts. I looked back again as the road curved once more and saw them dismounting to run to the aid of their fallen companions.

Our palfreys were winded and laboring, being unaccustomed to such usage, so I drew my beast to a walk and motioned Arthur to do likewise.

"What d'you suppose them fellows wanted?" Arthur said.

"Our lives."

"Oh... why so?"

"Because someone fears that I am closer to finding who hired the murderer of Sir Giles Cheyne than I am."

"Mayhap you are closer than you think also," Arthur said.

His suggestion gave me pause. If I was closer to discovering a murderer than I thought, what fact was I overlooking which some other man – or men – thought I recognized?

Alan Tonge did not know of his brother's death. His home was not far from the Aldersgate and it would be but a short detour to visit the man and tell him of the murder.

"'Twas that valet what argued with 'im," Alan said. "The man must have discovered where Arnaud had hidden himself and found 'im out."

"Nay," I said. "This was done to silence your brother. I have no doubt of this. And to save the murderer a few shillings. Your brother was hired to poison a knight in Prince Edward's service. Now he is dead he cannot name the man who employed him or collect his pay."

"'Tis hard for me to believe that Arnaud did such a thing," Alan said, a bewildered look upon his face. "He said..."

"Pay no heed to what your brother said. He used you falsely to flee London and has now met the Lord Christ with the death of another man on his hands."

"I will pray for his soul," Alan said.

"Such prayers will do him small service," I replied.

"If I do not, his soul will suffer purgatory for thousands of years, so the priests do say. I'll pay a vicar of St. Michael le Querne to say prayers for him as well."

I did not reply. I have spoken unwisely of purgatory in the past, and came near to calamity when an archdeacon learned of my views. If the prayers of men can spring open the gates of heaven to admit a murderer, then no man need ever see hell. So Alan will pay his parish priest to pray for Arnaud's soul, the priest will profit, and Alan will believe he has saved his brother. At least the money laid down will purchase some comfort for Alan, if nothing more.

London's streets were raucous, as always, and caused me to think fondly of the peaceful calm of Bampton. But even there men will do mischief, else why would Lord Gilbert require a bailiff? If men were honorable I would be unemployed but for surgery, and even that occupation would decline as men would seek my service only for harm they had done to themselves, less so for harm others had done to them, in a world where no man sought to harm another.

Perhaps the noisome streets of London are the reason Prince Edward prefers the bucolic surroundings of Kennington Palace, as his brother John does the Savoy, his palace at Westminster.

Arthur and I crossed London Bridge grateful to have escaped harm upon the road. I had not sought safety before the journey upon my knees, but we are told in Holy Writ that the Lord Christ knows our need before we ask. Perhaps even if we fail to ask. I must not fail to be thankful for our escape.

Grooms were erecting tables and benches in Kennington's hall when we arrived at the palace. Prince Edward had made it clear that he wished to be informed of my progress, or lack of it, in seeking Sir Giles's murderer, so I went directly to his privy chamber. He was not alone.

The valets who stood at the door announced my arrival, and I heard the prince tell them that I was to be admitted. Three of his knights attended him in the privy chamber, and their conversation ceased when I passed through the doorway. One of these I knew to be Sir Arthur de Lisle, Sir Giles's rival for the hand of Lady Juliana Pultney.

I bowed to the four seated men, and Prince Edward spoke. "You returned to that village today, did you not? What is it named?"

"Hornsey, m'lord."

"Ah, just so. What have you learned?"

"To ride a faster horse next time I must travel there."

Prince Edward returned my gaze with a puzzled expression. I did not wish to speak of the events of the day before these knights, especially Sir Arthur. I hesitated, and glanced to the prince's companions. Prince Edward discerned my hesitation.

"Master Hugh has matters to discuss with me," he said. "We will speak more of this matter at supper."

I wondered what matter that might be, but gave the statement no more thought. The business of great men seldom intrudes upon the life of a bailiff. Or a surgeon. So I thought.

"As you know," I began, once the prince and I were alone, "your valet was slain in Hornsey. The lord of the manor..."

"Sir Thomas Jocelyn?"

"Aye, m'lord, Sir Thomas, claims that Arnaud was caught in the act of hamsoken and his charter gives him the right of infangenthef."

"What of the coroner and the king's due?"

"He took flight when apprehended. So Sir Thomas said. A squire chased after him, and Arnaud turned on him with a dagger. The squire defended himself and Arnaud fell dead. Sir Thomas said he did not admit to this yesterday as he feared your wrath."

"You believe this tale?"

"Nay, m'lord. But I have believed wrong things and disbelieved true things often enough in the past that I consider my opinions suspect until I can prove them."

"What do you believe yet do not trust to be true?" the prince asked.

"I hesitate to say for fear of appearing foolish in your sight if I am wrong."

"Ah, but consider how wise I will think you if your opinion proves true. So speak."

When the Prince of Wales asks a man for his opinion the request is really a command. This was clear in the tone of his voice.

"'Tis my belief that Arnaud was paid but a portion of the promised remit before he placed the hemlock in Sir Giles's wine. He was assured that he would receive the remainder when he traveled to Hornsey. He was told to wait there, and the coins would be delivered. Why Hornsey, I cannot say.

"But rather than a purse full of pence and groats and perhaps a quarter-noble he found nothing. He waited for a day to receive his due. An ale wife of the village declares this. Then after dark three days past he was slain in the street, his corpse dragged away from the village so that, if Sir Thomas's word is to be believed, you would think Arnaud slain by highwaymen, not some man of Hornsey."

"What if the knight is not to be believed?"

"Then Arnaud thought he was to receive his reward from some man attached to the manor house of Hornsey. Why else try to enter the place in the night? If he did so."

"Sir Thomas?"

"Mayhap," I shrugged.

"Sir Thomas said that Arnaud attempted to enter the manor house in the night," I continued. "Did he, or was that a subterfuge on the knight's part to justify slaying Arnaud? Did Arnaud decide to seize goods from Sir Thomas because he had been promised payment which did not appear? Whichever may be true, if either, it means that Sir Thomas knows more of this business than he will say.

"And Sir Thomas knew Arnaud to be in your service before I told him," I continued.

"He misspoke himself?" Prince Edward said, pulling upon his beard.

"He did. And gave away his complicity in this, whatever it might be. He should not have known who Arnaud served before I told him. I did not bring the matter of his knowledge of Arnaud before him. He believes I did not perceive the error."

The bell signaling supper was sounded and I found myself escorted to the hall by the Duke of Cornwall. We were among the last to arrive, and I received many curious glances from all levels of society, from grooms to gentlemen. And their ladies. Some glances seemed more hostile than curious, but perhaps I saw what I expected rather than what was.

Once again I found myself seated upon a bench beside William Blackwater. He glared at me, which was a common enough greeting from other men in recent days that I was accustomed to the expression. Few men I had met recently received me with joy and smiles. I was unsure if I wanted to begin a conversation with the physician, and when uncertain if I should speak or not I find it wisest to hold my tongue. So it was Blackwater who spoke first, as we consumed the first remove.

"You will send the duke to his grave, you know," he began.

I looked to the prince and saw him enjoying a roasted capon. There seemed to be no boiled rooster anywhere in evidence. When I did not reply to his assertion the physician spoke again.

"Prince Edward has told me that he will have no more of my advice. Your herbs, he says, have improved his health. But any physician knows that such as he is now eating will upset his humors. The illness to come will be more grievous than that of the past. His diet of boiled roosters was beginning to mend his body when you foolishly told him to consume those ridiculous herbs. So now he charges me with preparing the herbs and claims for your absurd prescription the relief my diet has brought to him. He will soon relapse as his humors fall from balance, and you will be sent away. I pray 'twill not be too late to save the duke."

I glanced again to the high table and saw Prince Edward grinning at some remark of Lady Joan. The Fair Maid of Kent also seemed delighted by the fat capon. Indeed, her rounded cheeks and voluminous gown gave evidence that she took delight in most meals. But the prince does not seem to hold her corpulence against her. Indeed, if artists are to be believed, men prefer women who resemble wine casks to those who appear like a coppiced beech pole. For my own part, I prefer my Kate, amply fitted with curves but few bulges.

"I spoke to Lady Joan," Blackwater continued, as if he had read my mind, "about your interference. I advised her to speak to the prince concerning your malfeasance."

From what I had heard of the Lady Joan I had little doubt that if she thought it necessary to advise her husband she would not hesitate to do so.

"And what was her reply?" I asked.

"She does not understand the terrible gravity of the prince's condition."

"In other words, she paid you no heed."

"She will, soon enough, when his body fails him. I would not like to be in your place when that happens."

Nor would I, I thought to myself, and said a silent prayer that the remedies I had suggested would prove lasting. The bishops say that such unspoken prayers are of no value. Does the Lord Christ have ears? Must men pray aloud for their prayers to be heard? If so, the prayers of so many, especially upon a Sunday morning when 'tis time for the mass, must be a terrible cacophony in heaven. I should think the Lord Christ would prefer silent prayers, but priests do say prayers unspoken are also unheard. I must ask Master Wycliffe of this when next I see him.

A clattering of overturned benches and the sound of voices raised in anger interrupted my thoughts and William Blackwater's condemnation. I looked to the uproar and saw two squires pummeling each other. One of these had a flow of blood gushing from his nose, and as I watched he drew a dagger.

He clearly intended to use the weapon against the youth who had bloodied him, but was dissuaded from this when from the high table a voice bellowed for the combatants to halt. Both turned to see who had commanded them to cease. 'Twas Prince Edward who stood, fists upon the table before him. Anger reddened his face, and even in his frail state he was able to shout loudly enough that his tone overcame the anger of the brawling squires. They backed away from each other.

"What means this display?" the prince roared. Then, to his marshal, Prince Edward commanded, "Remove them. I'll deal with them later."

Sir Harold Shippen, Kennington's marshal, is not a large, brawny man. His strength lies in the authority behind his title. He hastened from his place at the high table, took each squire by the ear, and marched them from the hall. The lads made no protest to this indignity. Perhaps they understood that they deserved the opprobrium.

The marshal and squires disappeared through the screens passage, and those at supper who had stood from benches and chairs resumed their places and continued the meal. Conversations gradually resumed, although the topics discussed were surely different from those before the noisy altercation.

"Whose squires were those?" I asked Blackwater. The physician had attended Prince Edward for many years and I assumed he would know those who dined at the prince's table.

"The lad whose nose drips blood is Fulk de Driby, squire to Sir Humphrey Downey. The other is Roger de Clare, squire to Sir John Pedley."

"Do Sir Humphrey and Sir John dislike each other so much that their squires would come to blows in support of their masters?"

"Not that I've heard," Blackwater shrugged, "nor seen. Sir John and Sir Humphrey always seem amicable enough as regards each other. Must be the squires have had a falling out. Some lass at the bottom of it, I'd wager."

"Aye," I agreed. "A pert lass will oft cause bloodied noses and blackened eyes." And burned houses, I thought, as my mind turned to the ash heap which was the first Galen House after Sir Simon Trillowe gave vent to his wrath against me.

The exchange of fisticuffs in Kennington Palace hall had presented a new topic of conversation for those who, from high table to low, supped in the hall this day. Even William Blackwater lost interest in his previous condemnation of my medicine and spent most of the third remove exchanging thoughts with the man who sat upon his other hand, a minor knight of Prince Edward's fee.

"There is much talk," I heard this knight say to the physician, "of who gains most from the death of Sir Giles Cheyne." I heard little else of their conversation, for the hall was soon filled with folk expressing opinions of the squires' conflict, and the din drowned out his remarks.

Would the pugilistic squires have thoughts about Sir Giles's death and the gain such a felony might bring to other knights, as well as to their own masters? A conversation with each might resolve such a question, especially if the youths were reminded that Prince Edward has placed me in charge of discovering the felon or felons who sought Sir Giles's death.

The void was a compote of apples and pears, and as soon as Prince Edward stood from his chair at the high table and departed the hall, I left my bench and sought the marshal. I was not alone. The prince was there before me. He was not pleased.

The squires sat upon opposite ends of a bench at the entrance to the buttery. One of the lads had arms folded across his chest and a petulant scowl upon his face. The other occasionally wiped a finger across his upper lip, where drying blood had caked. The marshal stood before the lads, arms folded. He was silent, although I suspect he had not been until Prince Edward arrived.

"You disgrace my hall and Sir John and Sir Humphrey," the prince said as I came upon the scene. He heard my footsteps and turned to see who had interrupted his scolding of the squires. He saw 'twas me, then turned back to the youths to unburden his soul.

"Have you differences, you will henceforth settle them in some place other than within my hall. You are squires to worthy knights. Have you learned nothing from them? Should such a display occur again within Kennington Palace, you will no longer be welcome."

This threat surely caught the squires' attention. Neither Sir John nor Sir Humphrey would retain a squire who was unwelcome in Prince Edward's presence. Nor would such a squire find a place with some other knight, not even a minor knight unlikely to be called before the prince.

Prince Edward turned again to me, a question in his eyes. He surely wondered what interest I had in two misbehaving squires. There must be twenty or more squires attached to knights serving at Kennington Palace. The two who came to blows served knights who had had an intense dislike of Sir Giles. Was this coincidence or something sinister? Bailiffs, marshals, constables, coroners, and such like men do not believe in coincidences.

Prince Edward turned to his marshal. "Set these two to mucking out the stables tomorrow morning. Early." He then turned from marshal and miscreants and stalked from us.

The squires looked from the marshal to me, curiosity written upon their faces. I imagined they wondered why the man charged with discovering who had slain Sir Giles Cheyne stood there facing them. I enlightened them.

"There has been violence in Kennington's hall these past days," I said. "You know that the prince has assigned me the task of discovering who did murder in his hall. Lads who are quick to rage against one another may be of such a truculent nature that they would poison a man's wine, I think. I will discuss this matter with you. Separately."

I thought the squire whose nose had suffered might have spoken rashly and drawn the ire, and first blow, of the other. I told him to come with me, required of Roger that he remain where he was 'til I had need of him, then led Fulk through the kitchen to Lady Joan's privy garden. If Fulk had indeed said something to enrage Roger, he had behaved unwisely. Roger stood a hand taller than Fulk and likely outweighed him by two stone.

The lad did not accompany me willingly. He likely assumed I intended to ask him of matters he would have preferred to avoid. This is ever the case when searching out a felon. Questions which folk are willing to answer often provide no insight to whoso may be guilty, and questions they evade are those leading to a malefactor.

"What did you say or do," I began, "which caused Roger to bloody your nose?"

Fulk did not immediately reply, but gently touched his tender nose as if my words were a reminder of his condition.

"Prince Edward has appointed me his constable," I reminded the youth, and glanced down to my badge. "If you will not answer I must inform the prince of your recalcitrance. He will not be pleased. His temper against those who anger him is well known."

It is indeed. I saw Fulk blanch as I reminded him of Prince Edward's nature. The prince's disposition is much like that of other powerful men – and women – who become accustomed from childhood to obedience and react vigorously to insubordination.

"We spoke of Sir Giles's death," the squire said finally.

"Why should such a conversation lead to blows?" I said.

"Roger and I have differing opinions of the matter."

"Enlighten me. I will hear your opinion."

"All men know," Fulk began, "that Sir John held fierce resentment against Sir Giles for claiming that Sir John fled the battle at Crécy."

"Do you believe Sir Giles's charge to be true?"

The squire shrugged. "'Tis a thing all men know."

"But do all men believe it? Would Prince Edward have Sir John at his table if this tale was true?"

Fulk shrugged again. "Likely not," he said. "But mayhap the prince does not know the truth of the matter, busy with the battle as he was."

"You said this to Roger at table?"

"Not exactly."

"Then what, exactly, did you say which earned you a bloodied nose?"

"Roger said that of all of us who disliked Sir Giles, Sir Humphrey had the greatest reason to wish him dead."

"Why so? What reason for this did Roger give?"

"He said that many here at Kennington attended the joust where Sir Giles put Sir Humphrey upon his rump. Sir Humphrey likely heard others speak of it when he passed by and saw smiles behind upraised hands. The humiliation would gnaw at him until he could bear the shame no longer."

"Why did his claim bring you two to blows?"

"I replied to Roger that Sir John had as great a reason to slay Sir Giles as did Sir Humphrey. No man wishes to be reminded of his cowardice."

"You claimed Sir John a coward?" I said.

"Roger made it clear that he thought Sir Humphrey guilty of murder, and incompetent at the joust as well. I would not allow such a slur to go unchallenged."

"So you reminded Roger of the charge against Sir John's courage at Crécy?"

"Aye."

"He took the remark badly?"

"Aye, he did. But I would not allow Sir Humphrey to be slandered without reply."

"And you paid for his defense with a bloodied nose," I said.

"I did. But had not Prince Edward caused us to cease I'd have repaid Roger with my dagger." The lad spoke with such vehemence that I did not doubt it was so. Or that he would yet like to sheathe his weapon in Roger's belly.

"You heard Prince Edward. He will brook no more disturbance of this kind in his hall – nor anywhere else in Kennington Palace, I'd guess."

"Then Roger de Clare had best keep his opinions to himself."

"He would likely say the same of you. 'Tis known to most folks that neither Sir Humphrey nor Sir John are grieved that Sir Giles is no longer able to vex them."

"Aye," the squire agreed. "But they are not alone."

"So I am told. Sir Giles was not liked, I know."

I bid Fulk keep his temper under control and returned to the screens passage where I had told Roger to await my return. He had done so, unwillingly. I told the strapping youth to follow, and returned to the garden, where I might converse with him as with Fulk, away from prying ears.

"You accused Sir Humphrey of wishing Sir Giles Cheyne dead," I began.

"Aye, because he surely did."

"Did not Sir John desire this also?"

"No man believes that Sir John fled the field at Crécy."

This was not an answer to my question. The squire knew well why his master would be pleased at Sir Giles's death. His reply was proof of this.

"You did not answer my question. Is Sir John pleased that his nemesis is dead?"

"Probably. I've never asked him."

"If all men know that Sir John was no coward at Crécy, why would Sir Giles continue to repeat the charge? It seems to me that he would know soon enough that others did not believe his accusation. If it was known to be false."

"It was false, whatever men may say behind their hands."

"So then all men do not know the taunt to be false?"

Roger did not reply, caught in his own conflicting words.

"I know what you're about," the lad finally said.

"And what is that?"

"Prince Edward wants some man to hang for slaying his favorite. You seek his preferment and to get it will send some man to the scaffold, be he guilty or not."

"This is what knights and squires and pages here at Kennington say among themselves?"

"Aye, it is," Roger said firmly.

Here was troubling news. If Prince Edward's guests and retainers thought I was untrustworthy, seeking only to blame some man, guilty or not, for Sir Giles's death regardless of truth, I was not likely to learn from any man facts which would lead to the guilty. Rather, I was likely to be told that which would send me in pursuit of some man the questioned wished to impugn. If they thought I would not care who hanged or went to the block, neither would they. So long as 'twas not them.

Roger wore a dark grey cotehardie, nearly black, and a cap of lighter grey with a long, stylish liripipe wrapped twice about his head. I remembered with a start where I had seen a man in similar raiment. One of the four who had chased Arthur and me upon the road had been similarly garbed. The fellow had been one of the two who halted pursuit when he saw his companions fall in the newly plowed field. Until that moment he had been closing the distance between himself and me and Arthur while waving a sword above his head. The liripipe he wore then was wrapped about his face like a scarf so that it covered all but his forehead and eyes.

This pursuer had carried his sword in his left hand, with his beast's reins grasped in his right hand. I resolved that at the next meal in Kennington's hall I would watch to see which hand Roger de Clare used to feed himself.

Chapter 12

Roger used his left hand to eat his dinner the next day. Four other squires now sat between him and Fulk, creating an uneasy distance between the two. Fulk, I saw, had a darkened eye.

As I consumed my dinner I considered how I might learn where Roger de Clare had spent the previous day when Arthur and I were waylaid upon the road. If Roger was indeed one of those who meant us harm he would likely have been sent on the errand by Sir John. It would do little good, therefore, to ask Sir John of his squire's whereabouts a day earlier. He would claim the lad was at Kennington with him all day.

Prince Edward's marshal would know if Roger had required his horse a day past. I resolved to seek him when the meal was done.

Sir Harold Shippen was unsure of Roger de Clare's movements. Knights and squires and even pages were, he said, regularly seeking their steeds to travel hither and yon. He would ask of a groom.

"Aye," the fellow said. "Came for 'is beast about the third hour, perhaps a bit earlier."

"When did he return? Was he back for his dinner?"

"Nay. Returned the horse in the afternoon."

"About the ninth hour, would you say?" I asked.

The groom pulled at his beard, then replied, "Later. Near to supper."

"Did the horse seem ill used?"

"Aye, now you mention it. Sweat dried upon the animal. 'Ad to wipe 'im down."

"Was Roger alone when he departed Kennington yesterday, or when he returned?"

"Aye, by 'isself, both goin' and comin'."

If Roger de Clare was one of those who had set upon us on the road, where did he find three companions? Or did they, or one of the three, find him? And would he wear the same garb at supper as he had worn when pursuing me a few hours before? Would the squire not consider that I might recognize his clothing? Perhaps not. Grey cotehardies are common enough. And was the assailant upon the road truly dressed in grey? Might his cotehardie have been dark brown? The day was drear, and I was not at the time in a position to examine the hue closely. But the fellow upon the road was left-handed, as was Roger de Clare.

Perhaps Arthur would recall the event and its participants. I left the stables and sought him.

"Come to think of it," Arthur said, when asked, "one of them fellows *was* swingin' 'is sword with 'is left hand. But 'is cotehardie? Don't remember. Could've been grey, I suppose. Me thoughts was upon other matters. Only thing I remember about them fellows' dress was that one of 'em, him that took a tumble in that new-plowed field, wore a bright blue cotehardie."

"The squire to Sir John Pedley is left-handed," I said, "and wears a grey cotehardie."

"And Sir John's one of them that's not sorrowing now that Sir Giles is dead?"

"Aye. He'll not lie awake nights grieving."

At supper that night Roger de Clare wore a green cotehardie. Had he seen me inspecting him from across the hall while at dinner? Perhaps a young squire simply liked to change his attire upon occasion.

Musicians appeared when supper was finished, as was the custom at Kennington Palace. The tables and benches were cleared and stacked against the wall, and gentlefolk danced galliards and pavanes as the light from the windows faded and candles attempted feebly to dispel the gloom.

I enjoy music, but am no dancer. I have not the feet for such sport. So with Arthur I leaned against a wall and watched as knights and their ladies bowed and swirled in time to the tooting and plucking. Sir Giles's daughter Amabil and Sir Geoffrey Paget were among the dancers, and I noted a remarkable contrast in their demeanors. The maid smiled and threw herself into the galliard with near abandon, while Sir Geoffrey's face was joyless, his steps stiff and without grace. Perhaps he suffered from an incompetence like my own.

Kennington's hall is not as large as might be expected for the residence of the heir to the throne. The hall at Berkhampstead, I am told, is larger, and Prince Edward prefers that castle to Kennington except that it is farther from London and the seat of power. So because the dancers were many and the hall was modest in size there was the occasional bumping of elbows, which was generally followed by a bow and reciprocal requests for pardon. But not always.

Roger de Clare danced a tune with a lass I had seen about the palace – the daughter, I had assumed, of a knight in Prince Edward's service. I discovered later that she was the daughter of Kennington's butler: a valet who was wed, which is a rare thing in the service of a great noble. She would bring no land and little wealth to a husband, but her inordinate beauty would make the lass popular until the subject of marriage arose.

Roger and Fulk, their attention diverted to their partners, collided, turned to beg one another's pardon, saw who it was they faced, and thoughtlessly renewed the brawl they had begun the day before. Rather, I should say that Roger renewed the quarrel. Fulk bowed slightly and, although I could not hear his words, gave evidence of apology in his manner.

While Fulk's head was down, his eyes upon the tiles, Roger balled his fist and struck Fulk about the ear. Fulk dropped to his knees, then toppled to the floor. Several women shrieked and the musicians ceased their playing. Pandemonium ensued.

'Tis not meet for a surgeon and bailiff, even if made constable to a prince, to push his way through a throng of gentlemen and their ladies, so by the time I reached Fulk he had regained his wits and was being helped to a sitting position.

Prince Edward, however, may push through any crowd, and he did so. He had left his chair upon the dais, and as I approached Fulk I saw him shove other gentlemen and their ladies aside so as to approach the scene of combat. His choler was up, his face red. But his step was unsteady. No doubt the reason he and Lady Joan had chosen to observe the dance rather than participate. I wondered if my herbs were failing the prince and he should return to a diet of boiled roosters.

"Begone," he roared. Where he found strength to speak in such a manner I know not. "You were warned! Out of my sight. You are confined this night to your chambers, and will depart Kennington at first light, never to return."

With this command he stalked to the stairs, evidently having lost interest in watching others prance about his hall.

I did not want Roger away from Kennington Palace until I had had the opportunity to observe his behavior more closely and perhaps question him again. I followed Prince Edward to the stairs and then up to the privy chamber. The valets serving at the door had not yet closed it behind him when I drew near, so he heard me ask entrance, and spoke from the darkened chamber that I was to enter. His voice was weak. I could only just hear his words. His rage in the hall had reduced his strength, and I wondered that he had found sufficient stamina to climb the stairs from the hall.

As I entered the privy chamber the prince called to a valet to place more logs upon the smoldering fire on the hearth, then sat heavily upon his chair and bid me sit upon another.

"What is it? Have you new information of Sir Giles's death?" he began.

"Some," I replied. "Whether or not the knowledge is important I cannot yet say."

"Well, let's hear it."

I looked to the valet who tended the fire. I preferred he not hear what I had to say. If he did, I knew that within a few hours a dozen or more valets and grooms would know my thoughts. Prince Edward followed my eyes, saw them resting upon the kneeling valet, and nodded. We sat in silence awaiting the valet's completion of his task, and while we did Lady Joan entered. I stood. The lady smiled and motioned me to return to my seat, then went to a chair beside her husband.

Only two candles lighted the privy chamber when I entered. The prince commanded the valet to light several more when his work at the hearth was done, then bade the man leave us and shut the door behind him.

"What news have you?" Prince Edward said when we were alone.

"Little news, but I do have a request."

"Oh? Let's hear it."

"Do not send Fulk and Roger away. Not yet."

I saw the prince redden as he considered the scene in his hall. Perhaps it was the candlelight. Then again, perhaps not. Lady Joan reached out a hand and placed it atop her husband's.

"Why not? Such squires are a disgrace... to Sir John and to Sir Humphrey and to me."

"Fulk did not begin this new brawl. The two rubbed elbows accidentally. I saw it all. Fulk bowed to apologize, and while he did so Roger smote him. 'Twas uncalled for. If any should be sent from the palace it is Roger only, but I wish for him to remain. For a few days."

"Why so?"

"Yesterday we were called to supper before I told you of all the day's events," I said. "Returning from Hornsey Arthur and I were set upon. Four horsemen appeared from a wood near the road and gave chase. We managed to escape, either through good fortune or the grace of the Lord Christ. One of those who pursued us held his sword in his left hand and wore a dark grey cotehardie. Roger de Clare wears such a hue, and ate his dinner this day with his left hand. He saw me watching, I believe, for this evening, at supper, he wore green."

"You believe that squire one of those who would have slain you on the road?"

"Mayhap. I asked a groom of the marshalsea this day if Roger took his horse from the stables yesterday. He did so, and when he returned, after the ninth hour, the beast had been ill used and was covered with dust and dried sweat."

"I would have thought," Lady Joan said, "you'd want the fellow far from you if you suspected he was one of those who accosted you upon the road."

"I must be careful in the squire's presence, I think, but if he is sent from here I will no longer be able to observe his deeds, nor will I be able to speak more to him of Sir Giles."

"What has this business upon the road from Hornsey to do with your warrant to discover the felon who slew Sir Giles?" the prince asked.

"I cannot say of a certainty, but I believe there is a man, perhaps men, who believes me near to untangling this knot."

"Are you?"

"Nay, but some man believes it so and desires my death."

"And so sent men to slay you upon the road as you returned from Hornsey. If one of these was Roger de Clare this may mean that Sir John sent Arnaud to poison Sir Giles's cup. Shall you arrest him? I will be sorry to learn this of Sir John. I thought him a virtuous knight."

"He may well be. Roger may have been employed by some other if he was one of the four who gave chase upon the road, which I suspect but cannot say of a certainty. If you send the squire away I may never know."

"What is it you wish of me?"

"Put Roger to mucking out the stables for a fortnight and forbid him from taking meals in your hall. But do not send him from Kennington."

"As you wish. But I will not have the squire in my sight. See to it that he knows what is required of him. And when you do discover who has done murder in my hall, send him off then. If he is not guilty of the felony, that is. Meanwhile he will not only muck out the stables, he will sleep there. Tell Harold Shippen to see to it."

"I believe him innocent of Sir Giles's death," I said, "as I have found no reason for Roger to hate Sir Giles enough to slay him, other than loyalty to his master. But he may have intended murder upon the road yesterday."

"Would Roger serve Sir John so loyally that he would slay a man to protect his master and thereby risk a noose?" Lady Joan said.

"He might," Prince Edward replied, "if he thought Sir John had enough influence with me that I would absolve him of the crime. But I would pardon no man who slew my appointed constable."

"Roger will be unsure of his place after this evening," I said, "even after he is told that he need not leave Kennington. I will go now and press him about his recent conduct while he is worried about the trouble he may have brought upon himself by striking Fulk."

"Frightened men may speak more than they would otherwise like to, eh?" the prince said.

"Just so."

I bowed my way from the privy chamber, having become adept at backing from the room and finding the door without ever seeing it. I had discovered an augury which told me, as I looked down, that I was near to my target. A tile about one pace into the privy chamber from the door had a chipped edge. When my eyes passed directly over this blemish I knew I was little more than an arm's length from the door.

I went from the privy chamber to the chamber where the squires and pages of the knights who attend Prince Edward are lodged. Fulk was there, but Roger was not. I peered into the dim corners of the quarters, but he was not to be found. If Prince Edward learned that Roger had disobeyed his command he would surely send the squire from Kennington regardless of my desire to keep the lad near until I had learned more of his role, if any, in the felonies before me.

Fulk was sitting upon his bed, a morose expression upon his face, thinking, I am sure, that on the morrow he would have no position and no home, unless he could return in disgrace to his own father and manor. A thing he would shudder to consider. I sat beside him.

"I saw Roger strike you during the dancing," I began. "Prince Edward knows you are blameless and that Roger instigated the fight. You will not be sent away tomorrow, although if I were you I would seek to avoid Roger at all cost. The prince's patience should not be tried overmuch."

The squire brightened, his bent shoulders straightened. Then I spoke again and his glum expression returned.

"Where is Roger? Prince Edward told both of you to repair to this place."

Fulk shrugged. "I don't know. I came here as commanded. I've not seen Roger since I left the hall." From the tone of Fulk's voice I don't believe Roger's absence dismayed him.

"Where would he go of an evening? Most other pages and squires will likely yet be in the hall dancing," I said. I glanced around the chamber. There were seven other lads within, all giving me and Fulk their attention, straining to hear our conversation. I raised my voice and addressed them all.

"You were all in the hall an hour past and heard Prince Edward direct Roger to come here. He did not do so. Has any man seen where he did go?"

In the dim candlelight I saw the lads look to each other, shaking their heads. One spoke, taking upon himself the responsibility to answer for all.

"Roger was not here when we came from the hall. Fulk was, but not Roger. And he's not entered since."

If none of his companions knew where Roger might be I thought I knew of a man who might. I left the squires' chamber and sought Sir John Pedley and his lady.

Sir John and Lady Ardith occupied a chamber upon the ground floor of the palace, a privileged location. I approached the chamber by passing through the hall, where I saw that Sir John and his lady were no longer present. Neither were most of Prince Edward's guests. The prince's eruption against Fulk and Roger had choked off the amusement as surely as a man with a bowstring tightened about his throat will stop breathing. The musicians were packing away their instruments. Candles were burning low in their wall sconces.

I rapped upon Sir John's chamber door. There was no response. I thought the residents might have already sought their beds. I banged my knuckles against the door again, more firmly this time. If Sir John and his lady were abed they would not thank me for this disturbance. No matter – Prince Edward's wishes outranked theirs.

The second thumping upon the door produced the same result as the first. If Sir John and Lady Ardith were within they did not wish to be disturbed. Or perhaps, I thought, they were sound sleepers.

A third time I belabored the door. Chamber doors in Kennington Palace are oaken and substantial. Their hinges are well made, so even when struck firmly the doors do not rattle and they make little noise. When the third pounding produced no response I gave up, assuming that I could learn from the knight next day where Roger might be found.

I sought my own chamber, where I found Arthur already snoring. This is not conducive to my own slumber, but wakefulness upon my bed can be a useful thing if it allows me to review what I have learned, and what next I might seek to learn, of felons and their misdeeds. So I lay awake for a time, considering hemlock and Hornsey and horsemen riding from a wood.

Prince Edward and his knights and their ladies were to go hawking next day, so an early dinner was laid on. Fulk appeared, but Roger did not. I assumed that Sir Harold had been told that the squire was not to take meals in the hall, and had so instructed the youth. Oddly enough, Sir John and Lady Ardith were also absent. I thought that perhaps they were so ashamed of their squire's deportment they did not wish to be with other folk.

Prince Edward seemed in high spirits during the meal. He has ever enjoyed hawking and the hunt, as does Lady Joan. Although if the duchess continues to enjoy nourishment as much as she does, she will soon find it difficult to sit a horse. Perhaps I should not write of such matters.

When the gentlefolk had departed the hall for their sport I collected Arthur and we went to the marshalsea, where I felt sure I would find an unhappy Roger de Clare, perhaps with a pitchfork in his hands. I did not.

Prince Edward's marshal was present at the stables. While the gentlefolk were away with their beasts he could direct repairs and alterations to the stalls. I interrupted his work and asked of Roger.

"I've not seen him since that business in the hall last eve," Sir Harold said. "Prince Edward told him to go to his lodging and leave Kennington at dawn this day. I suppose he has done so."

"Prince Edward has not spoken to you since yesterday concerning Roger?" I asked.

"Nay. Last I knew he and that other lad were sent away. I saw the other at dinner, though, a short time past. Did the prince change his mind?"

"Aye. Prince Edward relented when he learned that Fulk was not the aggressor last night. And Roger is no longer required to leave Kennington, but he must assist in the stables, and sleep there, for a fortnight, and may not take meals in the hall."

"If I see him I will inform him."

Perhaps Roger had departed Kennington the previous night, preferring to escape any further ignominy. I asked of his horse.

"Just four stalls that way," the marshal replied.

"The beast is yet here?"

"Aye. If Roger did as Prince Edward demanded, he walked. Not likely, that."

I agreed, thanked the marshal for his time, and sought the squires' chamber again. It was empty. The squires and pages, even Fulk, were with their lords at hawking. What lad would choose to neglect an opportunity for such sport? Where, then, was Roger de Clare? For that matter, where was Sir John Pedley? Neither Sir John nor his lady had been at dinner. I had not been able to rouse the knight from his chamber last eve. Was he hawking with the prince on an empty stomach? I should have asked of his horse at the marshalsea.

"Sir John's beasts are stabled, all four of them," Sir Harold replied when I returned to the marshalsea. "Neither he nor his lady asked to have a horse prepared for use this morning."

Arthur and I exchanged puzzled glances. Something was very much amiss. I told Arthur that I intended to again seek the knight and his lady at their chamber. He accompanied me there.

"You suppose they took ill an' lie dead in their beds?" he offered. "There's been poison about this place."

"This has occurred to me."

Again I thumped vigorously upon the chamber door and again received no reply. I was reluctant to enter a knight's chamber uninvited but thought Prince Edward's warrant would, under the circumstances, sanction entry.

I tried the latch, but it did not move. The door was locked. I knelt and peered into the keyhole. I should have seen light in this chamber, as all those assigned to Prince Edward's knights had glass windows and the afternoon was bright and sunny. The keyhole was blocked. The key was yet in place.

If Sir John and his lady had locked their chamber door before they sought their bed they were yet in the room. No one leaves a chamber with the door locked from the inside, unless they depart through a window. This I thought unlikely. Lady Ardith was as buxom as Lady Joan, and Sir John was past the age when a man might easily climb through a window.

Since pounding upon the chamber door did nothing but cause me sore knuckles, I had to think of another way to enter the room.

"Remain here," I said to Arthur. "If any man approaches explain your presence and tell him I will return anon. If Sir John or his lady should appear, tell them I must speak to them upon an urgent matter."

I left Arthur and went in search of a stick. I needed something about the diameter of my little finger and as long as my hand. A brief search at the verge of a wood beyond Lady Joan's privy garden brought me a slender green shoot from a coppiced beech stump. With my dagger I also cut a longer shoot about the length of my arm.

"What's that for?" Arthur asked when I returned to him and held my prizes before him.

"Watch."

I took the smaller of the beech twigs and pushed it into the keyhole. When I met resistance I twisted the shoot one way and another, all the while pushing gently upon the key. I felt the blockage suddenly give way and a heartbeat later I heard the clang of the iron key upon the flags. I dropped to my knees and pushed the longer of the two coppiced shoots under the door. I swept the twig about until it made contact with what I assumed was the key. It was, and with the shoot I worked it to and fro and under the door. Kennington Palace's carpenters had left a space nearly the width of my thumb between the floor and the bottom of the door, else I would not have been able to slide the key from inside the door to the outside.

The key was nearly as large as the palm of my hand. I pushed it into the keyhole and twisted. I heard a satisfying "click" and when I lifted the latch the door swung open on well-greased hinges.

Nearly all of the knights and their ladies and squires, valets, pages, and such were hawking, or observing the sport, so Kennington Palace was silent but for my gasp as I saw what had become of Sir John and Lady Ardith. Sir John lay bloodied upon the chamber floor, his wife was dead upon the bed. Both were fully clothed. They had been slain before they could disrobe for the night.

I held out a hand and told Arthur not to enter the chamber. He did not need to do so to see the carnage there. I could not know if there was evidence in the chamber to explain who had done this evil deed, or why. I wanted no more folk than necessary in the bloody place until I and Prince Edward's marshal had had a chance to view it closely.

And bloody it was. Lady Ardith had but one wound which I could see. She had been pierced through the heart. Her blood, now dried, had soaked the bedclothes. Sir John was another matter. His arms and hands were slashed, and a gruesome laceration laid bare a cheek. Spatters of dried blood flecked the stones of the chamber wall and the flags near where the knight lay. He had fought his assailant. His dagger lay near him, and I saw blood dried upon the blade. Perhaps some of the blood specks I saw came from whoso had done these murders.

Did they not cry out when their lives were taken from them? Was the oaken door so stout that a lady's screams would not penetrate it? Or did they retire from the dancing before all others, humiliated by the violence of their squire Roger, so that no others were nearby to hear the shrieks and curses of combat and murder?

I dropped to my knees to better see what I might of Sir John's corpse. The day had dawned bright, but now, past noon, clouds obscured the sun, and the window above the dead man did not offer much illumination.

But there was light enough to see that 'twas Sir John's right cheek which had been so cruelly gouged, and his right arm was lacerated in four places, whereas his left arm bore but one wound. As with his wife, the fatal blow was a thrust to the heart. This stroke had pierced his cotehardie from near his right arm. Whosoever slew Sir John was likely left-handed. And where was Roger de Clare?

Did Sir John berate his squire so that the headstrong youth lost his temper and slew both knight and lady? I dismissed the thought. Had Roger done such a thing he would surely have fled. And not afoot. His horse, Sir Harold said, was yet in the stables. No man, be he ever so witless, would slay two others and wait near the scene of his felonies to be apprehended. But where was Roger?

Prince Edward must be told immediately, and the marshal also. Sir Harold must allow no man to enter the chamber until the prince was able to see what had happened, and heard my view of these felonies under his roof.

I assigned Arthur to remain at the chamber door and see that no man entered. It was unlikely that anyone would try, as all but grooms and a few valets were hawking, and no groom would come unbidden to this part of the palace. But Arthur frowning in the passageway would guarantee no disturbance.

I found Sir Harold with a groom and a farrier dealing with one of Lady Joan's amblers. The beast, the marshal said, was old but a favorite of the duchess. It had been off its feed, and one hoof was oozing pus.

But I had not sought the marshal to discuss his duties at the stables. He had other duties to perform, and when he finished his brief summary of his concern for Lady Joan's ambler I told him of them.

"Sir John? Dead in his chamber?"

"And his lady wife," I said. "Both slain. My man stands at the door so that no one will disturb the scene of the felonies. Come, I will show you. Meanwhile, send a stable groom to seek Prince Edward. He must know immediately of murders under his roof."

Sir Harold did as I suggested with alacrity. A youthful groom hastily saddled a runcie and set off after the hawkers, while the marshal followed me to the bloody chamber.

"Put up a fight, did Sir John," the marshal said when he inspected the corpses. "Whoso did these murders may have a wound or two himself."

"I agree," I said. "See where Sir John's dagger lies upon the flags. There is blood upon the blade. 'Tis possible but unlikely that Sir John slashed himself.

"And see where most of the wounds are," I continued. "What do you make of their location?"

Sir Harold considered Sir John's corpse, chin in hand. "He fought off his assailant with his right hand – so the cuts upon his arm say. He would have had trouble defending himself and striking a blow with his dagger at the same time… Ah, I see what you are thinking. His slayer was left-handed, else 'twould be his left arm slashed."

"So I believe, although we cannot know this for certain. What knights or squires or valets who dine at the prince's table are left-handed?"

The marshal scratched at his beard for a moment. "None that I recall. Mayhap one or two that I've not given heed to."

"I know of one," I said. "Roger de Clare."

"Sir John's squire?"

"Aye. And he is now not to be found."

"Prince Edward commanded that he leave Kennington. Perhaps he fled the palace before the prince in his wrath could punish him more."

"You said Roger's beast is yet in the stables."

"Oh, aye. Not likely he'd depart without his horse. The lad must be somewhere nearby. You suppose he did these felonies?"

"If he did he is a great fool. Would he flee these murders afoot? No. I think that only if he stole some other man's horse has he left Kennington. Is any beast missing from the marshalsea?"

"Nay. All are accounted for."

"I left the hall last evening behind the two squires and the prince," I said. "You were in the hall. What transpired after Prince Edward went to the privy chamber? Did all or most then depart the hall, or did some remain and dance to a few more tunes?"

"Most stayed. Few danced. Stood in circles and talked of the squires' quarrel and Prince Edward's anger. Best not to experience that, I can tell you."

"What of Sir John and his lady? Did they also remain in the hall to dance and gossip?"

"Nay. Followed the squires from the hall."

"Did any other follow them?"

"Not that I recall. Not on their heels. Some folk forsook the hall soon after, but not immediately. Not that I remember."

The sound of a multitude of hooves upon packed earth and cobblestones interrupted our conversation. The din came clearly to our ears through the window, to which I had paid little attention, the two corpses heretofore occupying my thoughts.

The window was cracked open about the width of a finger, allowing the sound of returning hawkers to fill the chamber. Here was how the felon had escaped the place of his crime. He had withdrawn through the window, then from the outside pushed it nearly closed, but of course could not latch it as he was outside and the latch was inside the chamber. He likely considered that a door locked from inside the chamber would allow him more time to escape than a window closed and latched. I wondered why the felon had not simply closed the door and locked it behind him. Perhaps he thought some other might then appear in the corridor and see him leaving the place. Or perhaps he was not thinking at all.

I heard further clattering of hooves and shouted commands through the window. I listened intently for Prince Edward's voice, but could not hear it above the others. Perhaps the hawking this day had taxed his strength.

It had. I awaited the prince at the door to the chamber, Sir Harold at my side. When the prince appeared it was with two valets at his elbows, keeping him upright. They were needed. He tottered as he approached, and I feared he might need to return to his diet of boiled roosters.

"I am told Sir John and Lady Ardith are slain," he said in a voice so soft 'twas little more than a whisper. "Is this so?"

"It is, m'lord."

"Under my own roof, another of my knights slain!" The prince staggered, but whether this was due to his illness or to murder I cannot say.

Lady Joan had followed her husband to the chamber. Her face was creased and drawn with worry. A poor cotter may fret for his poverty in a way that knights and gentlemen likely do not. But the wealthy are often troubled also. In this life all men, and women also, will one day find something to cause them anxiety, regardless of the weight of their purse. Did the Lady Joan's features reflect concern for her husband's weakness, or for murder in the palace? Perhaps both.

Standing at the entrance to the chamber, it was not my intention to obstruct Prince Edward's view, but I did so. He reached out a hand and motioned me aside, then brushed off the valets, reached for the jamb to steady himself, and entered the room.

From the door he walked unsteadily to a table which occupied a wall opposite the bed, rested his knuckles upon it, crossed himself, and stared at the corpses. For several moments no one spoke, awaiting the prince's opinion. When he spoke it was not to deliver a conclusion of his own, but to ask of mine. A chair stood next to the table. Prince Edward collapsed upon it, turned to me, and asked, "Was it you who found these murders?"

"Aye, m'lord. I sought Roger de Clare last evening, after we spoke, but could not find him, so came here to ask of Sir John if he knew where his squire might be. I pounded upon the door but could rouse no one. This morning I again sought Roger, then Sir John, but could find neither. I knew from your marshal that neither had gone hawking. Their beasts were yet within the stables. This chamber was locked from within, the key yet in the lock."

"How did you enter?"

"I found a twig, pushed the key from the keyhole, managed to drag the key under the door, unlocked the latch, and found this. All is as it was when Arthur and I entered an hour past."

"Tell me," the prince said, "what has happened here. What is your view?"

"Sir John and his lady were slain last evening, shortly after they came to their chamber, perhaps while we were talking in your privy chamber. They had left the hall immediately after Roger struck Fulk, so I learned, and had not begun to disrobe for the night. See where Sir John fought his assailant? His right arm is slashed. The man who did these murders is, I believe, left-handed."

"Roger de Clare is left-handed, you said," Prince Edward offered.

"Aye, and he is not to be found. But his horse is yet in your stables. If he did this, would he not flee?"

"Aye, and not afoot. How could these murders happen and Sir John and his lady not cry out?"

"All of your guests were yet in the hall when Sir John and Lady Ardith came here, embarrassed by Roger's behavior. No others were near to hear them call for aid. And the walls and door are thick."

"If the chamber was locked from within, how did the felon escape?"

"The window. He went through it, dropped some two yards to the palace courtyard, then pushed the window closed behind him. 'Twas dark when this happened. No man saw."

"If Roger de Clare did not do these murders," the prince said, "where is he and who could then have reason to do this?" He swept an arm over Sir John's corpse.

"I do not know the answer to either question, but I may hazard a guess."

"Do so."

"Roger is dead. Somewhere nearby his corpse will be found."

"Why do you say so?"

"Roger knew, or guessed, that I had identified him as one of the four who would have slain me and Arthur upon the road from Hornsey."

"Why would this lead to his death?"

"He spoke of this fear to another, likely one of the three others who accompanied him. To prevent him naming them if I confronted him, they slew him."

"But why also slay Sir John and Lady Ardith?"

"I am at a loss," I admitted. "Perhaps the felon thought Roger might have confided in Sir John."

"Confided in or admitted to," Prince Edward said thoughtfully. "Whoso did these murders, then, is likely the same who slew Sir Giles."

"Likely," I agreed. "Or one who is in the man's employ."

"One?" the prince said. "Mayhap two men, or more, did these murders and went through yon window."

"Mayhap."

"What will you do to discover the man, or men?"

Prince Edward had appointed me to be his constable to discover who had slain Sir Giles Cheyne. Now I found myself assigned to learn who had done two more murders. Three more, if Roger de Clare also lay a corpse. I wondered when I would see my Kate again.

Chapter 13

If, as I suspected, these murders were connected, solving one might also solve the others. Then perhaps my return to Bampton might not be delayed overmuch. Indeed, it might be hastened. More felonies meant more clues, if I could find and rightly interpret them.

Sir Harold had followed his prince into the chamber. I turned to him. "We must find Roger de Clare. If he lives he may be able to tell us what happened here. If he is dead, which I believe, his corpse may tell us something, however little.

"Send out Kennington's grooms and valets to search the palace grounds. Roger did not leave the palace with his horse, so I believe he did not depart at all, or if he did, 'twas against his will. Assign each man a place to search so that no place is searched twice and no place missed."

I saw Prince Edward nod approval. The marshal saw also and said, "'Twill be done."

"Immediately," Prince Edward said. "And call for my chaplain. He must give Extreme Unction and Sir John and Lady Ardith must be bathed and set before the chapel altar, as was done for Sir Giles. Tell Father Lawrence to come to me when he has done these things. Sir John would wish to be interred in his parish church. Arrangements must be made."

The prince pushed himself to his feet using chair and table to steady himself. Was this weakness due to the exertion of hawking, or the shock of two more deaths in Kennington Palace, or to his forsaking Dr. Blackwater's boiled roosters?

Prince Edward moved unsteadily to the chamber door, where Lady Joan took one arm and a valet seized another. Lady Joan is not hesitant, I have learned, to express her opinions. As she, the prince, and the valet departed I heard her unburden herself regarding her husband's decision to go hawking. From what I heard she had warned earlier that to do so would be unwise, and did he wish to make of her a widow? I could not hear the prince's reply.

Sir Harold sent a groom to fetch Father Lawrence, then he and I and Arthur put our heads together to devise a scheme for searching Kennington Palace and grounds. We had a goodly number of grooms and valets to do the search – nearly forty, as the prince keeps a great household.

Sir Harold and six stable grooms would search the marshalsea. We sent five other grooms to investigate Lady Joan's garden and the meadow and forest beyond. Past the meadow was a vineyard. I sent four grooms to prowl through the vines. The guest chambers must be examined, but tactfully, as knights and ladies who resided there would likely take amiss any demand that their lodgings be opened. I assigned myself this task, well aware of the opprobrium I might bring upon my head. I sent Arthur with six palace grooms and valets to search the kitchen, buttery, pantry, and outbuildings. When the bell rang to announce supper we would all return to the hall if Roger de Clare had not been discovered before then.

Most of Prince Edward's gentlefolk guests had gone from hawking to their accommodations, there to change from mud-spattered tunics and cotehardies. All knew of the reason for the prince's hasty return to the palace, and as I went from one chamber to another I saw concern writ upon titled faces. There was little hostility when I asked to inspect each chamber. Perhaps this was because my first words when each chamber door opened to my knock were to voice relief that the occupants were hale, and that whoso had slain Sir John and Lady Ardith had not visited them.

I watched eyes and faces as I spoke to each knight, seeking some sign that the man had no concern for his safety. Such an expression might mean that he did not fear an attack because he knew who had slain Sir John, and why.

I completed the circuit of Kennington's guest chambers without discovering even a suggestion of unconcern. Knightly brows were well furrowed and several greeted me at their door with hand resting upon dagger.

The bell calling folk to the hall for supper had not yet sounded, but I made my way there to await the other searchers. Two stable grooms who had searched the marshalsea with Sir Harold were already present in the hall, leaning against the wall. The marshal, they said, was detained but should appear shortly. No trace of Roger de Clare had been discovered in or near the stables.

More seekers began to appear. The five grooms sent to investigate meadow, forest, and Lady Joan's garden returned together. I doubted their search was thorough, but a few minutes later the insubstantial nature of the grooms' effort was rendered insignificant.

I heard rapid, heavy footsteps from the porch, and moments later the door from porch to hall burst open and Arthur, followed by a groom, burst in. He saw me at the opposite end of the hall and shouted, "Found 'im."

"Where?" I said, and hastened to meet him.

"In the larder."

"Dead or alive?"

"Dead as a man may be what's been stuffed head first into a barrel of pickled herrings. Come... see for yourself."

Kennington's larder was redolent of smoked hams and sides of beef. I was reminded of how hungry I was. The desire for a meal, however, soon passed.

Arthur led me to a large cask wherein salted herrings had been kept for fast day meals for grooms and other lesser folk.

"Noticed that the cover was askew," Arthur said as we approached the barrel and the grooms Arthur had assigned to remain with the corpse. "Thought a kitchen servant had left it dislodged, so when we finished lookin' around an' was about to leave I shoved the lid in place, but it wouldn't drop to a tight seal. Thought that odd, so lifted it to see what the obstruction might be. Folk don't want vermin getting to their herring."

As he spoke Arthur raised the lid and I saw why it would not close properly. A man's shoes and feet prevented the lid from seating.

"Reckon this must be that squire what's gone missin'," Arthur said as he set the lid aside. "Nobody else missin', is there?"

"Not that I've heard."

I turned to two of the grooms and told them to draw the corpse from the cask. This was odious work. As they lifted the corpse I saw that the man was richly garbed. Here was no groom or valet or even page. I was convinced Roger de Clare was found even before his face appeared.

We in the larder crossed ourselves as the grooms laid Roger out upon the flags. I peered into the cask to see if his cap was there, for 'twas not upon his head. I saw no cap, nor any other thing but a layer of salted herrings. Whoever had done this murder would know the corpse would be found soon. Wednesday was a fast day. Did this mean the felon thought one day enough time for him to escape detection, or did he not care that Roger would soon be found?

Five people who had lived or labored in Kennington Palace were now food for worms. Will worms consume a man who has been salted? The question calls for experiment, but what good can come of knowing the answer?

Prince Edward's chapel would soon receive another corpse. I hoped Father Lawrence would wash Roger's corpse well, else the fishy odor would overwhelm the place.

Prince Edward had assigned me the task of discovering a murderer. I had failed. So far. He would now demand of me that I find five murderers. Five, unless some of the dead were slain by the same hand. I began to despair of seeing my Kate and Bessie and John before Twelfth Night.

Perhaps my incompetence would so anger the prince that he would discharge me and I could return to Bampton. I entertained the thought with mixed emotions. To return to Galen House was appealing. To fail in such an ignoble manner was not.

Would Prince Edward wish to see the larder before Roger was taken from the place? I decided 'twould be best if the prince made that decision. I directed Arthur and two of the grooms to remain with the corpse. The other groom I sent to fetch Sir Harold and Father Lawrence. I hastened to the hall.

The marshal, the chaplain, and Prince Edward were all three in the hall when I entered. The prince was seating himself at the high table, and Father Lawrence was ready to speak a blessing upon the meal. I was about to ruin their appetites.

Prince Edward was yet unsteady and Lady Joan's face was

creased with worry as she watched her husband collapse into his chair, for collapse is quite an apt word for what he did.

The prince looked about after settling himself and saw me at the far end of the hall. Perhaps something in my approach told him that Roger de Clare was found. He raised himself from his chair, knuckles upon the cloth before him, and motioned me to come near. All within the hall saw this, and the place fell silent as I advanced to the high table and bowed to the prince.

"What news?" he said.

"The squire is found."

"Dead?"

"Aye."

"How? Was he slain? Where was he found?"

"I would rather speak of this in some private place," I said.

"Oh, aye… surely. We will retire to my privy chamber."

The prince began to push back his chair, but Lady Joan was too quick for him. She leapt to her feet, drew back the chair, then fixed herself to her husband's arm to assist him from the platform. She motioned for a valet to attend the prince, and together they helped him to and up the stairs. I followed. From the corner of my eye I saw Father Lawrence rise from his place, the groom I sent to him having delivered his message.

"Is your announcement so important that my husband must delay his supper?" Lady Joan said when we had entered the privy chamber. I suspected that the prince was not the only person in Kennington Palace who was hungry. The meal would surely be delayed until his return, or until he sent word to cooks and valets and butler to proceed without him. He made no move to do so, but slumped into his ornate chair. Lady Joan took her place beside him. He motioned for the valet to leave the chamber, then bid me sit upon a padded bench I had last seen occupied by the Archbishop of Canterbury. What would my parents have said had they known that their youngest lad's rump would some day occupy such a place? For that matter, what will my Kate say when she learns of it? I suppose I would not have to tell her of the incident. But I will.

Prince Edward interrupted my thoughts. "Who found the squire, and where?" he demanded.

"My man Arthur found Roger in the larder, head first in a nearly empty cask of salted herrings."

"He would not dive into such a place of his own will," the prince said. "What have you learned from the corpse?"

"I came straight to you when the lad was found. I thought you would wish to see where Roger was found and with your marshal examine the larder."

Prince Edward placed his hands upon the arms of his chair and made to rise, but Lady Joan placed a hand upon his to restrain him.

"Hawking," she said, "has drawn vigor from my husband. You and Sir Harold must study the larder and the dead. The prince needs his supper and rest."

As Lady Joan spoke I saw her nose wrinkle. A moment later I knew why. The prince had passed wind, and a foul odor came to my nostrils. The herbs I had suggested seemed no longer effective. Dr. Blackwater's boiled roosters may be Prince Edward's menu yet again, although I was troubled that a physic which had served for a time would become impotent.

Prince Edward sank back to his chair. He said nothing of the stench, but he surely noticed it. What man, be he prince or of the commons, would wish to acknowledge that he was the source of such pungency?

"Return to the larder and learn what you can. Call Sir Harold to join you," the prince instructed. "When your work in the larder is done, have Sir Harold and Father Lawrence take the corpse to the chapel to join Sir John and Lady Ardith. Roger must be taken to his father for burial... This is a sorry business." Prince Edward passed a hand over his forehead and sighed.

"You must eat," Lady Joan said firmly, "and none in the hall will have their supper 'til you appear."

"I will do so," the prince said, and stood slowly. "The cooks and butler," he continued, "will be told to hold back a portion of supper from the almoner until you and Sir Harold, and those with you have concluded your inquiry."

I bowed my way from the privy chamber and returned to the larder. The groom had fetched Sir Harold as instructed, and I found him kneeling over Roger's corpse when I entered.

"What think you, Master Hugh?" he said, rising. "Here is a felony, but who did this, and why? Do you suppose that other squire, the one he quarreled with, did this? I find no wound upon the corpse. Could it be he was turned into the cask while living?"

"If so," I replied, "surely more than one man did this. Roger was a strapping youth. If but one man pitched him while alive into the herrings he must be robust."

I knelt where the marshal had been and began a close scrutiny of the corpse and its clothing. I found no place where fabric was slashed. No dagger had pierced his cotehardie. I next examined the lad's skull. I felt a small swelling upon the rear of his pate, but this protuberance was so slight I could not be sure it had aught to do with his death. On the other hand, a blow which miscarried might leave little trace of its effect, especially if Roger's cap absorbed some of the blow. And where was the cap?

A blow to the skull will leave a man with a knob for a week or so, if he lives. What of a blow which is strong enough to slay a man? Will a lump grow upon a dead man's head? Galen did not address this, nor de Mondeville, nor any other surgeon I know of. And what if the blow does not stop the fellow's life, but some other event soon after does? Such as being stuffed head first into a cask of herrings and brine.

I stood from the corpse and at the corner of my eye saw a shadow darken the larder door. 'Twas Father Lawrence and his clerk. The priest stopped when he saw Roger, and he and the clerk crossed themselves.

"Sir John, his lady, and now his squire," the priest said. "Who could so hate a man he would slay his wife and squire also?"

"Sir John was not slain because some man hated him," I said.

"Why, then?" the priest said, his brow wrinkled.

"'Tis my belief that he and his squire were murdered not for what they had done, but for what they knew. Or what the felons thought they knew."

"What knowledge could be so dangerous that a man might die for having it? Ah," the priest answered his own question. "Some man thought Sir John knew him to have sought Sir Giles's death."

"Mayhap," I replied.

The chaplain began the prayer for the dead and we others faded back to the larder wall until the words were done.

There was nothing more to learn from the corpse. There had been precious little to learn at all. I was puzzled about the squire's missing cap. He had worn it last night while dancing. The murderers would not discard it. There could be no blood upon it, for there was no place on Roger's body where the skin was broken. Did some penniless fellow take the cap from Roger before he was dunked into the herrings? I thought back to when I had seen Roger de Clare: at dinner in the hall, at dancing last eve, and upon the road, chasing me and Arthur. His cap on all those occasions was of a light grey, the liripipe long enough to wind about his neck and face. 'Twas fashionable. A man unable to afford such a cap would prefer to see it upon his own head than have it preserved with the herrings.

Father Lawrence sent his clerk to fetch two servants and a pallet. He assured me that Roger's corpse would be thoroughly bathed and set with Sir John and Lady Ardith before the chapel altar. The marshal would now have three corpses to see transported to their places of burial. Roger's family had lands near to Tonbridge, not so far from Kennington. Perhaps he would be sent there.

By the time matters at the larder were concluded, the great hall had been cleared, musicians were plucking, and gentlefolk were dancing. Three of their number were dead since the day before. I thought this seemed not to vex them overmuch. I was mistaken.

I led Arthur and the grooms past the dancers to the screens passage. The pantler was there, and when he saw us directed us to a table laden with our supper.

My appetite was much reduced. I do not remember the fare before me that evening. I have seen much blood and many corpses in my posts as bailiff and surgeon. Perhaps one day I will become inured to death and gore. But not yet.

"What of that other squire?" Arthur said, half a loaf stuffed into his mouth. "The one what come to blows with Roger. Don't think he could challenge Roger alone, but 'e might've had help, you think?"

"Not likely, unless he followed Roger from the hall, slew him, and returned to his chamber in the time it took me to speak to Prince Edward in his privy chamber last night. And the other squires who share lodging claim that Fulk was in the chamber when they arrived from the hall, though Roger was not."

Why was Roger de Clare not present with the other squires when I visited their chamber? If Prince Edward found out that Roger had disobeyed his command, what greater punishment could he extact? Roger was already banished from the palace. The squire might have thought that he could go where he wished, in defiance of Prince Edward, and suffer no further penalty. If so, and some enemy found him, the penalty was greater than he could have conceived. Or perhaps he sought a friend, or a man he thought a friend, imagining no penalty at all.

Or was Roger apprehended as he departed the hall, before he reached the squires' chamber? Did some man seek him, rather than he seek another? If so, the fellow likely knew what he intended for Roger. Death. To silence him? I was convinced of this. I was now as near to certain as could be that Roger de Clare was one of the four who had accosted Arthur and me upon the road from Hornsey. If one or more of the others knew that Roger had got himself into trouble with Prince Edward, he might fear that Roger could be coerced into identifying the others who accompanied him in the attack.

How would Roger's accomplice know that the squire had annoyed Prince Edward? The felon must be close to Kennington Palace, or within, for Roger to have so quickly passed the news to him. Or perhaps the man was within the hall and heard Prince Edward banish Roger. Did Roger also tell this man that he had seen my gaze fixed upon him at dinner, and feared that he was identified as one who had descended upon Arthur and me from the wood, even though his liripipe covered all but his eyes and forehead?

Most men have an enemy or two. Even the Lord Christ, the only perfect man, had enemies. They crucified Him. Little good it did them. It is how enemies are made that sets men apart. Some make enemies of good men, others make enemies of the bad. I pray that I will always have the proper enemies.

Good men seldom slay their evil enemies – although they may contemplate doing so. Was Roger murdered because of the evil he had done, or because his slayer thought he might do good? What good could he do but speak of accomplices in the attack? If he had done so, he would have set me upon the path which would lead to the man who hired Arnaud Tonge to poison Sir Giles.

Immediately after Sir Giles was slain there was but one course I could follow to find his killer. That route led to Hornsey, but was soon obstructed. Now there were many paths to follow to find Sir Giles's murderer. If I could learn who pierced Sir John and Lady Ardith, or who plunged Roger de Clare into the herrings, I would shortly after know who paid Arnaud to poison Sir Giles. So I thought.

I lay abed listening to Arthur snore and musing about which direction would most likely lead me to a felon or felons. In the morning it might be as well to discuss matters again with Randall Patchett. He had been present in the squires' chamber when I sought Roger de Clare. Perhaps he had overheard conversations he might share – conversations that may have meant little or nothing to him at the time, not knowing that Roger was likely already a corpse, or soon would be.

I awoke next morning to the sound of activity in the palace yard. Men were shouting and iron-shod hooves were clattering upon the cobbles before the marshalsea. I splashed water upon my face and with Arthur departed our chamber to learn the cause of such clamor.

Men were loading wagons and carts. Grooms and valets and stable boys busied themselves hitching runcies to conveyances and covering the loads with waxed linen shrouds to protect from the rain which seemed likely to fall soon.

When all was prepared and the horses in place between the shafts, two ladies left the palace and were assisted into the wagons. Their knightly husbands mounted their own steeds. Prince Edward and Lady Joan had been standing to one side watching the process, and now approached the wagons to bid farewell to the gentlemen and their ladies who, with their squires, valets, and grooms, were departing Kennington Palace. Two knights and a lady had perished in this place. Sir John Berell and Sir Aymer Esty had decided to return to their own manors, choosing to request permission to leave the royal presence rather than risk adding themselves to the list of corpses accumulating in Kennington Palace.

"Have you spoken to Prince Edward yet about me serving him?" Randall asked when I found him after Matins.

"Not yet. Other matters concern me. It is about those other matters that I would speak to you. Walk with me in Lady Joan's garden again."

We passed through the great hall on the way to the garden. Arthur was in the hall, as I had instructed him to be. He nodded slightly as Randall and I passed. His duty was to watch if any man, or woman, took interest in my conversation with Randall. None did.

"When I came to the squires' chamber two nights past Fulk was there," I began, "but Roger was not. Had he been and departed, or did he never appear? You were present in the hall and heard Prince Edward banish him and Fulk from Kennington."

"I saw Roger and Fulk leave the hall in disgrace," Randall said. "I did not immediately follow, nor did any other squires or pages, I think. But the brawl drove away delight and soon several of us left the hall and the dancing and went to our chamber."

"How many?" I asked.

"Four or five. Didn't count."

"So some squires remained in the hall?"

"Aye. For a time."

"When you reached your lodging only Fulk was present. Is this so?"

"Aye."

"You said that after Prince Edward had banished them you remained in the hall for a time but soon departed. What does 'soon' mean? After a dance or two, or three?"

"After the next dance."

"As you walked to the squires' chamber did you see any man that might have been Roger in the passageway or elsewhere?"

Randall scratched his chin, which was an affectation, for he had no bristles there to cause an itch.

"I saw two men in the corridor, leaving the far end as I entered. Thought at first 'twas Fulk and Roger, but then knew it would not be, as the fellows did not seem to be antagonistic."

"It was too dark there to identify the fellows?"

"It was. I saw only shapes against a cresset at the far end of the passageway. And only a glimpse. They disappeared past the corner as I saw them."

"You believe they saw you and that caused them to be off?" I said.

"Nay. It didn't seem so. They were walking away when I first saw their shadows. Likely never saw me, though they might've heard our footsteps on the flags and our conversation. There were several of us. But if they did, it didn't change their direction or behavior. Not that I could see."

"Could one of these two have been Roger de Clare?" I asked.

"Could have been," Randall shrugged. "It was too dark to know, and they were walking away."

"In a comradely fashion, would you say, from what you saw?"

"Aye, just so. I saw no hostility."

A light grey cap might show against the darkened corridor, even in the light of but one candle.

"Roger wore a light grey cap which might be noticeable even in a dark place. Do you remember if one of these two wore some light-colored cap?"

Randall's eyes seemed to open a bit wider. "Aye," he exclaimed. "Now you mention it one of them did wear such a cap."

"And Fulk was alone in the squires' chamber when you and the others entered after having seen the two men at the far end of the passageway?"

"Aye, he was. And much in sorrow, too."

The bell for dinner rang and ended our conversation. We re-entered the hall and as we did so I saw Arthur from the corner of my eye shaking his head. No man, or woman, had tried to overhear my conversation with Randall. None that Arthur had seen.

From my place beside William Blackwater I could see Fulk de Driby toying with his dinner. The first remove was dighted crab, and the squire spent most of his time staring at the crab as if he expected it to rise from his trencher and smite him. Neither did he speak to either of his companions. Perhaps he had nothing to say to them. Or they had nothing they desired to say to him.

I suspect that Fulk showed no more interest in the second remove than he had the first, but I do not know this of a certainty. Dr. Blackwater wished to discuss Prince Edward's illness. More precisely, he wished to charge me with damaging the prince's health with my herbs.

"Had he continued my instructions and consumed boiled roosters at his dinner, his strength would not have failed him as it has. And Lady Joan has told me that his foul emanations are as abominable as they ever were."

I could not argue that point, having had recent experience of the prince's wind. "Aye," I agreed. "He is as malodorous now as he was when he consumed your boiled roosters at dinner. I worry that his ailment has worsened, so that neither your boiled roosters nor my physics will avail."

"Nonsense. 'Tis his humors remain out of joint. If he will again attend to my advice his humors will soon balance."

"If health were so simple," I said, "why do men die? All do. Can a learned physician like yourself not prescribe the food and drink which will balance all men's humors so that they will suffer no lasting illness?"

Blackwater snorted. "I'll suffer no instruction from a simple mechanic. Stick to stitching up men's wounds and mending broken bones and heads. Leave the cure of diseases and adjustment of humors to men who know what they are about."

It pained me to admit it, and I did not say this to Blackwater, but I thought at the time that he might speak true. Certainly the tansy, thyme, cress, and bramble leaves with oil of fennel root had lost their effectiveness. If they had ever been effective.

I was lost in speculations of medical matters and forgot that I had also intended to observe Fulk de Driby throughout the meal. The third remove, eels in bruit, and fruit and salmon pie, had been served when I next glanced at the squire. His face was as downcast as before, and he seemed to find no pleasure in the remove.

When the subtlety (a gingerbread castle in the form of Kennington Palace) and void had been consumed the hall was cleared. Gentlefolk and commons scattered to their duties and pleasures. I watched Fulk walk somberly to the corridor which led to the squires' chamber. Did he plan to spend the afternoon shut into that room? His fellows would be about the pleasures of youth: wrestling, discussing fair maids, exercising their horses, discussing other fair maids, gambling at Nine Man Morris, and discussing even more fair maids.

I found Fulk sitting upon his pallet, head in hands, a picture of disconsolation. I did not think my questions would lift his heavy heart.

The squire looked up when my shadow darkened the chamber door. He did not at first recognize me, I think, as the chamber was poorly lit and my form was but a shadow interrupting the light from the passageway windows. When I spoke, he knew who had entered, and were it possible, his face fell even more. He knew I was appointed to discover who had slain Sir Giles Cheyne. When a man given such authority suddenly appears, even the innocent will feel some dread. Constables, like bailiffs, have few friends, and most folk are more pleased to see them go than come.

In situations where I wish to ask information of a man who might be reluctant to yield it, I have discovered that standing, while the man I question is seated, is effective at prying such information from a fellow. But Fulk, I thought, was not now such a man. If he ever had been. I sat upon the cot next to his, our knees nearly touching, so cramped was the chamber.

"Randall Patchett has told me that after Roger de Clare struck you at dancing you came here alone, in obedience to Prince Edward's demand. Is this so? Did Roger not come here also as the prince required?"

"Roger left the hall with me. But when we came to our chamber he kept walking along the passage. He didn't speak more to me. I never saw him again."

"He went on through the passageway and out of the door?"

"I suppose so," Fulk said. "When I entered here he was yet in the passageway. Not alone, I think."

"Why do you say so?" I asked.

"Heard a voice. Speaking low, so as not to be heard. But I know – knew – Roger's voice, and the words were not his."

"You could not hear what was said?"

"Nay. I was about to go to the passageway to see who it was Roger was speaking to, or who was speaking to Roger, when Randall and some other squires returned. I never heard voices after that, and Roger never returned to this chamber. I heard what befell him. Do you think the man I heard speaking was him who slew Roger?"

"Likely," I replied.

"Why? I know some folk think I did the murder, then hurried back here before Randall and the others found me here. I had reason, they say, though I swear before God I did not do it. What cause would another man have to slay Roger? Has he done evil to others also?"

"Mayhap. From what I've learned of Roger 'tis likely. But I do not think he was slain for what he did."

"What, then?"

"For what he knew."

"For what he knew? Was he slain because he would not tell his murderer what he wished to know?"

"Nay. The other way round. The felon who put Roger in the herring barrel knew what Roger knew, and did murder to prevent Roger giving this information to me or any other man. So I believe. Since Roger's death was made known, have you heard other squires or pages speak of it?"

"Oh, aye. Often."

"What opinions have you heard?"

Fulk shrugged. "They do not speak of me having slain him – not when I'm present. But I know they do so when my back is turned. Mostly, when I can hear, they talk of suffocating in a cask of salted herrings and compare it to other manners of untimely death. Some make sport of it."

"Those who disliked Roger?" I suggested.

"Aye."

"Are there many who hold that view?"

"A few. Roger had both foes and friends."

"Who were his friends?" I asked.

"Friends? Why do you ask of them? Is it not a foe who would have slain him?"

"You said he was with some other man that night in the passageway, and that the other man spoke softly to him. So softly that you could not hear. Does that seem the behavior of an enemy? Would Roger consort in a darkened corridor with an adversary? And Randall Patchett also saw the shapes of two men in the corridor, and said they seemed affable. The man with Roger was perhaps the man who slew him. Likely with help. Roger did not go off from here with an enemy. So I seek the names of his friends."

"He was oft with Robert Waynflete and Stephen Corbet. Thomas Poer and John Stonor, also. And Geoffrey Paget."

"When Randall entered this chamber that evening, were any of those friends of Roger's with him?"

"Ah," Fulk said, "I see your drift. Were they with Randall they could not have been with Roger in the passageway."

"Just so."

Fulk furrowed his brow and thought back to that evening. For several minutes he did not reply.

"I was in a foul mood, I fear, when Randall and the others entered. I remember only John Stonor among Roger's friends who entered with Randall."

"Perhaps Randall will remember if there were others of Roger's friends who departed the hall with him," I said.

Chapter 14

I left Fulk as I had found him, staring glumly at his feet, alone in the squires' chamber. I walked the palace grounds seeking Randall Patchett and found him with several other squires and pages playing at bowls. I caught his eye and motioned to him to join me. He looked back to his companions, then reluctantly left his sport. Perhaps he had a few pence at risk in the game.

We walked some distance from the bowlers before I spoke. If he responded to my questions with a name or names of those who had been with him at bowls I did not wish for them to hear their names mentioned.

"When you left the dancing on the night of the murders and went to the squires' chamber, what others accompanied you?"

"You ask who else may have seen two men at the end of the passageway?" he said. "Do you not believe I spoke true?"

"I believe you. Have no concern of that. I seek the names of others who entered the squires' chamber for another reason."

Randall's features relaxed. No man likes to be thought a liar, especially when the man who might believe him to be has authority to send him to a gallows. He puzzled over the question for a moment, as had Fulk. "Stephen Corbet, Richard Daniel, Robert Waynflete were with me. John Stoner, Simon Ewes and Geoffrey Molyns, also."

"No others?"

"Nay. Those six. I'm sure of it."

Of the friends Fulk had named, Thomas Poer and Sir Geoffrey Paget were unaccounted for when Roger de Clare was slain. Sir Geoffrey I had seen dancing. But had he remained in the hall after Fulk and Roger had raised Prince Edward's ire? His dancing had not been enthusiastic even before the prince's eruption. Would the disturbance have caused him to abandon his fiancée, who was enjoying herself even if he was not, and leave the hall?

Arthur had remained in the hall when I followed Prince Edward up the stairs to his privy chamber. The upper rooms were forbidden to him. He had seen Lady Amabil and so might remember her partner at dancing.

I found Arthur playing knucklebones with other grooms. He seemed less reluctant to leave the game than Randall had been to leave his amusement. Perhaps the game had not been friendly and his purse the lighter for it.

"Lady Amabil?" he said. "She the lass what I saw following you an' that squire in the garden a few days past?"

"Aye. She and Sir Geoffrey were dancing when Roger de Clare struck Fulk de Driby. Do you remember seeing them?"

"Hard to forget a lass like that."

"Prince Edward told Fulk and Roger that they were banished from Kennington Palace and must leave on the morrow. He then went to the stairs and his privy chamber. I followed. When I was gone from the hall did you see if Sir Geoffrey was yet there when the musicians began again to play? Did you enjoy watching Amabil enough that you remember what her partners did?"

"Went off, didn't he? The lass was right vexed about it, too. Saw 'er stomp 'er foot when 'e walked away."

"Which way did he go when he left her?"

"Out through the porch."

"He did not go through the screens passage toward the squires' chamber?"

"Nay."

This puzzled me, but only for a moment. If he hurried, Sir Geoffrey could have passed from the porch outside the south wall of the hall, and entered the passageway door leading to the squires' chamber by the time Roger came there. Sir Geoffrey is not a large man. His form is much like Fulk de Driby's. If he disposed of Roger de Clare in a herring cask the squire must have first been rendered senseless, or Sir Geoffrey had help. I did not know Thomas Poer. Was he a brawny fellow? 'Twas time to find out.

I found Randall Patchett where I had left him, at bowls. I believe he had lost a few coins at the sport, for as I watched he lined up a toss with lips pursed tight. His ball did not come close to the target, and he threw up his hands in disgust. Some of his companions chuckled.

Randall turned from his bowling, a scowl embedded upon his face. Again I motioned for him to approach, and again we walked from the bowlers. Arthur followed.

"Who is Thomas Poer?" I asked when we were out of earshot of his companions. "Is he among the bowlers?"

"Aye, the large lad just about to take his turn... him in the russet cotehardie and the bluish cap."

Thomas was indeed a strapping fellow, nearly as robust as Arthur and a hand taller. He would have little trouble turning a man upside down into a barrel.

"What do you know of him? Who does he serve?" I asked.

"Sir William Vache."

I knew Sir William to be one of Prince Edward's household knights, a man who wore a large cap with a liripipe draped about his neck, but nothing more of him. Thomas Poer wore a light blue cap. At a glance, or in the dark, perhaps it might be mistaken for light grey.

"The cap that Thomas wears – have you seen him wear the same cap in the past, or is it new?"

Randall shrugged. "Don't recall. I think he's worn it before. Don't pay much attention to the color of caps. 'Tis a little soiled, I noticed."

Light blue and light grey might be confused. And a cap might become soiled if it was struck from a man's head by a blow which left him senseless and the cap in the mire.

"Who are Thomas Poer's friends among the squires?" I asked.

"He's thick with Robert Waynflete and Stephen Corbet."

"No others? What of Sir Geoffrey Paget?"

"Oh, aye. You could say they're close. Thought you wished to know only of the squires."

"Any others?"

"Simon Ewes, perhaps."

"Any enemies?"

"Nay. Thomas is a good-natured sort. Look at him. Sturdy as a castle wall, but not clever. A simpleton, actually, but do not say I said so. I'd not like to face his wrath, although, truth to tell, I've never seen him angry. Come to speak of it, Roger de Clare would often make sport of Thomas. Wouldn't say they were enemies, though."

"About his friends: does he lead them, or do they lead him?"

"Thomas is a follower. And faithful to his friends. There are those who will ridicule him behind his back, like Roger, and he knows that. So those who will not do so have his loyalty."

Would the robust young man be so willing to please a friend that he would assist him in a murder? I thought back to the afternoon when four horsemen pursued Arthur and me. Were any of the four as large as Thomas Poer? No, I thought not. If Roger de Clare was one of the four, he was not accompanied by Thomas Poer.

"A simpleton, you said."

"Aye."

"In the past day has his behavior seemed out of place?"

"Now that you mention it, when we heard of Roger's murder and how it happened Thomas shed tears. He was not fond of Roger, and surely knew Roger poked fun at him behind his back. And weeping before other squires is not a weakness to which even Roger's good friends would succumb."

Would a man of gentle disposition and weak mind be sorry for the part he had played in the death of another, even if 'twas a man he had no reason to care for? I thought it possible.

Sir Geoffrey Paget did not appear at supper. Amabil was present and if she was concerned that her intended husband was absent she did not give evidence of it. She showed joy, interest in her table companions, and took much pleasure in the interest of a young knight assigned to her left side. But Amabil was like the moon, I thought. There was a dark side that she showed to no one. I wondered if her father had glimpsed it.

As always my supper companion was William Blackwater. I believe he thought he had put me on the defensive at dinner, so was now determined to seal his victory.

"What will you do when the king learns that his son and heir nears death because of your stupidity?" he said with a mouthful of mushroom tart.

"We are all near death. You are nearer heaven's gate now than you were this morning. Although whether or not St. Peter will admit you is another matter."

"He will. And as I am older than you, when I greet him I will warn him of you."

"I'm sure," I said, "that the Lord Christ has advised His apostle concerning me. St. Peter will need no advice from you, and nor do I."

"Prince Edward must scorn your herbs and oils if he wishes to return to health."

"Do you serve as a physician to others, or only to the prince?" I asked.

"I serve only my prince."

"Before you came to his service did you attend other men, adjusting their humors and measuring their physics by their sign when born?"

"Indeed," Blackwater said pridefully. "Great men sought my knowledge and skill. 'Tis how the prince heard of me. Sir Thomas Ryland told him of my ability."

"Sir Thomas is dead, is he not? Three years past, I believe."

Blackwater said nothing.

"Did you mistake his sign, or assign foods for heat when he required cold? Wet, mayhap, when he should have consumed dry? How many others that you treated are now under the tiles of their manor church?"

"No man lives forever," Blackwater growled, "but he will live longer if he does as I say."

There was no way to counter that claim, or for Blackwater to prove it. But I did have a last rejoinder. "No man has perished from consuming the herbs I set before him, and when I sew up a man's wound or set a broken bone aright, I can prove that what I have done has improved the man's life. Show me your proofs of humors and signs in the heavens."

"The ancients knew that the planets and stars have great influence over men. Are you so vainglorious that you would challenge them?"

"The ancients also worshipped Thor and Athena and Poseidon. Do we not know better now?"

Blackwater swallowed deeply. He was readying a rejoinder, I believe, but thought better of it, took a bite of wheaten bread with honeyed butter, and turned from me to his other supper companion. We spoke no more that evening.

I had not noticed, but while the physician and I had jousted, a groom on the opposite side of the hall was watching. A man would have to be a dolt not to see that we were contending over some matter. The groom was Adam Trinkle, Blackwater's assistant and apprentice. He sought me after supper, as tables and trestles were being cleared for dancing. He glanced about the hall and over his shoulder as he approached, then looked back again as he came near. I followed his gaze and saw Dr. Blackwater in conversation with a lady, but his eyes followed his young assistant. Trinkle saw this also, and walked past me without ever looking in my direction. He had intended to speak to me, I was sure of it, but disregarded me when he saw Blackwater's eyes upon him.

After walking nonchalantly past me, Trinkle ended up against a wall of the great hall where other grooms and pages made chat. Arthur was among this cluster, and I watched as Blackwater's assistant sidled toward him. Trinkle seemed innocent of intention, but I thought appearances deceiving.

Blackwater no longer gave attention to his assistant, preferring his female companion. Trinkle leaned against the wall, his back to the physician, facing toward Arthur. He began to speak as the musicians launched into the first galliard. I saw Trinkle's lips move, but Blackwater was too far away to hear his words, and would have been even without the music. But Arthur heard him. I saw Arthur cock his head toward Blackwater's assistant and frown. A moment later Trinkle moved away and gave his attention to the dancers. I saw Blackwater glance at him, but he quickly returned to his conversation with the lady.

A short time later Arthur left his place along the wall with other grooms and sauntered toward me. When he reached me he stood silent for a time, hands clasped behind his back. When he did speak, he was careful to have his back to Dr. Blackwater, although this was likely an unnecessary precaution, as the physician was paying us no attention.

"That lad what serves yon leech – 'e says to tell you his master ain't doin' as you asked. 'E's not puttin' them herbs into the prince's wine like you asked. Hasn't been for four days. Said you ought to know."

Indeed I ought. No wonder Prince Edward was unwell. He consumed neither herbs nor boiled roosters. I wished to speak directly to Blackwater's assistant and considered how I might do so.

Beyond the screens passage lay another short corridor at the end of which was the small chamber given to me and Arthur. Two doors before that chamber was a larger room, much like the chamber where the squires made their abode, for the use of grooms who served their lords while at Kennington Palace. Blackwater would not think it strange if he saw his assistant make for the screens passage to go to this grooms' chamber.

I moved slowly clockwise about the hall, staying close to the wall, all the time giving attention to the dancers as if nothing that might happen that evening could be so diverting. When I reached the opening to the screens passage I halted my perambulation and tried to catch Adam Trinkle's eye without causing Dr. Blackwater to become curious about my behavior. After a few minutes beside the opening, the musicians struck up a new tune. This time the physician joined the dancers, accompanying the lady with whom he had been in conversation. He paid me no attention, but his assistant soon did.

Trinkle looked at me from across the hall. I tilted my head toward the screens passage, entered, and made my way to my own chamber, past the grooms' door. I waited at my door to discover if the lad had rightly interpreted my sign. He had.

Blackwater's assistant peered around the dark corner into the corridor and saw me, illuminated by a single cresset. The light was dim, but enough that Trinkle could see I was alone in the passageway. He hurried to me.

"I saw how Prince Edward's health began to improve after he consumed the herbs you advised," Trinkle said. "Dr. Blackwater required of me that I visit the fields around Kennington and collect what I could, and go to an apothecary for those I could not gather.

"I did so, and for several days I saw Dr. Blackwater put the physics into the prince's wine after I had pounded the leaves and roots to powder or an oil. But I began to notice that the stuff I had prepared was as great a pile in the evening as in the morning, when I readied the herbs for the prince's wine."

"You pounded fresh herbs each day?"

"Aye."

"Has Dr. Blackwater spoken to you of this?"

"Aye. He saw me this morning at the work of pounding more thyme leaves, and told me to prepare no more. The herbs were not effective, he said, so there was no reason to continue the physic. But this was not so. I saw Prince Edward grow stronger for a time."

"Did you say this to Dr. Blackwater?"

"And lose my position?"

"Nay. Of course not. I thank you for telling me of this."

"What will you do?" the assistant asked with some anxiety in his voice. "You'll not speak of this conversation to Dr. Blackwater?"

"Nay. Should I do so he would know 'twas you who told me of his iniquitous behavior. Bring me the herbs which are unused. I will prepare them myself. If your master asks what has become of them, tell him you disposed of them as he had no use for them. This will be no falsehood. Go now to his infirmary while he is dancing, get the pouches, and toss them beside the porch. I will go there before dawn and find the discarded herbs."

Trinkle did so, and before daybreak I searched in the darkness beside the porch and found four small leather pouches, and one large pouch for the fennel root.

I had no mortar and pestle, but I knew where they might be found. The cook and baker were at their work as light came to the eastern sky, and Kennington's cook supplied me with the instruments I needed. From the butler, also just from his bed and rubbing his eyes, I asked a ewer of wine.

The herbs and wine I took to my chamber and awakened Arthur with the grinding of tansy and thyme, cress and bramble leaves. I had lighted a single cresset to better see the work, although enough light now penetrated the window that doing so might not have been necessary. Arthur rolled upon his pallet, blinked, and saw what I was about.

"Thought that was the leech's work," he mumbled.

"It was, but he will not perform it."

"Hmph. That why Prince Edward's so wan?"

"I believe so. Blackwater's assistant told you of the doctor's perfidy, so now I must see to the prince's dose myself."

I finished pounding enough of the herbs for one day's remedy, stirred the powdery stuff into the ewer of wine, then left Arthur and our chamber.

I walked through the dim, empty hall, my footsteps echoing upon the tiles. No valet guarded the base of the stairs leading to Prince Edward's privy chamber, but I knew there would be two stalwart fellows at the privy chamber door. There were, and they were unsmiling.

Prince Edward, they said, was with his chamberlain, preparing for the day. I was about to ask one of the valets to announce me, and say to the prince that I was at his door upon an urgent matter, when one said, "Likes his bread and cheese alone in the morning, does the prince. John Chamberlain always brings this to the prince, then helps him with his attire an' grooming for the day."

"Please say to the prince, as soon as you may, that Master Hugh must speak to him. Without delay. I will await the prince's summons in my chamber."

'Twas more than an hour before Prince Edward called for me. John Chamberlain appeared at my open door to announce that the prince would see me.

"He is unwell?" I said.

The chamberlain shrugged. "No worse than has been."

"Did he break his fast with good appetite?"

"Nay. A few bites of bread and a small fragment of cheese. He's had little desire for food these past days. Lady Joan fears for his life."

I took the ewer of wine and mixed herbs from my chamber's small table and set off with the chamberlain for the stairs to the privy chamber. We were expected, and the valets at the prince's door pushed it open as we approached. Prince Edward was not alone. Sir William Vache was present – he of the large cap and imposing liripipe.

Prince Edward looked from me to the ewer I carried, a puzzled expression upon his face. Perhaps Dr. Blackwater's custom was to bring the prince his wine and herbs in a similar vessel each morning. His words confirmed this supposition.

"Where is Blackwater? Is he ill? I see you have prepared my potion for this day."

"Dr. Blackwater is hale," I said, "so far as I know. But I have decided to administer the physic myself. Dr. Blackwater is a busy man dealing with the ailments of your household."

"Is he? I suppose so. Well, pour some of the wine into the cup on yon table."

I did so, after swirling the wine about the ewer so to be sure the herbs were well mixed. Prince Edward drank the mixture, coughed as some particles of pounded herbs caught in his throat, then said, "Dr. Blackwater made a finer powder of the herbs. They did not chafe my throat as yours do."

I did not reply. The prince looked into the empty cup and tilted it for better light from the row of windows which now blazed with morning sunshine. He extended a finger into the cup and withdrew a few tiny flakes of pounded herbs. He stared at his fingertip, and as I watched, his expression became one of deep puzzlement.

"I saw nothing like this in the dregs when Blackwater served the physic. Why are you unable to make the herbs into such a fine powder as Blackwater?"

I was unsure as to how I should respond. As it happened I was not required to do so.

"Your potion has not been so effective as at first, and as at Limoges. And when Blackwater prepared the mix I saw nothing in the dregs as I do now. He has not done as he was charged, has he?"

"I have doubts, m'lord."

"Doubts! Ha, I have none."

Then, to one of the valets who guarded his door the prince shouted, "Richard, fetch Dr. Blackwater. Immediately."

The valet turned and I heard his running footfall as he disappeared through the corridor and down the stairs to the hall. I thought for a moment I might be called upon to set the fellow's broken leg when he tumbled upon the stairs. He did not.

Sir William Vache had stood silently during this conversation. Prince Edward seemed suddenly to remember his presence, turned to him, and spoke. "I am no king. Not yet. If my father's touch will not relieve you, mine surely will not."

The King's Evil! No wonder Sir William wore his liripipe wrapped about his neck. He suffered from a scrofulous sore, which folk do believe may be cured by the touch of a king. Evidently Prince Edward had sent the knight to his father, and there had been no good result.

"Perhaps Dr. Blackwater will suggest some remedy," the prince said. "He will be here soon, and is a competent physician even though he will not obey my commands. Well, he will do so in the future or he will seek other employment."

As if in response to these words I heard footsteps approach the chamber door, and a moment later Dr. Blackwater entered. His demeanor was that of a man confident of his place and value. Then he saw me and guessed, I believe, my knowledge of his transgression. He removed his cap and bowed deeply to his prince. "How may I serve m'lord?" he said.

"You may explain this," Prince Edward said, and again swept a finger through the dregs in his wine cup. Once again a few flecks of crushed herbs adhered to the finger. He held the finger before Blackwater's eyes. "What do you see?"

"Uh, ummm, some impurity has contaminated your wine, m'lord."

"Nay. Master Hugh, what is this? Can you identify the stuff?"

"A fragment of bramble leaf, I believe."

"And bramble leaves were to be among the herbs pounded and given to me in wine each day. Is this not so?"

"It is, m'lord."

Prince Edward turned again to Dr. Blackwater, whose face had turned quite pale. "Why is it that when you prepared my wine with the herbs Master Hugh advised I found no residue of bramble leaves or any other herb in my wine cup? What say you?"

"Uh... perhaps Master Hugh used too much. I, uh, was sparing of the physics."

"So sparing that the herbs did me no good. You wished me to have nothing but more boiled roosters for my dinner. Is this not so?"

"Your illness requires a diet which is dry and hot, m'lord. Nothing serves so well as boiled roosters."

"So you say. But before Master Hugh arrived here your roosters did me little good. You cannot be trusted. Master Hugh will prepare my draughts and we shall see if I need your boiled roosters. Or if I need you, for that matter.

"Now, on another matter, Sir William suffers from a scrofulous sore. My father, the king, has touched him, but to no effect. What say you?"

"When did this touch take place?" Blackwater asked.

"Last week," Sir William replied.

"And what is your birth date?"

"The fourth day of January."

"Ah, you are a Capricorn. The King's Evil can best be relieved if the sufferer is touched under his natal sign. For the king's touch to succeed you must wait 'til December, then visit the king again."

This assertion was new to me. Perhaps it was new to the quick-witted William Blackwater as well. He could assure the prince and Sir William that his knowledge of astrology would assist the knight in seeking a cure, and also buy time for the physician either to try some other remedy or hope Sir William would forget the claim. Or mayhap the knight would die of the affliction and Blackwater's explanation would remain untested.

Prince Edward turned suddenly to me. "What say you, Master Hugh? Must Sir William wait 'til the stars and planets agree before my father's touch will be effective?"

Hope is a valuable commodity. Perhaps for that reason it should be used sparingly. I did not wish to undermine Sir William's faith, but I knew it was unlikely that King Edward's touch would heal a man of anything. Physicians say such a thing may happen.

The world may end tomorrow in fire and the Lord Christ return. But probably not.

"I have heard of men recovering from scrofulous sores after a king has touched them," I said cautiously.

"Aye," Blackwater said. "'Tis common in France. King Jean once touched more than one thousand sufferers in one day."

"How many of these found relief?" I asked.

Blackwater shrugged. Here was answer enough.

"You are a surgeon, Master Hugh," Prince Edward said. "What can scalpels and such do for a scrofulous sore?"

"If it has not grown too large the sore might be cut away. But the surgery is not always successful."

"Not successful?" Sir William said. "How so? If you remove it may I perish of the wound?"

"Nay. But a scrofulous sore will often return."

"Often, but not always?" Sir William asked.

"Aye. No surgeon knows why this is so."

"So if you relieve Sir William of his sore he may be rid of it for good?" Prince Edward said.

"He may. But he may not. I can promise nothing."

"What say you, Sir William? Will you have Master Hugh deal with your carbuncle?"

"The king's touch failed, and Dr. Blackwater has said I must wait many weeks before it may succeed. The sore grows apace. I would have it dealt with now."

"Success is not guaranteed," I reminded the knight.

"But if nothing is done the sore will surely increase, will it not?"

"Aye," I replied. "That much can be guaranteed."

Dr. Blackwater had been silent during this exchange, but now he spoke. "'Twould be foolish to allow a mechanic with a blade to slash away upon your neck."

"You recommend that I wait until December? What if King Edward's touch fails me then?" Sir William said.

"I will prepare you so that it will not. Your diet must henceforth be warm and wet, and a poultice of pig fat applied to the sore twice each day."

"Have you treated other men with scrofulous sores in like manner?" the knight asked.

"Aye. A servant to Lady Margaret Chesham."

"Was he cured?"

Blackwater hesitated. "Nay," he finally admitted, but quickly explained the failure. "Lady Margaret presented the man to King Edward for his touch at the time when King Jean of France was held hostage in London. King Edward brought King Jean to touch the servant as well, saying that he was God's anointed also. But this caused the cure to fail, as the French king was no longer upon his throne – a regent governed in his stead."

"My father's anointing as king could be overcome by another king no longer upon his throne?" Prince Edward said. "Jean was yet king of France."

The prince's tone of voice caused Blackwater to retreat a step. Clearly Prince Edward was not pleased with the assertion that his father's powers could be rendered ineffectual by some other sovereign.

Sir William spoke. "'Tis sure that the sore can be removed?" he asked me.

"Aye, unless it has grown too large. I must see it to know."

Without another word the knight unwrapped the liripipe from about his neck. Doing so exposed a putrid lump the size of half a hen's egg oozing a small amount of pus and blood.

"What say you, Master Hugh?" Prince Edward asked.

"'Tis not too large. I can cut it away. But again I must tell you that it may return."

"Hah," Blackwater said. "With the proper diet suited to your unbalanced humors, and an appropriate salve applied daily, when the king touches you in December the sore will disappear and not return. Be patient, and under my care all will be well."

No man enjoys the thought of another man applying a blade to his flesh, even if the flesh is diseased. I watched as Sir William considered his choice and the possible consequences of the decision.

"You can provide no assurance that after you cut the sore away it will not return?" the knight said to me.

"None."

"If it does return, what then?"

"It may be that I or another surgeon can remove it once again."

"How much time must pass before I know if the sore is to return?" Sir William is a thoughtful man and was considering alternatives and results. He spoke again, and repeated his earlier decision. "I will have it dealt with now."

Blackwater snorted quietly to show his view of Sir William's resolve.

"Can you do this surgery soon?" Sir William asked.

"This day, if you wish it."

"I do. I'll not live with the sore any longer than need be.

"Perhaps Dr. Blackwater will assist you?" Sir William continued.

Blackwater had done no good service at the surgery tent when Limoges fell. I wanted him nowhere near an open incision. At Limoges his behavior made it clear that he desired nothing to do with blood and scalpels.

"Too many hands at work upon a sore will interfere with each other," I said. Blackwater seemed relieved that I had rejected the suggestion.

"After dinner, then?" Prince Edward said. "Where will you do this surgery? You may do it here if you think it suitable."

"The day is cloudy and I will need good light to see what I am about. Your privy chamber is not suited. A table set in the palace yard would serve."

"It will be done," the prince said. "After dinner, then."

Sir William nodded.

"I will prepare my instruments," I said, "and some herbs which will reduce the pain: crushed hemp seeds and the dried sap of lettuce pounded to flakes. But these will only reduce the hurt."

"I've been wounded twice in battle," the knight said. "What can your scalpel do to me beyond what swords have already done?"

Chapter 15

I forget what was served at dinner that day. My thoughts were upon other matters. Gossip had flowed through Kennington Palace and by the time dinner was done most folk, from high to low, knew why a sturdy table had been moved to the palace yard.

Following the meal I sought Prince Edward's butler and asked him to provide a ewer of wine and two cups. I intended to give Sir William a substantial dose of wine with hemp seeds and lettuce sap. The wine remaining I would use to bathe the incision. From the buttery I went to my chamber and armed myself with my medium scalpel, a needle, and a spool of silken thread. Also two pouches of the herbs I would dissolve in wine.

The hall was nearly empty when I returned to it on my way to the porch and palace yard. Those who remained ceased their conversations and watched me pass. They knew where I was going and what I was to do.

I was stunned when I turned the corner of the palace to the yard. I was to have an audience. The thought had not occurred to me when I suggested that the surgery be done outside where the light would be greater. Had I done the work in some room in the palace the curious could be excluded. But in the yard forty or fifty onlookers greeted me, both men and women. My first thought was to ask Prince Edward to send them away. My second thought was that he would not wish to do so, for he stood closest to the table, apparently eager to see blood flow. William Blackwater was not present.

Sir William stood beside his prince, appearing a little pale. His scrofulous sore was yet hidden under his liripipe. I heard footsteps behind me and turned to see the butler, in his hands a ewer and two silver cups. I took them from him, set them upon the table, and poured wine into one of the cups. Then into this cup I measured a heaping handful of crushed hemp seeds and flakes of dried lettuce sap. As I did this the spectators grew silent, watching, wondering. I saw no obligation to explain to them what I had done, but I told Sir William.

"These herbs will, as I told you, lessen the pain of the surgery. The hemp seeds dull a man's pain, and the lettuce will cause you to become drowsy. About an hour after you drink this wine, the herbs will take effect and I will begin. Are you yet determined to have me remove the sore?"

"Aye. More so than this morning."

I held the cup to Sir William and he drank it in two gulps. Those of the audience who stood nearby had heard my words, and passed the explanation to others who stood farther from the table. Upon hearing that no blood would be shed for an hour many departed. Perhaps they would return. But twenty or so remained, unwilling to risk missing a unique entertainment. Prince Edward did not relish standing while the herbs took effect, so called for a bench to be brought to him. While I waited for the hemp seeds and lettuce sap to do their work I threaded a needle with silken thread, ready to remedy the damage I was about to do to this man's neck.

Prince Edward's chamberlain stood at his master's elbow. There was one other item I needed which I had forgotten to collect before I entered the castle yard. I requested of the chamberlain that he seek a clean linen cloth of good size, perhaps a fragment of portpain from the pantler's store.

A moment after the chamberlain had departed to seek the linen, we who stood about the table heard the iron-shod hooves of horses and the clatter of cart wheels striking the cobbles of Kennington Palace yard. I looked to the marshalsea whence came the racket, and saw three men mounted, a wagon, and two carts. Two runcies drew the wagon, and a lady rode regally upon it, behind the driver.

As I gazed upon this scene Prince Edward spoke. "Sir Thomas Dod departing for Clovelly." The prince said no more, but I knew his thoughts and why Sir Thomas, his wife, squires, pages, and grooms were leaving. Sir Thomas was the third knight to abandon Kennington since the deaths of Sir John and Lady Ardith. A prince likes to show his wealth, but if I could not soon discover who had slain Sir Giles, Sir John, and Lady Ardith there might be no man remaining at Kennington Palace to enjoy Prince Edward's splendor and largesse.

A few more onlookers drifted away, bored, but some who had departed returned, so that an hour later I had as many spectators as ever. If this surgery succeeded, my name would be known throughout the realm. Of course, if I failed, my name would also be known.

Clouds obscured the sun, but even so the light was much better than it would have been within the palace. Sir William had been in discussion with Prince Edward and a few other knights when I noticed that he began to slur his words, as if he'd consumed too much wine. 'Twas time to begin.

I told Sir William to remove his cap and I would assist him to the table. His squire, Thomas Poer, stood nearby. The knight removed cap and liripipe, gave it to the squire, then climbed to the table, disdaining my assistance. This concerned me. I had placed enough hemp seed and lettuce sap in his wine that Sir William should have been unsteady. Too unsteady to mount the table, which was as high as my waist. I feared the draught did not stupefy him enough to ease his pain. 'Twas too late to do aught about it though. I would proceed, and trust to his courage proved in battle. Onlookers crowded closer to see Sir William's affliction, and several ladies gasped at the sight.

I took a length of the chamberlain's linen cloth, doubled it twice, and laid it under Sir William's head, neck, and shoulders. Prince Edward would not wish his table stained with blood.

Beneath the skin of a man's neck are many vital vessels which must not be severed nor punctured. For this reason I planned to make several shallow cuts about the carbuncle as I lifted the sore with the fingers of my left hand. But first I swabbed Sir William's neck with a linen fragment soaked in Prince Edward's wine. Washing a wound with wine will speed its healing, although no man knows why this is so. It seems to me that if bathing a laceration after the wound is made will aid its mending, then doing so before a scalpel is applied might also be of benefit, although this I cannot prove. I dipped the scalpel in wine for good measure.

Because I feared that Sir William might flinch when he felt the blade against his neck, imperiling vessels I must not slash, I assigned Arthur and Thomas Poer, his sturdy squire, to stand on either side of the table and grasp the knight's arms just below his shoulders. Poer gave Sir William's cap to one of Prince Edward's valets and did as I asked. I saw Randall Patchett nearby, called to him, and asked the lad to hold Sir William's head steady. I need not have concerned myself. Sir William was not the man who twitched when the scalpel was applied.

I heard a woman gasp when I sliced into the flesh of Sir William's neck. With my left hand I felt under the sore, found a vessel, and pressed it down so that I might cut more deeply under the growth without harming some vital vein or artery.

When my scalpel had sliced halfway under the carbuncle I moved to cut under the opposite side of the lesion. Before I could do this I heard a strange guttural sound and felt a shove against my back. 'Twas as well I had not placed the scalpel against Sir William's neck for a second incision. The jolt would have pushed my blade into places I did not want it to go.

What I had felt was Thomas Poer collapsing at my feet. I turned in time to see his head strike the cobbles, fortunately cushioned by a large, fashionable cap and liripipe. But the blow would be enough to render him senseless for some time. His eyes rolled back in his head and I glimpsed only the whites. I heard Prince Edward order two grooms to haul Poer's limp form from the table, and gave the stricken youth no further thought.

Sir William had lain motionless under my scalpel so I saw no need to replace the fallen squire. 'Twas but short work to slice under the scrofula from the opposite side of the first cut, and lift the lesion free of Sir William's neck. The carbuncle was little larger than a chestnut in circumference and as thick through as a finger.

I was somewhat surprised that the wound bled little. I wiped blood from the cut with a scrap of wine-soaked linen, took up my threaded needle, and began to stitch up the hole I had made in Sir William's neck. Six or seven stitches would have served, but the scar would be less conspicuous if I made more but smaller sutures. I closed the wound with twelve stitches, washed it again with wine, and declared the procedure finished. I believe some of my audience were disappointed that nothing tragic had happened.

Arthur helped Sir William to sit. This time he needed the assistance. The ample measure of herbs I had placed in his wine would no doubt leave him unbalanced for several hours. But the knight had enough wit to ask what salve I would apply to his wound.

As always in such circumstances I was required to explain that I follow the practice of Henri de Mondeville, late surgeon to the army of the French king, who discovered when patching together wounded soldiers that those whose wounds were left open, unbound, not treated with salve, healed most readily. Sir William nodded understanding, but his expression was skeptical.

"The stitches I have made to close the wound must not be removed 'til St. Edmund's Day. When you turn your head, the sutures will hold the cut close together. Removed too soon, the incision might open and be more difficult to close than at first. If I am no longer at Kennington" – and I dearly hoped I would not be – "any man with a steady hand and sharp blade may slice and draw the silk threads."

As I concluded these instructions I heard behind me a groan. 'Twas Thomas Poer awakening from his slumber. I turned to him. He lay yet upon the cobbles where the prince's grooms had deposited him. I was done with Sir William – I should now attend his squire.

I knelt over the lad. He blinked, then mumbled, "A terrible end... terrible end." I assumed he spoke of the surgery I had performed upon his lord which had caused him to swoon. Perhaps he thought the surgery would prove fatal to Sir William.

The squire's eyes closed again. I asked for a bucket of water from the well. One was soon provided, and I told Arthur to dash the water into Poer's face. The result was miraculous. The lad shook, spluttered, and raised himself to a seated position. His face took on a crimson hue, from embarrassment or the cold water I cannot say. Prince Edward found this humorous and laughed loudly.

The squire then staggered to his feet, swayed, looked about him, and seemed to shrink back against the palace wall. I thought he was about to swoon again. Not so. He stared into the crowd of onlookers, now dispersing. Fear was in his eyes, and his hands went to his neck. I thought this due to the surgery I had done upon Sir

William. Perhaps Thomas worried that his own neck might someday require such surgery. Scrofulous sores are common enough. Then I remembered that I yet held the scalpel in my hand. I turned from the squire and set the blade upon the table beside Sir William. This did nothing to allay the lad's fearful expression.

Poer paid me no attention when I rested the scalpel upon the table. He continued to watch the departing observers, then to Sir William he said, "What did I say?"

The knight was yet stupefied. "Say? When?" he replied.

"When I lay senseless upon the cobbles. What did I say? I remember speaking as I awoke."

"I don't know," Sir William said. "Paid you no heed."

These words did nothing to reduce the fear in Poer's eyes or stop the twitching of his hands about his neck. And his gullet swelled and shrank as he gulped air like a carp tossed upon the bank.

"You said, 'A terrible end,'" I said.

"Nothing else?"

"Nay. Just 'A terrible end.'"

The squire visibly relaxed, but his gaze never left the departing observers. I turned and followed his eyes to see what, or who, so entranced, or frightened, him. Several folk made their way from the palace yard in the direction of Thomas's vision. Among them were Amabil Cheyne and Sir Geoffrey Paget. Their backs were to us as they departed the yard. I dismissed them as the cause of the squire's fear. But of the other knights, ladies, squires, and grooms in the line of Poer's sight I could detect none who should cause a robust young man to quake with fear.

Thomas Poer regained his senses enough that he realized he should assist Sir William from the table and to his chamber. The two men lurched off toward the porch. I could not tell which was supporting the other.

All the while Prince Edward had stood watching the exchange between me, Sir William, and Thomas Poer. When they disappeared into the porch he spoke.

"There have been many terrible things happen in Kennington. I wonder which that squire spoke of."

I gave thought to the matter, but only for a moment. My attention and that of Prince Edward and the others who remained in the palace yard was diverted. A woman was shouting, and then a man, and then both together, each trying to surpass the other in volume. This was not a contest the man could hope to win.

Prince Edward scowled to hear such a din. The shouting came from beyond the marshalsea, so we could hear but not see the verbal combat. The prince turned on his heel and stalked toward the disturbance. I followed, and Arthur followed me.

The screeching female was Amabil Cheyne, and her antagonist was a well-dressed man I had not before seen at Kennington Palace. Two men stood behind this stranger, apparently willing to take his part in whatever strife might ensue. Sir Geoffrey Paget stood behind Amabil, seeking unsuccessfully to calm her wrath.

Much of the argument was incomprehensible, as Amabil and her adversary were shouting over each other. Prince Edward quieted the screeching and bluster. "Silence!" he roared. Where he found the strength for such volume I cannot say. Perhaps my herbs were already having an effect. Or anger gave stimulus to his voice.

"What is the cause of this unseemly display?" the prince bellowed. His voice was powerful enough to make both Amabil and the stranger quail before him. Sir Geoffrey seemed properly awed as well. He need no longer seek to calm Amabil. Prince Edward did so for him. After he wed the lass that obligation would be his alone. Better him than me.

"Who are you?" Prince Edward addressed the stranger.

The man doffed his cap and bowed. He was a thin-faced fellow, with a nose that protruded from his sallow cheeks like an axe blade. "I am Richard Rowell, mercer, m'lord."

"What business have you here?"

"I seek payment of a debt."

"Who owes you money?"

"She does," the mercer said vehemently, "and she will not pay."

"I owe the churl nothing," Amabil retorted hotly.

"Why do you say she does when she claims not?" Prince Edward said.

"Sir Giles owed me twelve pounds, four shillings, and eleven pence. I have learned that he is dead. His heir assumes the debt. 'Tis the law, is it not? His daughter inherits his lands and wealth; she must from the legacy pay her father's debts."

"My father's debts, not mine," Amabil said.

"I'll have no more shouting and cursing at Kennington. As for your debt," the prince said to Rowell, "hire a lawyer."

"Bah," the mercer said. "She'd rather bribe a judge, as would her father, than pay me what is mine. But I'll have my due," Rowell hissed at Amabil. "As for your scoundrel father, 'tis no loss to this world that he is now in the next. A fitting place for you, as well. Best look to your words or you may join him sooner rather than later."

Prince Edward scowled and said, "Away with you! I'll have no threats against my guests."

With that Rowell spun on his heels and stalked toward the gatehouse. His servants followed. The mercer did not look back, but as the three approached Kennington's gatehouse one of the mercer's men turned to Amabil and Sir Geoffrey, grinned, and drew his index finger across his throat. I believe Prince Edward did not see this gesture. But Amabil did, and reached a hand to her neck.

All I knew of Richard Rowell, mercer, I had learned in the past few minutes. He was a man who was ill-used, and he gave evidence of a fierce temper. Would he slay Sir Giles and then seek payment from his heir, assuming a lass to be a weaker adversary? If so, he had clearly underestimated Amabil. When St. Paul identified women as the weaker vessel he had not met Amabil Cheyne.

Arthur had stood behind me observing this confrontation, and now spoke.

"Seen that mercer before," he said.

"Where?"

"At the hangin'. The apprentice what stole his master's silk. That fellow was there. Stood by the cart, arms folded across his chest, lookin' satisfied. I'd not forget a face like his."

Prince Edward did not know Richard Rowell, which meant that this was likely the mercer's first visit to Kennington Palace. So I thought. Then how could Rowell have to do with the murders of Sir

John and Lady Ardith? Or of Roger de Clare? Were these deaths all unrelated to that of Sir Giles Cheyne? I could not believe it so. But Rowell's tempestuous behavior a few moments earlier indicated a man willing to dispense his own justice if he saw no one else able or willing to provide it. Did Richard Rowell do business with Alan Tonge? A skinner would need silk to line the fur coats he made for gentlemen, and also for fur coverlets made for a lady's bed. In the course of business with Alan, had Rowell met Arnaud?

I sought Sir Harold and asked him to assign one of his constables to accompany Arthur and me to the Shambles. The fellow he chose was not pleased with the duty, I think, for a chill mist had settled upon London and made the streets even more disagreeable than normal. But the miserable weather meant that the streets were nearly empty, so no throngs impeded our journey to Greyfriars' Church – although the mud was not helpful.

The afternoon had become dark, with low clouds, so that some folk had candles or cressets lit. Windows of oiled skins glowed dimly. The windows of Alan Tonge's house were dark, but as we made our way behind his house two windows showed that the skinner was at work in his shop, his labor lighted by a cresset or two.

I thumped upon the workshop door. His apprentice opened to me, took a hurried glance at Prince Edward's badge, and stepped back, open-mouthed. Perhaps he remembered my face. He surely remembered the badge.

"Who's there?" Alan called.

"'Tis Master Hugh," I replied. "Upon Prince Edward's business."

In the dim light of the workshop I saw the skinner bent close over skins he was carefully stitching together, as assiduous in his labor as I had been over Sir William Vache earlier. When I spoke, Tonge stood, blinked, rubbed his back, and asked, "You have news of who slew my brother?"

"Nay, no news. A question."

On a shelf beyond the table where lay the furs being assembled I saw fabric folded carefully. This material had a dull sheen in the light from cressets and window. Not linen but silk was stored on the shelf. No wonder the workshop entry door was so heavily barred. I pointed to the stuff.

"You use that for lining the coats you make for gentlemen?"

"Aye."

"And with winter near you are at work on a coat?"

"Aye. For Sir Robert Bray."

I walked to the table where the garment was being constructed and felt the fur. Even in the dim light I could see glimmers of a reddish hue in the grey.

"Fox, is it not?"

"Aye."

"A man would be pleased to don such a coat, I think. The silk you will use to line the coat, from whom will you purchase it?"

The question brought a puzzled look to Tonge's face. "Whoever provides the goods I need at lowest price," he replied.

"Surely. Wise business. Is the price not set by decree?"

The skinner was silent for a moment. "It is," he finally said.

"But not all mercers and drapers hold to the ordinance, I suppose. Who among those who sell silks will offer bargains when you seek their goods?"

The puzzled look remained upon the skinner's face, and even deepened. What, he surely wondered, was I about, asking who offered silk at a reduced price?

"Henry Estes is my usual supplier." Tonge glanced to the shelf. "The silk you see there I purchased from him. I'd not wish to see him troubled for offering an occasional bargain."

"I have no interest in the price of silk," I said. "Any others that you buy from?"

"I have done business with Thomas Gryce… Do you seek silk?"

"Nay. It's not that. Have you purchased goods from Richard Rowell?"

"When I must."

"When you must? Explain."

"If Henry or Thomas does not have what I need, nor any other mercer, I have sought silk and linen from Richard."

"Why only when you could not find goods from others?"

"Rowell charges the set price. And will deceive a man who is not vigilant."

"How so?"

"Have you met the man?" Tonge asked. "He is short in stature. When he measures out a yard of silk the distance from his thumb to his nose is briefer than most men's, but he sells the length as a yard and cheats the buyer."

"And will offer no discount on the ordinance price? Yet men do business with him?"

"When they must. His goods are of quality, that must be said, and he has many colors from which a man might choose."

"So folk who seek quality and care little for cost seek his goods?"

"Aye. Gentlemen and knights and folk of rank."

"Did your brother know Rowell?"

"Aye. We both learned the skinner's trade from our father. I am oldest, so will inherit. Arnaud understood this and so when he came of age he left to seek his own way in the world. Did well, did Arnaud. Became valet to Prince Edward."

"So Arnaud knew the mercer Rowell. Were they friends?"

"I'd not say so. And 'twas five years past when Arnaud went his own way."

"He might have remained known to Rowell," I suggested.

"Aye, might've. Likely."

"How did Arnaud come to find employment with the prince?" I asked. "Did he leave this business because he was offered a position at Kennington Palace?"

"Aye. We'd made a fur coat for Sir Gilbert Flynt. Whilst Arnaud was fitting the garment he heard Sir Gilbert telling his squire of Prince Edward's intention to employ more grooms at Kennington. Arnaud made so bold as to ask Sir Gilbert if he'd speak to Prince Edward's marshal for him. Not a fortnight later he went to the palace."

"And did good service, so was made valet?"

"Aye. I suppose he must have served well."

"When did you last do business with Richard Rowell?" I asked.

Tonge pulled at his beard for a moment. "Two years past. I

needed crimson silk to line a coverlet for Lady Margaret Beston. There was none to be had in the hue she demanded from any other mercer in London. Rowell demanded nine shillings a yard. Robbery!"

"You've not seen the man since?"

"Nay."

"What of Arnaud? When you saw him did he ever speak of meeting with Rowell?"

"I didn't see much of Arnaud. Duty at Kennington kept 'im there, I suppose. That's why I was surprised when he came to me a week past, seeking to escape London. Is that why you're asking of Richard Rowell? You think he knows something of what Arnaud was about, and who the felon is what did away with 'im?"

"It may be so. But many things which may be so are not. Possible does not mean likely."

I bade the skinner "good day" and with Arthur and the groom set out for London Bridge and the palace. The foul weather quickened our pace, but even so the gloom of the day had become the dark of evening before we reached Kennington Palace gatehouse.

Chapter 16

Dr. Blackwater was not interested in conversation during supper. This was good. Neither was I. I chewed and thought of what I had learned from Alan Tonge. And I also thought of what I had not learned from the skinner.

I had detected no reluctance in Tonge to tell of his dealings with Richard Rowell, or Arnaud's association with the mercer, once his mind had been set at rest that I had no interest in seeing he had followed the law to the letter in plying his trade. If Alan Tonge thought there was some business between Arnaud and Rowell which needed to be disguised he indicated no intent to do this. But could the mercer really have become so furious at Sir Giles that he would consider murder to avenge his unpaid debt? And did he know of Arnaud's service at Kennington Palace? Likely he did. Word of such an advancement would be a matter of pride, not concealed.

One man who had reason to harm Sir Giles Cheyne was now dead. Another now sought redress from Sir Giles's daughter. The man who slew Sir Giles was now himself slain, in curious circumstances, and in a village where folk seemed determined that I would learn no more of the death than I had thus far been able to discover.

Prince Edward, I noticed, attacked his supper this day with enthusiasm. Perhaps this was due to the continuing absence of boiled roosters from the removes. Most of the prince's guests at supper appeared light-hearted. The deaths in Kennington Palace seemed forgotten. Or perhaps those who brooded over the murders had departed the palace, leaving only the unconcerned and those who knew of no enemies. I knew of three knights who had fled to their own shires.

I saw only one morose man. Sir Geoffrey Paget nibbled at his portions, staring at the wall across from his table, barely speaking to Amabil Cheyne, who had suffered no loss of appetite from her exchange with Richard Rowell. The lass consumed her fare with much cheer and ignored her dour companion.

My eyes occasionally rested upon Thomas Poer, who seemed recovered from his swoon. The squire conversed freely with his companion. At first. As the third remove was served, a jelly de chare and fraunt hemelle, Poer caught my eye resting momentarily upon him, and his visage fell. Why? What had I done to cause him melancholy? I had relieved his master of a grievous sore. For that, I thought, he should be joyful this night. As I consumed the third remove I noticed that the youth never again looked to me, nor did his countenance resume the sanguine appearance with which he had begun the meal.

My thoughts wandered to the squire's words as he awoke from his swoon. "A terrible end." What did he find so terrible about surgery to remove a scrofulous sore and what end did that involve? Or was it some other terrible thing of which he spoke? Certainly there had been terrible things happening in Kennington Palace. More terrible than the blood of a surgery. Did Thomas Poer speak of these? One of them? "A terrible end," he had said. One end was terrible. One only. What other dreadful things that had taken place at Kennington Palace in the past fortnight did not strike the squire as terrible?

I lay abed considering Richard Rowell. If 'twas he who paid Arnaud Tonge to put hemlock into Sir Giles's wine then it was likely he who slew Arnaud, or paid some other man to do so. Why would such an arrangement lead to the hostility I found in Hornsey when I was seen to be curious about Arnaud's death? Why would anyone of the village care?

Did Sir Thomas Jocelyn know Richard Rowell? Had he purchased silk and linen from the mercer? More to the point, did he owe Rowell for some of his fabrics, and what might he do to see his debt to the mercer forgiven? With the sonorous accompaniment of Arthur's snoring I fell to sleep thinking that another visit to Hornsey was required. But this time I would first seek Sir Harold and travel with a small army of his constables.

I awoke to the same suspicion as had occupied my mind before Morpheus claimed me. But what of Roger de Clare? What could he have to do with an unpaid debt to a mercer? Was he in the party of young men who were hired to halt my inquiry? If Rowell paid four men to accost me upon the road, and paid Sir Thomas – or forgave a debt – to have his henchman slain, he would have small profit from the debt owed him by Sir Giles, even if he could recover the obligation from Amabil.

Arthur and I broke our fast with loaves hot from the palace bakehouse and cups of fresh ale. I did not need to seek the marshal, for Sir Harold also sought a loaf and ale. I told him that I required six men with horses enough for them and Arthur and me. The marshal knew of the assault Arthur and I had escaped, so guessed our destination.

"You travel to Hornsey again?" he asked.

"Aye, and I do not wish to be overcome upon the road."

"Eight armed men should be enough to persuade malefactors to turn their attention elsewhere. I'll be one of them. You wish to depart soon, before mass?"

"Aye. The journey to Hornsey is not far, but I may be detained there seeking information from those unwilling to part with it."

The marshal wolfed down his wheaten loaf, swallowed his ale in one gulp, and hurried to the stables. He advised me that he and his constables would be ready shortly.

Prince Edward breaks his fast in his privy chamber. I went there with a cup of wine from the buttery, laced with the herbs I hoped would ease the prince's ailment. The valets attending the privy chamber door announced my arrival, and from within I heard, "He may enter."

The prince's chamberlain was about the business of preparing him for the day. But when he saw the cup of wine in my hand the prince waved the man away, took the cup, and drank it down.

"Dr. Blackwater," he said, "is angry."

"I am sorry to hear it."

"Bah. Let him rage. What will he do? Leave my service? Where else will he find a man willing to pay him forty pounds each year to sniff his piss? This wine – had it more of your herbs?"

"Aye, m'lord."

"Good. I am somewhat stronger already, I think."

"I am setting off for Hornsey," I said. "Your marshal and six others will accompany me."

"No more surprises upon the road, eh? Unless it be a surprise for those who seek to do you evil. You think the answer to the wickedness overspreading Kennington may be found in that village?"

"It may be so."

"Report to me immediately upon your return, even if the journey is a waste of time. You may tell me then of what you learned, or of what you hoped to learn but did not."

I thought as I left the privy chamber that 'twas likely I would do the last rather than the first. Most of my investigation into the death of Sir Giles Cheyne had involved matters I had hoped to learn but had not.

I left the palace porch and hurried to the marshalsea. Sir Harold's promise was kept. He and Arthur, along with five constables and serjeants, stood ready at the main stable door. The beasts were saddled and bridled, casually flicking their tails. Arthur held the reins of two beasts and I was pleased to see that one of these was one of Prince Edward's best amblers. The journey to Hornsey would not be as unpleasant as it might have been, and although the day had dawned overcast and dim, the sun was beginning to regard the realm through breaks in the clouds.

The marshal and three of his constables had swords dangling from their side. The Lord Christ commanded that His followers were not to recompense evil for evil. This is a difficult charge. I seek to do no man evil, but is it evil to bring felons to justice, or to employ a sword or dagger to prevent an evil which has not yet occurred, but which will if not forestalled? I must ask Master Wycliffe of this when next I see him.

As always London Bridge was thronged with those whose business took them into the city. We eight were an hour on our journey before we passed through Aldersgate and departed London. The road was nearly dry and the sky bright when we came to Hornsey. Along the way men and oxen were at work in fields, plowing fallow ground for planting rye. Swineherds guided their charges in forest pannaging. All peered at our party with suspicion as we passed. Four swords were visible, and when men so armed travel the roads it usually means no good thing.

I raised my hand to halt my companions when our party reached the priest's dwelling. A priest generally knows all there is to know of folk in his parish, although he may not wish to share the knowledge if the lord of his manor has the power to appoint his priest, or if the information came at the confessional box. His housekeeper answered my rapping upon the rectory door and said that her employer had gone to a village house where a grandmother lay dying, there to administer Extreme Unction. The woman provided directions to the house, but I was loathe to break in upon so solemn a matter. I would first seek Sir Thomas Jocelyn.

The lord of Hornsey was at home, and when his servant announced that I and Sir Harold and six others stood before his door he appeared quickly. The marshal to a duke will have such an effect on men.

We were invited into the hall and provided with ale before Sir Thomas's curiosity drove him to ask our business.

"The death of Prince Edward's valet in the road before this house vexes me," I began, "as it does the prince. He will not rest 'til the matter is resolved."

"I told you all. The man was discovered doing hamsoken and when pursued he turned on my man who then slew him."

"Have you or your wife a silken tunic or cotehardie?" I asked. "Or perhaps a silk-lined coverlet for your bed?"

Sir Thomas stared open-mouthed at me, startled at the change in the conversation. "Why would you ask such a thing about my domestic arrangements?"

"There is a reason. Answer my question and I will make the matter clear."

"Aye. Lady Beatrice owns two silken gowns. In winter my bed is provided with a fur coverlet lined with silk, and my wife also has such a coverlet."

"Was the silk purchased in London?" I asked.

"Aye. Where else would a man find a mercer who deals in silks?"

"Where indeed. From what mercer did you buy the silk for your wife's gowns?"

Sir Thomas's puzzled expression remained. He could not understand this interest of mine. "From Thomas Gryce. The Pagets always took their custom to Thomas, so when I wed Beatrice we continued to give our business to Thomas."

"Your wife was a Paget when you wed?" I said. "Is she sister to Sir Geoffrey Paget?"

"Cousin," the knight replied, and seemed to grow red in the face. Here was an interesting connection, but likely of no consequence. If Sir Thomas had purchased no silk from Richard Rowell he would have no debt to the man. So my journey this day to Hornsey also appeared to be of no consequence.

We were silent on the return to London and Kennington. Those who accompanied me knew that the journey had not been fruitful, even if they were unsure why this was so. Richard Rowell may have seen his apprentice hanged, and he may be furious about Sir Giles's unpaid debt, but I could not tie him to Sir Giles's murder, nor to any other felonies. This did not mean he was innocent of the slayings. But if he was guilty I had not the wit to discover it.

The journey to Hornsey and back caused we who had traveled there to miss our dinner, even though the distance to the village is not great and our stay there was brief. I had seen no reason to question Hornsey's priest before leaving the place, and he was yet occupied at the hovel where the crone was fighting the approach of death.

Prince Edward had demanded that I report to him directly upon returning from Hornsey, so I left Sir Harold and the others at the marshalsea and went to the privy chamber. I found the prince seated at a table before the window, reading from his Book of Hours. This was a magnificent creation, as befits the possession of a great lord.

"Come… What have you learned this day?" Prince Edward asked when I was announced, raising his eyes from his book.

"Very little. I believe Sir Giles's death had not to do with his debt to the mercer Richard Rowell, but this I cannot prove. 'Tis mere supposition."

"Have you exhausted your list of suspects? Are there yet men you believe might have hired Arnaud?"

"Sir Giles was not much admired. There are surely men I have not considered who might have wished him dead."

"And perhaps women also," the prince said, pulling upon his beard. "A wife who has seen her husband maligned or who believes him cheated might consider murder."

Here was a thought which had not occurred to me. I realized in that moment that the list of suspects – those who would be pleased to see Sir Giles Cheyne receive what they viewed as his due punishment – had become longer. A woman may as easily employ one man to poison another as any man. But what woman?

Sir John and Lady Ardith Pedley were dead, slain in their chamber. Was some other man, unknown to me, also seeking whosoever had slain Sir Giles? And did that man learn that Sir John, or Lady Ardith, had hired Arnaud? Was the slayer correct? If so, he had surpassed my feeble attempt to discover Sir Giles's killer. And Sir John had had good reason to be satisfied that his antagonist was in his grave.

But who would have reason to seek revenge for Sir Giles's death? He was disliked. Who would take up his cause? His daughter? Her suitor? I could think of no other. And, if revenge against Sir John or his lady wife was sought, why also slay Roger de Clare? Did the squire have to do with Sir John's death?

These thoughts flashed through my mind as the prince spoke.

"Kennington has become a nest of vipers. You and Sir Harold must clean it out. I have confidence you will do so." I felt grateful for his patience as the stain of violence spread through his household.

Roger de Clare had been among the four who had attempted to slay me and Arthur upon the road from Hornsey. Of this I was confident. If Sir John or Lady Ardith had paid Arnaud Tonge to slay Sir Giles 'twould make sense that – if they thought I was near to finding them out – they would assign Roger to find three others who could accost me returning to London. For the proper fee. But before I could find evidence of their guilt some other had done so, and had all three put to death.

Who could that man be? And what had Hornsey and its lord to do with the matter? Lady Beatrice was a Paget. What, if anything, did the relationship have to do with murder?

But yet, why had Arnaud traveled to Hornsey? What was there that he should seek the place after fleeing London? And, when he was pierced, why had Arnaud's slayer said "Here's what is owed you"?

I left Prince Edward to his book and descended the stairs to Kennington's hall. Valets and grooms were setting tables upon trestles, readying the hall for supper. As I crossed the room scents from the screens passage came to my nostrils and my stomach growled in response. How many dinners had I and Arthur missed in Prince Edward's service?

During the meal, I could not keep from glancing to Amabil Cheyne and Sir Geoffrey Paget. The hall grew dark as the removes were presented, but candles and cressets gave light enough to see that Amabil enjoyed her meal and, as before, Sir Geoffrey did not.

The man was to wed a wealthy heir to a sizeable estate. If she was not the most beauteous lass in the realm she was near so. Amabil was a shrew, but Sir Geoffrey knew that before the banns were read. If he thought her character so unpleasant that he could not enjoy his supper in her presence, why seek her as a wife? The estate she now possessed! A man will endure much for gold crowns in his purse. And why would Amabil be content with Sir Geoffrey? Was his estate so great that she would overlook his faults and weaknesses?

If Sir John Pedley or Lady Ardith had employed Arnaud to poison Amabil's father, the couple had set Amabil on her way to wealth. Did she now seem pleased with life because of the inheritance, or because she had discovered who slew her father and seen them punished for the deed? Or both?

I chose not to remain in the hall for the music and dancing which followed, seeking rather my bed and sleep, which I hoped might clear my head for the next day. Arthur followed, and joined me in slumber. For the first time I can remember when sharing a chamber with Arthur I fell to sleep before he did. Whether or not this influenced my thoughts the following day I cannot tell.

Prince Edward had assigned his marshal to organize a stag hunt on Saturday in the deer park to the south of Kennington Palace. I awoke before dawn to the sound of barking hounds and the conversation of their fewterers. Neither Arthur nor I would have business with the hunt, but curiosity drove me to observe preparations. I took with me a pouch of pounded herbs for Prince Edward's morning dose.

Knights and ladies were served loaves fresh from the bakehouse ovens slathered with parsley butter, and cups of wine, before they mounted their steeds and departed the palace yard. The sun was not yet above the forest to the east, the riders in shadow, but I thought as I watched the hunting party depart the palace that one rider lagged behind and turned away to the east as all others thundered on to the south and the prince's deer park. The baying of the hounds was soon lost to my ears and I decided to seek one of the fresh loaves. I would not accompany the loaf with Prince Edward's malmsey. Ale would suffice. But it was fresh-brewed.

For want of anything better to do I wandered to Kennington's chapel while Arthur sought other grooms to discover if some might be willing to risk a few pennies at Nine Man Morris.

Sir John, Lady Ardith, and Roger de Clare were gone, their corpses removed from before the altar and transported to their respective village churches for burial. I was alone in the quiet place, the only movement being the flickering of candles. Multi-hued light penetrated the chapel through stained-glass windows. 'Twas a place where a man might lose himself in meditation.

Does the Lord Christ wish malefactors brought to justice? The apostle wrote that He came not into the world to condemn men, but that they might be saved. Men must not be punished unless they have first been judged and condemned. But if the Lord Christ will not condemn a felon, what man may do so?

But the Lord Christ also said that the way to destruction is broad, whereas the path to salvation is narrow and few find it. If He does not wish to condemn men, yet they are bound for ruin, it must be that they condemn themselves. Here is another question for Master Wycliffe.

Chapter 17

Perhaps my post as bailiff to Lord Gilbert Talbot at Bampton has instilled within me a suspicious nature. Seated there in Prince Edward's chapel, I could not forget the horseman who, an hour before, had galloped from Kennington Palace with the hunters, then fallen behind and turned away. Had the fellow so little interest in chasing the hounds that he would seek some other entertainment? Did he ride to Southwark and the stews? A man could do this any time. He would not need the subterfuge of a hunt to do so. Perhaps he wished others to believe he was doing one thing when he was doing another. Few knights or their ladies would concern themselves about who was riding beside them. If the man said later that he had enjoyed the chase, who would gainsay him?

I departed the chapel, found Arthur at his game, and told him we would seek our palfreys at the marshalsea. I explained why. We would seek to follow the track of a man who wished to seem at one place when he was at another.

With many beasts gone from the stables our palfreys were soon saddled and we set off in the direction the hunting party had taken. The lone rider had turned aside at a place where a wood came near to the disturbed meadow grass where three dozen or so horses had galloped. We looked for his track, but saw nothing, so with only conjecture as my guide we turned our beasts into the wood where I thought the single rider might have gone.

I guessed correctly. A hundred or so paces into the wood Arthur spotted a pile of fresh dung. A few paces beyond was a place where last year's oak leaves had been newly turned, and two hundred paces beyond that we departed the wood and found ourselves upon the road between Kennington Palace and London Bridge. Perhaps the fellow was bound for Southwark and the stews after all.

Many horses had traveled this way, and if we came near to the bridge we would find even more hoof marks in the mud. The mysterious absconder could not be followed farther. I told Arthur we would return to the palace and there await the return of the hunters. And dinner.

The hunt was successful. Prince Edward appeared in the palace yard with a broad grin splitting his face. I saw nothing of the weakness he had displayed after hawking. William Blackwater would not be pleased, I thought. Weary hounds and mud-spattered knights and ladies followed Prince Edward, and lastly came two grooms, a pole stretched between them, resting upon their shoulders. Suspended from the pole was a fine stag. There would be venison for dinner next week, for some, after the flesh had been allowed to age properly in the larder.

I watched as the hunting party dismounted and dispersed, but could not identify any man of the palace missing from the group. Perhaps, I thought, he had rejoined the hunt and my curiosity was foolish. Other, much more weighty, matters should be occupying my time and thoughts.

'Twas not 'til dinner that I learned who was absent from hunt and hall.

Amabil Cheyne occupied her bench alone. Sir Geoffrey was absent. What grave matter would persuade him to miss his dinner, and the pleasures of the hunt? I had been required to serve Prince Edward and in so doing missed several dinners. I would not have chosen to do this, but important matters required it be so. What great business took Sir Geoffrey from the hall this day, I wondered?

Always before at dinner or supper Amabil had exhibited a light heart, even when her future husband did not. But I noticed this day that the young woman was subdued, not seeking conversation with those who sat on either side of her, and answering their chat with brief comments. Nor did she consume her meal with enthusiasm, as she had done in past days. Something was amiss. Could it have to do with her father's murder? I thought not. This behavior was new to her. Perhaps, I thought, Sir Geoffrey had tired of Amabil's biting wit and tiresome character and retreated to his own manor, content with his bachelor's life and his income, if to remedy any lack of funds meant a life with Amabil.

I have been wrong before.

Wherever Sir Geoffrey went this day he returned for his supper. The journey must not have been pleasant, for his long face matched Amabil's at dinner. And his return did not seem to bring her joy. She was as morose as she had been earlier. They spoke little during the meal, and did not remain for dancing, but departed the hall immediately after supper.

My mind was becoming fixed upon the idea that Sir John Pedley, perhaps with the help of his squire, had slain Sir Giles, and that Amabil and Sir Geoffrey had discovered this, while I had not. If this was so they had surely sought aid against Sir John and Lady Ardith, and Sir Geoffrey alone could not, I thought, have placed Roger de Clare in the herring barrel.

Sir Geoffrey and Amabil did not depart the hall for their chambers. Rather, they left the palace through the doors to the porch, and disappeared into the night. I decided to follow. I did not think the two of them off for some romantic tryst. Not with faces so doleful. Perhaps I might overhear some incriminating conversation.

Arthur saw me walk to the porch doors and made to follow, but I motioned him to remain in the hall. I needed stealth, not strength.

When I opened the great door from hall to porch I knew that light would escape from the hall into the night, so cracked the door only enough to allow me to slip through and hoped the departing couple would not notice. I waited on the porch for my eyes to become accustomed to the darkness, and listened for Amabil and Sir Geoffrey.

Moments after I had closed the door behind me I heard a soft squeal, as of rusted hinges. I knew the sound. My quarry had walked the length of the palace and entered Lady Joan's privy garden through the gate between garden and palace yard. I followed.

But when I arrived at the gate I did not open it. It would surely announce my presence as it had Sir Geoffrey and Amabil's. I am not so youthful and agile as in years past, yet nimble enough to vault over a gate little more than waist high.

When my feet touched the path inside the gate I crouched low and listened for the couple. Their voices were muted and I could not discern what they said, but I could follow the sound and draw near.

I approached the pair from the opposite side of a yew hedge. They had not moved, but stood in one place while they argued. And argument was what I heard, even though their exchange was hushed.

"We have no choice," Sir Geoffrey said.

"He has his five pounds," Amabil said. "I'll not pay five more."

Was it Richard Rowell they spoke of? Five pounds? Sir Giles had owed the mercer much more than that. I listened intently. No words from Sir Geoffrey, but his betrothed had more to say.

"What can he do if we refuse? If he speaks of what he knows to Prince Edward or that nosy bailiff, he will confess his own part in the matter. You should have hired a man more competent than Roger to slay that bailiff," Amabil hissed. "Had you done so we would not be here in this place, in the night, having this conversation."

"Sir Thomas would still demand five pounds more, whether Roger de Clare had succeeded in his mission or not," Sir Geoffrey now replied.

"But you would not have had to slay him and Sir John and Lady Ardith. This business has become expensive. I'll not send your cousin another five pounds."

"Then we must devise some strategy to avoid discovery," Sir Geoffrey said. "Sir Thomas will surely have some scheme in mind to deflect Prince Edward's wrath if he chooses to make known what we have done. We must do so as well."

"If I pay him five pounds more, he will demand another five or ten before Candlemas. And more yet by Whitsuntide. We will never be free of his claims."

"You should have paid Roger his fee, even though he failed," Sir Geoffrey said. "He would not then have threatened to go to Sir John, and we would not have been required to slay them."

"I'll not suffer extortion by any man. And 'twas less dear to do away with Sir John and Lady Ardith than to grant Roger his demand."

Silence followed. When next Sir Geoffrey spoke he was some distance away. The pair had walked on before resuming their conversation. I could barely hear Amabil's next words.

"Send that oafish squire to persuade Sir Thomas to keep silence, since you were unable to do so."

"Thomas Poer?"

"Whatever his name. Make clear to him that he is implicated in this matter, and tell him he must do as you require else he will find himself upon a scaffold, or at a block."

"As may we," Sir Geoffrey whispered.

They walked on, but I did not follow. I had heard all that was needed. Amabil and Sir Geoffrey had indeed seen Sir John and Lady Ardith murdered. And Roger de Clare also. But not for the reason I had thought. I crept away, careful in setting down my feet lest I snap a twig or stumble upon a stone.

My mind traveled back to the first time I had walked in the garden, with Randall Patchett. All became clear. Sir Giles had been about to wed a fecund young widow. She would likely bear him children, perhaps a son. A lad would displace Amabil. To remain Sir Giles's only heir her father must not wed Lady Juliana Pultney. He did not.

I left Lady Joan's garden as I had entered it, over the gate, then returned to the porch and hall. I now had the truth, or at least most of it, but how to gain proof of it? If I went to Prince Edward with what I now knew, surely Sir Geoffrey and Amabil would dispute my accusation. Would the prince and his knights believe me, a mere bailiff?

Arthur saw me re-enter the hall, and was quick to leave his place along the wall with other grooms and approach when I motioned to him. I wished to have him near when I spoke to Thomas Poer.

The squire was a competent dancer, for all his bulk. I watched until the galliard was done, then approached Thomas and asked him to follow. He did, and Arthur walked behind him.

I led the squire to the chamber he shared with others of his rank. The place was dark and empty, lit only by a pair of smoldering cressets. I bid the lad sit upon his bed and stood over him.

"When I dealt with Sir William Vache's scrofula, you swooned. When you regained your senses you spoke. 'A terrible end,' you said. I thought then that you spoke of the blood of Sir William's surgery. But not so. 'Twas of other blood you spoke."

The lad said nothing.

"Did you help slay Sir John and Lady Ardith, or only Roger de Clare?" I asked.

Thomas spluttered a denial and began to rise. Arthur put a firm hand upon the squire's shoulder and pushed him down.

"'Tis of no use to protest your innocence," I said. "Sir Geoffrey has named you."

"Sir Geoffrey? But 'twas he..."

"He what? Finish what you began. Truth may save you from a gallows."

"Sir Geoffrey said 'twas an evil thing, the way Roger put me to shame. Said he'd help me end it. I didn't know he meant to slay him."

"You struck Roger a blow to his head, then tipped him into the herring barrel."

"'Twas Sir Geoffrey who smote him. I thought that was all he intended. But then he told me to carry Roger to the larder. Didn't want to put him with the herrings, but Sir Geoffrey said that when Roger awoke he'd be more wicked to me than ever before."

"Did you also aid Sir Geoffrey in slaying Sir John and Lady Ardith?"

"Sir Geoffrey did those murders?"

"Aye, likely with help."

"Nay. He never bid me do so, and I'd not have. Sir John never troubled me as Roger did."

"Tomorrow, or soon, you will be required to travel to Hornsey. Do you know the place?"

"Aye. Why must I go there?"

"Sir Geoffrey will send you there. He will tell you to threaten violence against the lord of the manor and his wife, Sir Thomas Jocelyn and Lady Beatrice."

"But why must I make such a threat? And will Sir Geoffrey demand I travel alone?"

"Aye, likely. But you will not do so. Arthur and I will accompany you. We will meet you at the Aldersgate. Wait there for us on the morrow, or next day, or when Sir Geoffrey sends you. As we travel to the village I will tell you why we do so, and why you are to threaten

Sir Thomas Jocelyn. Meanwhile, tell no man of this conversation if you value your life."

I left the despondent squire sitting upon his bed and returned to the hall. Whether or not to tell Prince Edward of discoveries this evening perplexed me. He had always required of me that I inform him of any progress I made, however slight, in finding Sir Giles's slayer, yet I hesitated to do so 'til I could prove all and not be challenged. I decided I would tell the prince what I had learned, as he would wish, and beg of him not to act upon the knowledge until I had accumulated more proof.

The hall had become heated, with candles and cressets, the hearth and dancers all adding to the warmth. Prince Edward and Lady Joan were rosy of cheek when a pavane ended, and rather than join the next dance they took seats upon the dais. Some time passed before I caught the prince's eye, made a slight bow, and nodded to the stairs leading to Kennington's upper story and his privy chamber. I then crossed the hall toward the stairs and glanced over my shoulder to learn if my message had been received.

It had. I saw Prince Edward lean toward his wife, speak to her behind an upraised hand, then rise and stride across the hall. All eyes followed.

I awaited the prince at the base of the stairs. He nodded slightly, then ascended. I followed. Prince Edward gave no sign of toppling backward upon the stairs. I heard behind me the musicians begin another tune.

The valets at the privy chamber door heard our approach and swung open the doors when we came near. A fire burned low upon the hearth, providing the only light. The prince commanded candles to be lit, and when a valet had done so and departed he turned to me.

"What news?" he said.

I told him.

"So the lass and her swain have slain four in this place to save her inheritance?" Prince Edward concluded when I had completed the tale. "And blackened Kennington Palace and my name also."

"So I believe. But they will declare it not so. My word against theirs before the king's judges."

"A judge will accept your testimony if I tell him to do so," the prince replied. "But I take your point. It must be clear to all men that Sir Giles's daughter did this evil, else men will gossip that she was unjustly punished. You travel to Hornsey tomorrow, you say, with the doltish squire – what was his name?"

"Thomas Poer."

"Ah, yes. Sir William's squire. The one who dropped to the cobbles when you put a blade to Sir William's scrofula."

"Aye, the same."

"And he is to threaten the lord of Hornsey? For what?"

"Arnaud Tonge was told to flee Kennington and London after he poisoned Sir Giles. He was instructed to travel to Hornsey and there await payment for his foul deed."

"Ah," Prince Edward said. "But he received a dagger rather than a purse full of coins."

"Just so. Sir Thomas is wed to Sir Geoffrey Paget's cousin, the Lady Beatrice. I know not the wealth Arnaud was promised to place hemlock into Sir Giles's wine, but Amabil and Sir Geoffrey found it less costly to pay a relative to slay the valet than to keep their bargain with Arnaud."

"Five pounds then to slay Arnaud. And now Sir Thomas requires five pounds more to hold his tongue."

"Aye."

"And will likely ask more in the future," Prince Edward concluded. "So Thomas Poer is to somehow persuade the lord of Hornsey that his demands must end?"

"Aye."

"How would he do so?"

"You've seen the lad. He could wring a man's neck with his bare hands."

"Likely. But would he?"

"Mayhap, if he was persuaded 'twas needful to do. And the squire is dull and easily led."

"I have a thought," Prince Edward said. "I will dress as a

commoner tomorrow and accompany you and the squire to Hornsey. I will hear with my own ears what Sir Thomas has to say of his cousin."

"But m'lord, the roads may be dangerous. And you are not well."

"'Tis true enough," he sighed. "I am not well. But," he brightened, "I am better now that I consume your herbs each day. Well enough to ride to the hunt is well enough to ride to Hornsey."

"We will not know if Thomas Poer is sent to Hornsey until he seeks his horse at the marshalsea. Arthur and I then intend to have our palfreys made ready, follow, and meet Thomas at Aldersgate."

"Simple enough. I will tell Sir Harold to accompany us, also garbed as a commoner. A simple brown cotehardie, I think, and chauces of wool, not linen. What say you? I will wear a hood against the cold. Even folk in London will mistake me for a minor burgher. Few will have seen my face, and no man in Hornsey will recognize me. Not even Sir Thomas. I've never met the fellow."

"Your scheme troubles me," I admitted. "I would think better of it if we had also with our party half a dozen grooms, armed."

"Very well. Speak to Sir Harold." Prince Edward rubbed his hands together and grinned. "We shall soon have the truth of the evils which have befallen Kennington."

Chapter 18

I awoke next morn well rested, for as I lay my head upon the pillow I thought it sure that I would soon return to Bampton and my Kate.

At dawn I sought the marshal and learned that he had already been told of Prince Edward's scheme. If Thomas Poer sought his horse this day Sir Harold would be told immediately, would send a message to me and Prince Edward, and we would follow the squire to Aldersgate. I worried about whether Thomas Poer could be trusted to keep the bargain.

He could.

Prince Edward's nondescript cotehardie hid his royal person well. The garment was even a little threadbare and I wondered which of his grooms he had acquired it from. No man gave us a second glance as we rode through the city, even though several of us wore the prince's badge. Such men are common enough on London streets as to raise little curiosity. The most difficult part of escaping London had been leaving the palace, and even there, with the hood drawn low, Prince Edward was able to pass undetected.

Poer recognized Sir Harold, but until the prince threw back his hood a mile and more beyond the Aldersgate he did not know he was in the company of Prince Edward. The knowledge caused the squire to shrink in his saddle.

When we came to Hornsey I stopped our party and explained a scheme to trap Sir Thomas into disclosing the truth. We who wore the prince's badge would hold back from entering the village. Thomas Poer, the prince, and the marshal would approach the manor house and demand to speak to Sir Thomas. Prince Edward would again don his hood, to be more certain that Sir Thomas would not know him.

It would be Thomas Poer's duty, I said, to threaten the lord of Hornsey as Sir Geoffrey had planned. Prince Edward had a different scheme. He did not, I believe, think the squire capable of believable dissimulation.

"Nay, Master Hugh. This Sir Thomas does not know me. We've never met. I will tell him that Sir Geoffrey and Amabil refuse to pay another five pounds. When he hears this he will likely reply in some way which will incriminate both him and them. If he does not, I will then play ignorant and ask why he believes Sir Geoffrey and Amabil owe him the five pounds they refuse to pay. A messenger only – that is what I will be. And Thomas behind me will add emphasis to my words."

The scheme seemed likely to succeed. The lord of Hornsey would perhaps assume that these "messengers" knew some of what had transpired between him and Sir Geoffrey and Amabil, and would see little reason to keep his part in the business a secret.

So I tied my palfrey to a sapling at the south edge of Hornsey and with Arthur – Sir Thomas might recognize him – sat at the base of a tree while Prince Edward, Sir Harold, and Thomas Poer entered the village and approached the manor house. What next transpired I learned from the prince.

When Prince Edward came to the manor house he had no need to smite the door. Sir Thomas was in the yard, saw the three visitors approach, and walked to meet them. His greeting, the prince said, was curt.

"I give you good day," Prince Edward replied. To this greeting the lord of Hornsey made no comment, but stood with arms akimbo, waiting to be told by his unwanted callers their reason for appearing before his house. The prince did not disappoint him. Not immediately.

"We come from Sir Geoffrey Paget and Amabil Cheyne," Prince Edward said. "We bear a message for Sir Thomas Jocelyn. Are you the man?"

"I am. What message do you carry from my cousin? If 'tis a message only, you may as well turn your beasts and be away. You might return to London in time for your supper."

"What is it we might bring you in addition to a message?" said the prince. "Never mind, I believe I know."

"Then you may return with a message for Sir Geoffrey. Prince Edward will be told why Amabil paid five pounds to a man of this manor."

"A man? Amabil did not pay you this sum?"

"Oh, aye, as you likely know. She did. But I will say 'nay,' and 'twill be but her word against mine. She wished the prince's valet dead, and dead he is. Caught at hamsoken. He can tell no tales, nor can he seek more coin from Amabil. But I live, and can tell tales, and will have five pounds more of her to remain silent."

"Five pounds now, and likely five more before St. Stephen's Day," Prince Edward said.

"Aye," Sir Thomas laughed. "Mayhap."

Prince Edward turned to his marshal and spoke. "We have heard enough, think you?"

Sir Harold nodded. "Aye."

"Enough for what?" Sir Thomas said.

"To hang you and Sir Geoffrey and Amabil Cheyne."

"You serve Sir Geoffrey and Amabil," Sir Thomas exclaimed. "Will you betray them?"

"I serve no man but my father, the king."

"Y-your father? The king?" Sir Thomas stammered.

"You speak to Edward, Duke of Cornwall," Sir Harold said, "and I am his marshal. You will return with us to London."

"Bah," the lord of Hornsey replied. "How do I know you speak true?"

Sir Harold drew off his modest cotehardie to reveal under it a black tunic with Prince Edward's badge embroidered upon it.

Sir Thomas was silenced.

Before the sun was overhead I saw four mounted men approach. Sir Thomas Jocelyn rode in the midst, his features downcast. Well might they be.

I enjoyed my supper that evening, for I knew I would soon depart Kennington Palace and be once more at peace in Bampton with my Kate and our babes. Sir Geoffrey and Amabil were not at their usual places for the meal, and those who knew why soon informed others, so that before the second remove was brought to table all knew of how Sir Giles Cheyne had been slain so that Amabil could keep her inheritance.

The journey to Hornsey did tire Prince Edward. After supper

he forsook the hall. Shortly after, I was summoned to the privy chamber. Lady Joan and the child Richard were also present. The prince waved to a bench and bade me sit.

"You have done me good service," he began. "You have found who slew my loyal companion, and have eased my bellyache. You will be rewarded. I intend to grant you a knighthood. You shall henceforth be Sir Hugh, not Master Hugh."

"This is an honor I do not seek."

"Hah!" Prince Edward turned to Lady Joan. "A modest man." He then turned to me. "Will your wife not be pleased to be Lady Katherine?"

"Aye. I suppose she will."

"Good. There is no time like the present to begin the ceremony. Tomorrow is All Hallows' Eve. You may seek the chapel. I will have my chaplain make ready. In the morning you will bathe and I will complete the rite."

So it was that I spent that night in prayer, prostrate before the altar on the cold tiles of Kennington Palace Chapel. Prince Edward was true to his word, and at dawn I was led, stiff with cold, to the prince's copper-lined tub, where I could wash filth from my body just as I had swept impurities from my soul before the chapel altar.

I no longer needed the authority of Prince Edward's livery, so I donned my own chauces and cotehardie for the investiture. The prince and Lady Joan wore their finest robes, of gold cloth, and the chapel was crowded with knights and their ladies as Father Lawrence spoke the mass. I was offered bread and wine, then brought to kneel before Prince Edward to receive his sword upon my shoulders. I felt no different from the man I was a day, even a year, before – but now I was Sir Hugh.

Amabil was the daughter of a knight, and Sir Geoffrey was a knight, so neither faced a noose for their felonies. Amabil was permitted to enter the nunnery at Rosedale, in Yorkshire, where she would awaken each morning aching with cold to remember her sins. Sir Geoffrey went to the block upon Tower Hill. As for Sir Thomas Jocelyn, he was able to convince the King's Eyre that, whatever part he had played in the business of Sir Giles's death, he had the right of hamsoken and could not be charged with the death of Arnaud Tonge. Thomas Poer was absolved as being the unwitting accomplice of men who used his simple-mindedness for their own purposes. Perhaps my testimony before the judges and jury helped spare the lad's life.

I remembered to speak to Prince Edward of Randall Patchett, and he took the lad into his service as a squire.

As there was now no heir to Sir Giles Cheyne's estate, his lands – but for one manor the revenues of which were given to Rosedale Priory for the maintenance of Amabil – reverted to the crown. As a reward for my services to his son, King Edward assigned a sixth part of the revenues of Sir Giles's remaining lands to me. I am sure Prince Edward had influence in the matter. No doubt the prince thought this a great favor to me. But the Lord Christ said that 'tis difficult for a wealthy man to enter His kingdom. Has the prince done me a favor, or harmed me? Surely he believes the former. All men, I suppose, wish for greater wealth than they possess. Would they if they thought the coins would send them to hell? Perhaps they believe that their wealth can be used to hire priests and monks to pray them out of purgatory. The Lord Christ said nothing of this – that a man's wealth might save him rather than condemn him.

The prince retained William Blackwater as his physician, but only after Blackwater humbly promised to provide tansy, thyme, cress, bramble leaves, and oil from the root of fennel for the prince's wine each day.

Prince Edward decided to depart Kennington Palace for Berkhampstead Castle. Kennington, he said, reeked of calumny and death, and he wanted to be away from the odor.

As Roger de Clare was dead he could not name the men he had hired with Amabil Cheyne's money to accost me upon the road. They were never found out, nor did I seek them. Doing so would have kept me in London – a place I had no wish to be. I even lost interest in the scoundrel of the bright blue cotehardie. The Lord Christ may deal with him!

Arthur and I mounted our palfreys on the eleventh day of November and set off for home. Prince Edward's grooms and valets were busy dismantling his household for the move to Berkhampstead as we departed.

At Stokenchurch we halted before the house of the babe whose wound I had stitched. 'Twas well healed, and as I had half suspected might be the case, the child's father had not dared cut away the silken threads. I did so, the little lad protesting the business mightily all the while. 'Twas but a matter of minutes to accomplish this and did not much delay our return to Bampton.

We spent the night with the Cistercians at Thame Abbey and rose early from our beds, both of us eager to be at home. Where Church View Street meets Mill Street I dismounted, sent Arthur on to Bampton Castle with the beasts, and walked to Galen House with my instruments bag over my shoulder.

My Kate was as pleased with my return as I had hoped she would be, and Bessie hugged my knees while bouncing with joy. Infant John was unimpressed with my appearance and slept through the greetings and questions and replies.

'Twas a fast day, so only a pottage of peas and beans bubbled upon the hearth. But I thought it a meal fit for a king. Or for a knight.

Afterword

Kennington Palace was located in what is now the Vauxhall area of London, in the triangle between Kennington Road, Sancroft Street, and Cardigan Street (see map).

From the late 1340s to 1363 Prince Edward built a hall at Kennington, with a chamber and wardrobe, a kitchen, bakehouse, and pastry cook's house. The hall was oriented east-west, and measured approximately eighty-eight feet long by fifty-three feet wide. An undercroft was sunk about three feet under the hall; a stone-vaulted roof supported the floor of the hall which was about six feet above ground level. In 1531 Henry VIII demolished most of Kennington Palace to provide building materials for his new palace at Whitehall.

The main parts of Kennington Palace, including the hall, great chamber, kitchen, and stables, were excavated between 1965 and 1968.

Prince Edward did not live to become King Edward IV, dying in June 1376, before his father. His second son, Richard, became king when yet a child. Edward was known in the fourteenth century as Edward of Woodstock (his birthplace), or as the Duke of Cornwall, not the "Black Prince." That name was not commonly used for him until the Tudor era. The "Black Prince" sobriquet was supposedly given to Edward because of his black armor, although there is no contemporary evidence for this. His crest featured an unusual black background, so may have been the source of the nickname.

Historians differ as to the nature of Edward's lingering and debilitating illness. Amebic dysentery and malaria are usually at the top of the list of suspected maladies. Dysentery seems the most likely culprit.

Bampton Castle was, in the fourteenth century, one of the largest castles in England in terms of the area contained within the curtain wall. Little remains of the castle but for the gatehouse and a small part of the curtain wall, which form a part of Ham Court, a farmhouse in private hands. The current owners have done extensive restoration work, and even restored a part of the moat.

Many readers have asked about medieval remains in Bampton. St. Mary's Church is little changed from the fourteenth century, when it was known as the Church of St. Beornwald. The late May Bank Holiday is a good time to visit Bampton. The village is a morris dancing center, and on that day holds a day-long morris dancing festival.

Village scenes in the popular television series *Downton Abbey* were filmed on Church View Street in Bampton, and St. Mary's Church appeared in several episodes. The town library was transformed into the Downton Hospital.

A scrofula is a tubercular swelling of the lymph system in the neck and these seem to have been not uncommon in the fourteenth century.

An extract from the twelfth chronicle of Hugh de Singleton, surgeon

Chapter 1

June and July are hungry months. Hogs slaughtered and smoked and salted at Martinmas have been consumed, and unless a man is adept at setting snares to poach his lord's coneys and hares he and his family will go without flesh upon their trenchers.

In the June of 1373 corn was also in short supply. The harvest had not been bountiful the last year, so most folk in Bampton village had lived with hollow bellies and prayed for an abundant harvest this year.

Two of my Kate's hens had gone missing since Whitsunday, so we were without their eggs to feed ourselves, Bessie and John, and Kate's father. I was angry that some villager had made off with the fowls, but what would I do if my babes were crying with hunger? Would I steal to spare them? Or to keep them alive? I pray that I may never be brought to such an impasse.

Men sometimes wonder how they might conduct themselves in a crisis. Such a question can only be answered when a crisis visits. It is better, perhaps, to never know the answer to such a question, for to know means that evil has come.

No man had made off with Kate's rooster, so the creature awoke me as he greeted the dawn on Tuesday, June 21. I remember the day well, for before the sun dropped below Lord Gilbert's wood to the west of Bampton Castle my employer, Lord Gilbert Talbot, assigned me the most vexing task I had yet undertaken in his service.

I am Hugh de Singleton – Sir Hugh, since Prince Edward saw fit to award me a knighthood for my service to him some months past – surgeon and bailiff to Lord Gilbert Talbot at his Bampton manor. My post often requires that I seek out miscreants who trouble the peace of Lord Gilbert's villeins and tenants. As I have had success in such duty, Lord Gilbert has sometimes seen fit to charge me to assist friends who require the services of a sleuth to unravel some knotty trouble.

I broke my fast with a fragment of stale maslin loaf and a cup of ale, then set off for John Prudhomme's house. John has been reeve of Bampton Manor for several years, and this day we must divide our duty: one to oversee haying, the other the ploughing of a fallow field of Lord Gilbert's demesne. I sent John to watch over the ploughing, to be sure that the ploughmen turned the sod deeply so that the roots of weeds were exposed, and went to observe the haying.

Ten of Lord Gilbert's villeins, with their wives and older children, arrived at the meadow shortly after the sun had dried the dew. The men set off with their scythes while the women and children followed, turning the hay to ensure that it dried evenly. My presence as observer of this labor was not really required. A successful hay crop means that more animals can be kept over the next winter for fresh meat, or breeding stock, or sale. So the men at their scythes swung them close to the ground, and the women and children were careful to leave no clumps which would mold if the weather turned wet.

The day became warm, so that the haymakers had stripped to their kirtles by the fourth hour, and sweat mingled with dust upon their brows when the Angelus Bell rang from the tower of the Church of St. Beornwald, signaling noon and a break for dinner. The work was arduous, but the laborers grinned as they went to their meals. The hay crop was good.

As I turned from Bridge Street to Church View Street on the way to my own dinner, I saw Adela walking ahead, returning to Galen House from the baker with three loaves in her arms. Adela's father is a poor cotter of the Bishop of Exeter's lands in the Weald. My service to Prince Edward last year included discovering who had slain Sir Giles Cheyne, the prince's companion at the Battle of Crécy. For this labor I had been made Sir Hugh, and also awarded a sixth part of the revenues of the murdered knight's lands. I was prosperous enough that I could hire a servant to assist my Kate, who was now Lady Katherine to the folk of Bampton and the Weald.

Dinner this day at Galen House was a porre of peas and loaves yet warm from the baker's oven. Kate had found some bits of pork to flavor the pottage.

"Have Lord Gilbert's guests arrived?" my father-in-law asked as we ate.

"Nay, but Coleshill is not far distant and the roads are dry. Sir Aymer should arrive before supper."

The care and feeding of guests at Bampton Castle is not part of my duties to Lord Gilbert, but his instructions for the cook, chamberlain, valets, and grooms regarding the forthcoming visit of guests were soon known to me and most others in the village.

Sir Aymer Molyns, the expected guest, was wed to Philippa Felbridge, cousin once removed to Lady Petronilla, Lord Gilbert's wife. Lady Petronilla had succumbed to plague when the disease reappeared four years past. The Lady Philippa was Sir Aymer's second wife; his first bride, Lady Alyce, having also perished during the return of plague in 1369.

A man with a scythe is expected to mow an acre of hay in a day. As there were ten men at work in the hayfield, and the field was little more than half a yardland in size, the work was nearly complete when, at the ninth hour, I saw riders, two carts, and an elaborately painted wagon approach the castle from Cowleys Corner. Here, I thought, are Sir Aymer and Lady Philippa.

A painted canvas stretched over hoops covered the wagon. As this had been a day of bright sun I assumed the Lady Philippa was travelling under the canvas so as to keep her complexion pale. Most gentlefolk consider this a mark of beauty. And status. A tanned visage is the mark of a woman of the commons, who must labor in the sun. My Kate is usually tanned by Michaelmas, but this does not diminish her beauty. Not to me. Why is it, I wonder, that the summer sun will cause skin to grow darker and hair to become lighter? Here is another question for my mystery bag to be opened when the Lord Christ welcomes me into His kingdom. Surely He will know.

When I first came to Bampton in Lord Gilbert's employ I was surprised to learn of a practice which I had not seen before. At the end of a day of haying, men are permitted to take for their own as much of the lord's hay as they can carry from the field upon their scythe. But they must not be overly greedy. If any hay falls before they carry it from the field, all they have piled upon the scythe is forfeit.

I watched as the villeins stacked remarkable mounds of hay upon their scythes and carried the fodder away, then departed the hayfield and walked to Bampton Castle forecourt. Lord Gilbert's visitors had but moments before passed under the portcullis and into the castle yard. Arthur and Uctred, two of Lord Gilbert's grooms, who had in the past been of service to me in seeking felons, were among the servants who took Sir Aymer's beasts in hand as he, his squire, and a dozen or so grooms and valets dismounted.

I had no business at the castle, no reason to greet Lord Gilbert's guests, so I was about to retrace my steps to the forecourt when I heard raised voices. I did not at first comprehend the words, but as I turned to see from whence the din came I heard Sir Aymer roar, "Empty, by heavens! Where is she? She entered the wagon this morn. Why is she no longer within?"

The knight addressed these shouted questions to an elderly, wispy-haired man who had, until a moment earlier, been mounted upon the first of the three runcies which drew the wagon. The fellow was frail, and glanced from Sir Aymer to the wagon with an open mouth and a startled expression.

Lord Gilbert drew aside the canvas enclosing the rear of the wagon, and as I watched he peered inside. The roads were dry. The wagon was closed front and back to keep out dust. When my employer withdrew his head his bluff features registered puzzlement. Apparently Sir Aymer's wife – for who else would travel in such a conveyance? – was nowhere to be found.

This disappearance soon had tongues wagging. Sir Aymer's grooms and valets put their heads together, and Lord Gilbert's servants did likewise. Meanwhile, Lord Gilbert stood, arms akimbo, studying the wagon, while Sir Aymer continued to berate the hapless postilion rider.

The curious spectacle caught my attention. I stood near the castle gatehouse to watch and listen. How could a lady disappear between Coleshill and Bampton, a distance of but nine miles? This question was about to be assigned to me, for as I watched Sir Aymer berate the wagon driver Lord Gilbert's eye fell upon me. A moment later he gestured vigorously that I was to approach him.

"Here is a puzzle," Lord Gilbert said over the clamor of competing voices as various folk pronounced opinions regarding the vanished lady. "The Lady Philippa and her maid went into the wagon this morning at Coleshill, but are no longer within. I fear some evil has befallen the lady."

Sir Aymer, meanwhile, left off castigating the hapless postilion and stalked over to where Lord Gilbert and I stood.

"My wife has been taken," he concluded. "My men and I will ride back the way we came to see if Lady Philippa may be found."

"I will join you," Lord Gilbert said. Then, to me, "You come also. Arthur, Uctred, saddle my ambler and three palfreys. We four will accompany Sir Aymer."

Arthur and Uctred hurried to the stables to do Lord Gilbert's bidding, while my employer hastened to his hall. He returned a moment later buckling a sword to his belt.

"If there are felons about who stole the lady 'twill do well to be armed. Have you your dagger?"

I touched the hilt of my weapon in reply.

Sir Aymer, his squire, and five of his grooms and valets, along with Lord Gilbert, Arthur, Uctred, and I clattered across the castle drawbridge a few moments later. We rode past Cowleys Corner, across Radcot Bridge, and beyond Clanfield, all the way to Faringdon. We saw no trace of the missing lady, nor any sign that any felony had taken place along the road. Sir Aymer often called Lady Philippa's name. Silence was the only reply.

We occasionally saw men working late in fields along the road, and once passed two travelers afoot. None had seen a lady and her maid. At Clanfield we questioned several folk. A woman of the village remembered seeing Sir Aymer and his party pass by earlier in the day. Lady Philippa's wagon would naturally be remembered. Since then, she said, only a cart and men afoot had traveled the road before her house.

'Twas near to midsummer's eve, so we had ample light to inspect the road and verge. Nothing was amiss. Lady Philippa and the maid had vanished.

The sun had set by the time we returned to Bampton Castle.

For six hours we had sought Lady Philippa without success. But the search was not ended.

As he dismounted, Lord Gilbert turned to me and spoke. "Hugh, I wish for you to discover what has befallen Lady Philippa. It may be that she was taken whilst upon my lands, near to Bampton. If so, I'll not have a guest so ill-used. Come to the castle early tomorrow and we will decide what must be done."